I0661700

The Sinclair Seven

INKED COWBOY

GEMMA SNOW

ENTWINED PUBLISHING

Inked Cowboy
ISBN # 978-1-80250-253-4
©Copyright Gemma Snow 2025
Cover Art by Erin Dameron-Hill ©Copyright June 2025
Interior text design by Entwined Publishing
Published by Entice, an Entwined Publishing imprint

Published in 2025 by Entwined Publishing, United Kingdom.

Entwined Publishing is a division of Totally Entwined Group Limited.

INKED COWBOY

Chapter One

Shit.

Saint sent up a silent apology to the grandmother who had done her very best to steer her away from profanity, and pounded the heel of her hand against the dashboard.

The fuel gauge didn't budge.

The ancient sedan had gotten her several hundred miles from Seattle, packed with Saint's entire life, but while the gauge normally jumped a notch or two when she turned the engine over, this time all she got was a slow, steady whine. She had pulled off the interstate to try to find cheap gas, hoping to make it at least to Helena for the night, but what difference would it have made? She had less than forty bucks to her name — in cash, at least — and she couldn't keep playing *guess how much gas is in the tank* as she navigated the windy, isolated mountain roads.

Washington had been a natural, wild place, but she had grown up in the city. Montana, from what little she had seen of it, was a place out of time, barely inhabited, and very much at the mercy of Mother Nature.

As if listening to her thoughts, a dark cloud rolled over the soft yellow of the late afternoon sky, and thunder cracked loud and echoing just beyond the mountain ridge.

Don't panic. Take a moment to breathe. In one Mississippi, two Mississippi, three Mississippi, and out one Mississippi, two Mississippi, three Mississippi.

She'd been prone to panic attacks as a child, after she'd gone to live with her grandmother, and she reached for Gram Violet's mantra now, breathing in the soft smell of her grandmother's quilt, folded on the seat beside her, an old coffee she'd been nursing for the better part of a day, the soft patterning of cold rain against the bare trees just beyond her windows.

She breathed. In and out, just like she'd been doing all her life.

The car probably wasn't damaged beyond repair. She'd need to get the fuel gauge checked, or she ran the risk of seizing the engine or something equally permanent, and since she'd been using the car for both transportation and shelter for the last three days, that was a non-starter. She took stock of her surroundings, just as Gram had taught her to do when she needed grounding, and caught sight of a neon bar sign just down the road, the entrance to the parking lot not far from where she had pulled over at the first sputter.

Please start.

She willed the engine to turn over, and after a moment, it did, though not without voicing loud, squealing protests. Chances were, she was dealing with more than low fuel. She'd been pushing the car too hard and too fast the last few days, and it hadn't been in great shape to begin with.

But Saint hadn't had a choice.

It seemed she hadn't had a lot of choices in a very long time.

By some act of God, if Saint still believed in that sort of thing, she was able to cover the distance to the parking lot entrance, making it just far enough to slide into a spot at the far end of the lot, before the engine stalled out in a shuddering, frame-shaking sigh. Saint put the sorry thing in park, not that it would make a damned difference, pulled the keys from the ignition, and let out a long, shuddering sigh of her own.

She was stuck.

In…

Where the hell am I?

After days on the road, she'd lost track of the states and towns she'd driven though, one eye on the rearview mirror, with the goal of putting as much distance as possible between her old life and whatever came next.

New York City.

Gram Violet's dream.

And still thousands of miles away from the small town in the Montana mountains where her car was stalled and out of gas, and she didn't have the money for a hotel, let alone a new fuel gauge.

Somewhere in the car, there was a box of day-old donuts, and she turned to search through the piles of belongings in the back seat, nearly bumping her head on the roof when another crack of thunder crashed loud and hard through the air, immediately followed by the sharp dagger of bright lightning that split the sky around her.

Fuck. This.

She didn't bother to apologize to Gram that time. Violet would have told her to spend a few of those precious dollars she had left on a hot meal and some temporary respite from the biblical storm bursting free around her.

So Saint grabbed her coat, purse and keys, and darted out into the rain.

It took two seconds flat before she was soaked to the bone, the November chill seeping into her skin and promising to stay, her hair matted against her back, and her fingers already going numb at the tips. But before she could die of hypothermia, she was through the door and into the warm caress of the bar.

With the exception of the friendly waitress who gave her a nod and held up a menu from the other side of the room, no one paid her much mind. The floor was wet, and muddy boot prints crossed the entryway, indicating that she wasn't the only one who'd been caught in the deluge. Whatever big-city fear she'd had about attracting too much attention, like she'd walk into the saloon in a one-horse town, and everyone would turn her way, quickly evaporated. It was warm and cozy in the bar, with a soft golden glow from hanging bistro lights, and the inviting smell of grease and salt, and a sudden wave of hunger washed over her. She'd been surviving on donuts, granola bars and truck stop coffee for three days, and she was absolutely starving.

And tired.

So, incredibly, tired.

"Sit anywhere, hon," the waitress called. "I'll grab you some water."

Saint felt like she was moving in slow motion, but she finally settled into a booth at the far end of the bar, the worn cushion soft under her tired legs. She'd been stuffed into the little sedan for so many days now, she was certain her butt was permanently imprinted on the seat, and her lower back ached from the worn springs and long-gone padding.

And from the clenching of her muscles for three days straight.

I need a plan.

This wasn't going to work. Not without a strategy. Running for the hills — or away from the hills, as the case was — had felt like the right idea at the time, the *only* idea at the time. But she'd coasted into town on luck and adrenaline, and with an all-but-dead car in the parking lot of a sleepy mountain town, in the middle of a torrential storm, she was fuck out of that luck, and coming down from her adrenaline in a very serious way.

"You must be freezing, hon." The pretty waitress sidled up to the booth, pulling Saint from her moment of self-pity. Food first, then strategy. "I'm Maisie. Let's get you started with something warm. How about a coffee? Or maybe something stronger?"

"Do you have green tea?" Saint asked, her voice unused and unfamiliar after days alone on the road.

"Coming right up," Maisie replied. "Let me see if I can't find you some paper towels in the back too." She twirled away with the expertise of a long-time server, collected two bottles of beer from the table to her left then disappeared through the back door to the kitchen. It was such a familiar scene, a type of movement so ingrained in Saint's own muscles, that she could practically smell the chicken parm and simmering red sauce from the restaurant back home.

Not that she had a home anymore.

But she did have skills, skills that might just get her out of a sticky spot.

Sticky spot. *Ha.*

That was putting it mildly. She needed a strategy, and it was staring her dead in the face. Stay here in this

Montana mountain town. Just until she could get back on both feet. Just until she could figure out her next steps.

So, when the waitress came back with a hot tea and a few dry dishrags, Saint did the only thing she could do. She swallowed her pride, opened her mouth, and asked, "Any chance you're hiring?"

Chapter Two

Lia left town.

Dante watched the three little bubbles pop up on his phone and took the brief moment of peace before the storm to sip at his beer. Normally, he reached for the whiskey — he was damned good at picking out whiskey. But he was alone — lonely — on a dark, stormy night, and starting with hard liquor had felt like asking for trouble.

Of course, he *was* talking to Bastion, so he was, almost literally, asking for trouble.

Dante might have looked the part, ink covering every inch of bare skin, long hair, piercings in his ears, his lip, lower...but Bastion Kane was the rock and roll star, and when he raised hell and fought for revolutions, he meant it with every fiber of his being. Dante, Dante was just a part-time bartender, full-time inker, who was completely and pathetically alone now that his receptionist had taken off for greener pastures.

Why not go up to The Ranch tonight? came Bastion's reply. *Blow off some steam.*

Because they both knew Dante barely played these days. It wasn't that he didn't love and appreciate everything about the intimate club he'd built with six of his best friends in the wilds of the Montana mountains. He did. The Ranch, which was the hidden, secret part of a mountain lodge for tourists, was built on the land they'd been left from the one man most of them had been able to call a father, Beau Sinclair.

Beau had mentored them all in one way or another since he'd inherited the lot of seven rowdy, amped-up teenagers that one summer. Teenagers who had needed friendship and a hearty meal more than discipline and rejection. The Sinclair Seven—Caleb, Reece, Gabriel, Rafael, Bastion, Donavan. And Dante. It had been them against the goddamned world that summer.

And when Beau had died, he'd left them another gift, a gift that had tied them all together for good, even after they'd been scattered to the winds of the world. His ranch. They'd converted part into a lodge, but turned the other, the part that only approved visitors ever got to see, into a club for people like them, with similar wants and desires, hidden needs in hidden mountains.

Normally, Dante would be up at The Ranch right now, slinging drinks and flirting with anyone in a pair of cowboy boots, and shooting the shit with the men he thought of as brothers. But in the past year, three of those brothers had found themselves women worth settling down for. Dante couldn't have been happier for them. Skylar, Morgan, and Emerson made his friends the best versions of themselves. They brought light and joy into all their lives, and Dante knew they were all heading off their own adventures.

It was just...

Fuck, sometimes it was just hard to watch. It wasn't that he was jealous. Except sometimes it was hard to return to his shop after a night shift at The Ranch, cold and empty, from the warm, glowing light of the lodge. Especially on a night like this one, where the rain turned to sleet before it hit the ground, and he was, as of eight that morning, officially on his own running the shop.

Not in the mood.

He wrote back. Not that Bastion wouldn't jump on it. Despite a grueling touring schedule, with their lives barely interacting when he was on the road, Bastion knew Dante. Maybe better than anyone.

Too many happy couples?

Too many happy couples.

It wasn't like he'd been interested in Lia. But there was something to be said about greeting another living soul when he walked into work. She hadn't been great at the job, but he'd needed the help running his one-man ink operation, and she was able to book appointments and manage payments well enough. But she wasn't meant for small town Montana, and less than a month after arriving, she'd caught the first bus to Helena.

You could find someone. You're not that hard to look at.

Despite himself, Dante chuckled. They'd both been hellions in their youth, and that hadn't been limited to hand jobs in the barn while the others mended fences or helped train horses. At the time, it had seemed like such rebellion, such a *fuck you* to the small town that had raised them, mind, body, and soul, and it had taken Bastion years of rock star life to finally put words to it. It had taken Dante longer. Now, occasional flirtation aside, they had the solidarity of their identities to keep them warm at night.

You're only being a brat because I'm a thousand miles away.

I'm only being a brat because you're notoriously not a brat tamer, Bastion wrote back. *And I'm serious, what's stopping you from finding someone?*

Dante was about six GIFs deep of middle fingers, when the conversation at the booth beside him snagged his attention.

"Is there any chance you're hiring?" the woman asked Maisie. "I have serving experience."

"You know what, let me ask in the back," Maisie said. "I'll get you some more tea, too."

"Oh." The woman's voice sounded small, sad even, and Dante felt that familiar rush he always did to *care*, to lift the burdens of the world off the shoulders of those in his orbit, if only for a moment. "That's all right."

"It's no charge," Maisie said, though Dante knew for a fact that Hal's diner and bar didn't do free refills. "You're still shivering. Be right back."

Before the mystery woman could protest again, Maisie had walked away from the table, and as she walked past his booth, Dante caught her eye.

"Put it on my tab," he said, without much thought. It wasn't like Maisie had the means to go around covering bills this way and that, even for something as simple as a hot tea. After year of listening to Gabriel's expertise on high yield savings accounts and portfolios and diversification, Dante was more than set. And business was good. Surprisingly good for a small-town shop, but he had a loyal cadre of followers and fans who often trekked into the mountains for art, and who he was more than grateful for. He could afford to be generous. "And throw in a slice of apple pie."

"You're a good man, Dante Castiglione," Maisie said. "Listen, I'm going to ask Hal in the back, but I already know what he's going to say. There's no extra shifts here, and that poor girl looks like she could use the mother of all breaks. Do you have any room at the shop?"

Dante. Bastion pinged his phone again. *Don't ignore me when I'm trying to talk about your love life.*

Dante didn't answer. He just slid the phone into his pocket and walked over to the booth at the far end of the bar. He'd learned long ago that life wasn't fair, and the universe didn't hold the scales of justice up to every soul for weight and measurement. So when a gift did fall into his lap, well, he wasn't about to walk from it. No way. He was going to take that sucker all the way to the bank. And it had absolutely nothing to do with Bastion's ribbing or his dark apartment and lonely shop or the fact that all his brothers had found the women of their dreams.

Nope. Nothing to do with that, at all.

Chapter Three

Saint bounced her leg as she watched Maisie walk back toward the kitchen. She didn't mean to, but a sudden bout of nerves had taken over in the minute since she had opened her mouth, and adrenaline and nauseous panic were flooding her system too quickly to manage, making her jittery and sweaty, even with the sleeting rain and mountain cold just outside.

Nerves and a desperate need to survive had gotten her this far, but she couldn't make it across the country without an influx of cash, at least enough to get the gas gauge fixed. More than that, she was exhausted, unable to get a good night's sleep in her car, in desperate need of a shower and already burned out on truck stop coffee and stale snacks. All of a sudden, in a way she didn't want to acknowledge, but it seemed her body already knew way too well, Saint needed this job.

A job she was fairly certain, given the amount of time Maisie was spending in the back, she wasn't about to get.

Maybe in the next town.

She tried to calm herself, using the technique Gram had shown her several lifetimes ago. But counting to ten and deep breathing wasn't going to find her a warm place to sleep for the night, and it certainly wasn't going to put more money in her pocket.

Her knee bounced so high it hit the bottom of the table and made the teacup jangle against the saucer.

"Whoa there, cowgirl." She heard a man's voice before she saw the long line of his shadow across the table. "You keep bucking that hard and someone's liable to get hurt."

The addition to her pity party was so unexpected that it actually made Saint's knee jerk mid-jump, and for a second, maybe two, the panic ebbed.

Sometimes all you need is a second.

Gram Violet, always in her ear.

Right now, she needed a hell of a lot more than one second to assess the situation, why a strange man was approaching her table, and exactly how much danger she was in. She was alone. In a bar in a small town in the middle of a sleet storm with a car that was completely out of gas, and not enough cash to get her back on the highway.

So. A lot.

"I'm not looking for company," she said, proud to hear her own voice coming out steady and strong. She didn't need anyone to know she was worried about how this situation might go, especially the man who was currently standing in shadow, his large size blocking the lamp swinging over her booth.

"I'm sure you're not," he said. "But I did hear you might be looking for a job."

That made Saint's head snap up, and her heart pound so loudly she was sure the strange man could hear.

"Let me start again." He pulled a chair from a nearby table and spun it around, before sitting down, his arms draped over the back of the chair.

His very tattooed arms.

Tattooed *everything*. His fingers, wrists, forearms, they were all covered in ropes of ink, some intricate and detailed, the finest work of a master artist, others bold and unapologetic, a declaration from someone fearless, or someone afraid and not willing to let the fear take over their life.

So not me, then.

She'd been afraid for twenty-three years. She was still afraid.

"I'm Dante."

She looked at him then, really looked at him for the first time since he had appeared above her, and Saint's heart beat and her knees trembled for an entirely different reason.

If there was any truth to be found in the pages of scripture, it was that Lucifer had been a beautiful angel.

The man before her was nothing short of a fallen angel, beauty at celestial crossroads with his devilishness, his pitch-black hair swirling in perfect curls against his shoulders, his storm-blue eyes rimmed with black halos and framed with coal dark lashes. He was sinew and strength in his easy, almost lazy stance, and his bare forearms were corded with thick muscle below the twining ink stories.

"Dante?" she repeated, because it almost felt absurd, that a man who could so easily lead to sin and temptation would be named for the poet who descended into hell's very depths.

"My mother had her reasons," he said, cocking his head to the side, as if trying to read her thoughts. She'd love whatever information he was able to discern, because at the moment, she couldn't be certain which way was up. "What would your name be?"

Saint hesitated. She was here for a reason. A damned good reason, as far as reasons went, and the last thing she wanted to do was draw attention to herself by using an uncommon name in a tiny town while on the run for her very life.

"Violet." Her grandmother's name slipped from her lips. Violet was common enough. Violet made her feel safe and protected, like Gram was still there to wrap her arms around her, thin and cool as they had been toward the end, and tell Saint it would be all right.

Nothing is ever going to be all right again.

But, fallen or not, this strange man was, in the moment at least, the angel offering to save her butt, and she had to hear him out. She didn't have a choice.

"It's nice to meet you, Violet," he said, the name lingering on his lips a moment too long, like he was tasting every word with the tongue that a second glance told her was double pierced down the middle. "Welcome to Duchess."

"I didn't see a sign when I pulled in," she said, not sure why she was offering any more information than strictly necessary, and not quite able to stop herself. With the exception of Maisie, who had kindly brought her towels and tea, she hadn't had a friendly ear in three days. So much longer than that, if Saint were being honest with herself, which she really didn't feel like being in the moment. "My gas gauge is... I thought I had more time to find a place to fuel up."

With all forty bucks I have left.

"Your car is in the lot?" he asked, and Saint nodded.

"Well, I happen to be pretty good with my hands." The words sounded like an innuendo they shouldn't have been from a man who looked like *that*, dark and promising and disappearing behind the curtain of sin and decadence, a curtain Saint had never stepped through herself. But she got the distinct impression that he genuinely meant them, especially when he added. "You can leave it there tonight and I'll take a peek in the morning. If you want to, that is."

"I don't think I have much of a choice," Saint admitted. "I rolled over here on fumes." In more ways than one.

"Hence the job?"

She looked down at her lap when she asked, "What kind of work are you offering, exactly?" How far exactly was she willing to go to get out of here? To get to New York and to start her new life? The job situation was dire, but when did she cross lines she hadn't realized were drawn in her own heart and soul?

Apparently, her war wasn't entirely internal, because Dante spoke again.

"Hey there, none of that. Nothing untoward."

He reached out, but he came just short of touching her, for which Saint was grateful. At this point, it wouldn't take all that much to melt the hard exterior she'd built, and there would be no one to put the pieces back together when she fell apart. "I know you're probably in survival mode right now, but I think I can help you. If you'll let me."

Bastion had always said that Dante picked up strays. He'd saved more than one box of kittens and lost, raggedy dog on the side of the road, he'd admit. And he did tend to see lost souls wherever he went. Maybe it was because he'd been that raggedy dog on the side of the road once upon a time. Maybe it was because he didn't just scene as the caretaker and pleasure Dom, but he'd lived his life that way since he'd first understood his desires were a little more specific and intense than most. Maybe he'd never really know, but the one thing Dante knew for fucking certain was that the woman in front of him needed help.

The beautiful young woman.

Young. *Young.*

She couldn't have been more than twenty-two or twenty-three, putting more than a decade between them, and giving him all the more reason to set some very sturdy boundaries out of the gate. Especially since she looked ready to rabbit the very first chance that she got, and in this weather with a car that needed work, she wouldn't get very far.

"I can give you room and board," he added. He'd been planning on offering it anyway, since that had been what he offered Lia, but it was all too apparent that this girl needed to know the terms were good before she agreed to anything. "And plenty of hours."

"What's the job?" she asked after a moment, her eyes still downcast, and her shoulders hunched around herself. He knew survival mode like he knew every line of ink he'd painted on his own hands.

"Reception and admin for my shop," he said. "My last receptionist quit yesterday."

"Why'd she quit?" She narrowed her eyes at him, piercing, bright blue eyes that couldn't hold a secret or hide an emotion. They made him want to confess to things he wasn't sure he'd done.

"We had a torrid love affair and when I begged her to marry me, she ran off with the strong man from the traveling circus," Dante said drolly. She blinked at him, those long coal lashes so dark against her pale skin. "I'm kidding. She wanted to live in a bigger city, so she moved to Helena."

She scoffed, as if enjoying a private joke with herself, then squared her jaw.

"One month," she said. "And I'll need to be paid in cash."

Yeah, this girl was in survival mode. She was definitely running from something, most likely an ex-boyfriend who'd been responsible for the skittishness and the dark circles under her eyes, and the white knight instinct flared deep and hot in his chest.

"I can do that," he said. "For a month. If you want to stay longer, you'll be on the books."

"I won't," she said, more to herself than to him. "But thank you."

The genuine gratitude in her voice threw him, and Dante took a deep breath to keep from reaching out and gathering her in his arms. She'd bolt, no matter what he offered to pay her, if he did that, and the overwhelming desire to protect this woman was settling deep into his bones like a familiar, old friend. Instead, he stood and moved the chair back to the neighboring table, then held out his hand to her.

"Should we shake on it?" he asked, hoping that the terrified look in her eyes would fade with time. Hoping, very much against his better judgment, that he'd be the one to help warm her back to the world.

"As long as I don't have to sign anything," she said. Then she took his hand and shook. Slight, pale fingers, rough at the tips like she'd worked service or labor for too many years, a single silver band on her index finger, tipped with an opal, each detail softening and framing her in a way Dante knew would leave lasting damage if he got too close. One month, that was what they were shaking on now. One month and he'd never see this woman again.

"Come on, let's get your stuff from the car," he said, pulling back and trying not to think about the way her small but steady hand felt against his own. Anything but that.

"I still have to pay for dinner," she said, reaching for her bag. Before Dante could say anything, Maisie sidled up to their table.

"Your new boss already took care of it," she said, handing Violet a to-go bag with her food and the slice of apple pie he'd ordered. "Left me a twenty-five percent tip, too, so you don't need to worry about that."

Violet turned to him with narrowed eyes. "And if I hadn't accepted the job?" she asked.

"Then you would have had a good hot meal and a warm place to enjoy it," he replied. "But you did, and we shook on it, so it's too late to back down now."

He stepped away from the booth, but not so far away that he didn't hear Maisie loudly whisper that Violet would be safe with him, and that she could always call if she needed anything. Out of the corner of his eye, he watched Maisie write her number on a slip of paper and pat Violet on the shoulder before taking off for her next table.

"She says I can trust you," Violet said, coming to stand next to him. She was taller than he expected, huddled as she had been in the booth, but even with the extra inches, she barely came up to his chest, and not for the first time, he was acutely aware of how fragile she looked, how terrified and strong all in one.

"You can," he said. It should have gone without saying, but it very much seemed like this woman needed him to say it. "I won't hurt you."

As for him getting hurt, well, Dante wasn't nearly so sure about that.

Chapter Four

Saint woke in a panic.

Her skin was slick and hot, her breath caught in her chest, part sob and part scream, and she was tangled in the sheets.

Sheets.

She hadn't slept in a bed in days. This wasn't the cramped passenger seat of her little compact. This was...

Where am I?

She took a deep breath and looked around the room. Light streamed in from behind the blinds on the far wall and cast the room in a soft golden glow. Her duffel bag and backpack were piled on the large chair in the corner, and she had a glass of water on the table beside the bed. It was too warm and inviting to be a motel, and it was all-too clear that someone had taken care to create a space worth staying in.

Not just someone.

The man from the bar.

Dante.

Her new boss.

After Maisie had assured her that Dante Castiglione was safe, despite his very dangerous outward appearance, Saint had led him to her car in the sleeting rain and grabbed her necessities. She'd expected to drive somewhere else, but Dante had led her around the back of the building and up a flight of stairs to his apartments, where he'd shown her to her room.

Her room. For the next month, at least.

She'd been so grateful to have a real bed, to have a plan in place that would get her back on her feet, that she hadn't lasted five minutes before completely passing out into a dreamless, dark sleep, the kind her body had been craving for days.

She felt refreshed, awake, and was thinking clearly for the first time since leaving Seattle. And the very first thing she wanted to do was take the longest shower in history.

To her delight, the door off the bedroom led to a private bath, and it wasn't long before she was steaming up the room and scrubbing the road off her skin. Washing her face in truck stop bathrooms hadn't exactly done the trick, and she took her time, enjoying the way the hot water seemed to cleanse her soul as much as her body. There was something to be said about feeling confident, and when she stepped out of the shower, her skin pink and her hair clean and fresh, she felt more like herself than she had in so long.

And she had him to thank for it.

A twinge of guilt prickled at the back of her mind. No doubt, Dante knew she was in some kind of trouble. He seemed the type to want to go around saving people in dire straits, and she would have been more peeved about that if her own straits had been less dire. Still, staying in one place was risky, even if she didn't have any other choice, and if the things she was running from turned out to chasing her, well, he might just get caught in the crossfire.

I'll tell him if I need to.

So far, she hadn't seen any indication that she was being followed, nothing that made her hair stand on end or her neck prickle, and Saint had to wonder if it was somehow possible that she'd gone far enough fast enough to be out of the direct line of danger. And to keep danger from his doorstep.

My doorstep, for now.

She kissed her Gram's ring and made the promise a second time, a practice she'd picked up a million years ago. *A promise to yourself is just as important as a promise to a friend,* Violet had said. *Sometimes more. Make it official.* So, Saint kissed the ring and said quietly to her reflection in the mirror, "I'll tell him if I need to."

If something happened. If she got the slightest inkling that danger was headed her way, she'd let him know. Or she'd leave. But she wouldn't repay his kindness with pain of any kind.

With that in mind, she dressed for her first day on the job—whatever the job was. In all the chaos of the night, she wasn't entirely sure what his business was, or what she'd be acting as a receptionist for. Not that she could dress the part, even if she did know. Most of her clothes needed to be washed, and she only had the one pair of shoes. Still, she wanted to feel confident in whatever the job was, so she pulled on her last clean pair of leggings and an oversized pink sweater to stave off the chilly morning, then wrapped her hair in a long ponytail and dabbed on a little mascara for the first time in weeks. Then she followed the scent of brewing coffee with her head held high.

Gone was the little scared rabbit from the bar. The woman who stepped into his kitchen was confident, bright and smiling, no trepidation behind her blue eyes, no closed off shoulders or hunched back. She had a spring in her step that made her...

Well, it made her something Dante definitely shouldn't be thinking, not as her boss and not as the man ten years older than her. Beautiful. Glorious. Enticing.

Innocent.

Too, too innocent with that waterfall of blonde hair and the soft pink sweater and the touch of gloss on her full lips. Inside him, a war waged, to protect and care for this little sprite who'd fallen into his path, or to wreck her makeup and stain her cheeks, the prey caught in his web.

He did neither.

"Coffee?"

"Please." She settled at his kitchen counter, and he was struck by how right it felt to see her there, like she'd been sitting down to breakfast with him for as long as he could remember. Maybe he was lonelier than he thought.

"You look refreshed this morning," he said, pouring her a cup and indicating to the cream. When she nodded, he poured some in. "Did you sleep well?"

"By sleep well, do you mean completely pass out the second my head hit the pillow?" she asked, accepting the coffee with a smile that seemed to somehow burst inside him. "I did, thank you. And if I didn't say it enough last night, thank you for all of this. I don't know what I would have done without your help."

He'd gotten that impression the night before, that she was in a mess of some kind, and he'd gone ahead and welcomed that mess into his life. His home. Because people deserved to be helped, even when it wasn't easy or convenient.

"What kind of trouble are you in?" he asked, regretting the question when her back stiffened and the glow left her pretty blue eyes. He shook his head. "I'm not going to change my mind about hiring you. I told you, Violet, you can trust me."

"Can you trust me?" she asked. "Even if I don't tell you why I'm here?"

"That depends," he replied. "Is your ex-boyfriend going to show up at my door with a shotgun?"

"No ex-boyfriend," she said quickly. "Nothing like that."

"Then what is it like?" he asked. "I would like to know how prepared for trouble I should be."

Not that he hadn't spent his entire life prepared for trouble. For good reason.

"It's best you don't know," Violet said. "But if that changes, I promise I'll tell you then. Okay?"

He looked at her across the kitchen island, held those blue eyes and searched for deceit, for any sign of dishonesty, and found none. All Dante could see was a woman in trouble, and a way to help her.

"Okay," he said. "But you'll tell me. If you're scared, if something happens. And if the time comes for me to ask questions, you'll answer them." He hadn't meant for that to come out with the dark Dom tone normally reserved for nights at The Ranch, but the words were this side of demanding, this side of intense that triggered the harsh, carnal part of him. He wanted to *care* for this woman, in a visceral and overwhelming way, and the animal side of his brain was having a very hard time finding the difference between helping a stranger get on her feet and helping a sweet little sub lose the ability to stand.

"I will."

He even thought she might mean it.

"Now, we've got a big day ahead of us, and my guess is you haven't eaten enough in the past few days," he said, filling a plate with toast and eggs from the pan on the stove. "So eat up."

"I realize I never asked last night," she said, and to his pleasure, she didn't argue about the large plate of food. "What kind of business do you run?"

Dante grinned and flexed his fingers, the ink rippling along the corded muscles and strong bones.

"A tattoo shop, of course."

Chapter Five

Saint walked down the stairs from Dante's apartments to the studio below, her heart in her throat. *Of course* he ran a tattoo shop. He was covered from his knuckles to his throat in bands of black and green and purple ink, snatches of stories she'd confess only in the dark to wanting to read. What else could he do, but own a tattoo shop, with black earrings looped into each ear, and that daring glint of silver that flashed every time he spoke. This morning, in fact, he'd added another looping ring to his lip, and rather than making him look feminine or delicate, which could have been all too possible given his jaunty cheekbones and purple-gray eyes, it made him look dangerous. Made him look....

Tempting.

Not for her. Saint wasn't tempted, not by this strange man who had walked into her orbit and given her a life preserver when she'd needed it most. It was...interest, that was all. Interest and curiosity. She'd grown up in the backs of restaurants, and line cooks and chefs alike were tattooed and ripped around the edges, but there was something altogether more intense about Dante than any of the men she'd known back in Seattle.

It should have scared her.

He should have scared her, especially as she watched him settle into the studio with such incredible ease and grace, born to the space and the world it represented. But he didn't. Not now, after everything she'd been through. Desperation really did make strange bedfellows, it seemed, and Dante Castiglione was the strangest of all.

Not bedfellows. *Not* bedfellows.

Bosses and employees. Boss.

She'd do well to remember that next time she stared a little too long at the ink lines on his muscled forearms. To remember that he was her lifeline out of here, and not some incarnate fantasy of boss and secretary playing out in real time.

"Welcome to Inferno Tattoos," he said, gesturing to the studio.

"Isn't that a little on the nose?" she asked, turning around in a circle to look at the space, as Dante flipped on lights and opened the blinds to let the winter light stream in. "Really leaning into the levels of hell thing, there."

"Well, the source material is *right there*," he joked, chocking himself against the front desk. "And it makes for some great inspiration."

Inspiration was right. The entire studio was covered in art, from delicate fine line work to bold and thick designs, classic, iconic characters, and totally unique illustrations she'd never seen anywhere else. It was a crash course in alternate media she would never have studied, even if her life had gone a different way, and for the first time in so long, she felt a brick on the wall of creative blockage shake.

"These are incredible," she murmured, more to herself than anything. When was the last time she'd seen an artist with such a range of talents and skills? Never. "You're a master…"

Dante stiffened, the move unexpected and strange from this man she'd only known for a handful of hours, but whom she'd seen only loose-limbed and jovial since their meeting.

"Maybe master isn't quite the right phrase," he said. "At least not for that. But thank you."

She filed that strange comment away for later and stepped up to an image of a cherry blossom tree that took up a large section of the wall. "Can you do all kinds of flowers?"

"I can do anything you want."

Those words sent a burning ember of heat from her lips to her belly, bursting a little too bright to see, and a little too hard to ignore. But ignore it, Saint did. She needed to ignore everything burning between them if she wanted to make it through the next month as his receptionist — and that was the only way she was going to survive.

"I might have a commission for you," she said, hoping he wouldn't notice the husky edge to her voice. "But first, show me the ropes."

Dante let out a low laugh and shook his head, as if he knew a secret it would be dangerous to share, then indicated for her to sit at the front desk.

"Here's everything you need to know."

* * * *

The day went by in a blur, but for the first time, Dante wasn't dead on his feet by the time he locked the front door and turned the sign. Lia hadn't been great at her job, whether from incompetence or disinterest, he hadn't had time to figure out, and he'd spent half of his days correcting simple mistakes she'd made between appointments.

Violet, on the other hand, was a natural. She took to the daily tasks with grace, placing orders, posting payments, and setting his schedule for the following week. She took pictures of his clients' tattoos and posted them to his long-ignored social media channels, and she had a granola bar and coffee in hand when there was a lull in his back-to-back appointments. But most importantly, she put people at ease. It was the mega-watt smile that welcomed in newbies with nerves in their eyes, and softened the gruff on the inked-up dudes looking for one last patch of bare skin to tell their stories. She answered the phone with genuine joy, answered all the questions she could and directed the remaining ones to him, and brought something to the shop that he hadn't realized had been missing. Sunshine. Brightness. A sense of togetherness he hadn't felt in too long.

And that was dangerous for all its own reasons.

But Dante wasn't about to look a gift horse in the mouth, and if this woman made his life a little easier for the next few weeks, he'd take what he could get.

Only in the most obvious sense. The rest of it, the way she so blithely used words that made his carnal self want to take control, that part was firmly off-limits and locked away hard and fast behind closed doors. And would remain that way.

Even if the word *master* on her lips was something out of his most depraved fantasies. For a thousand reasons, she could never know what kind of man he was.

"Pizza or burritos?" he asked, as they climbed the steps to the apartment. "My treat."

"That's not necessary," Violet replied. "Just take it out of my pay."

"Boss makes the rules," he said. "And boss wants to pay."

"Does boss pick the movie we watch too?"

He'd watch just about any made-for-TV Christmas romance movie to keep that smile on her face. But he *did* have a reputation to uphold.

"Boss picks the genre."

She grinned and scampered up the stairs, swishing that long blond ponytail before him. Dante reached for the banister and held tight, just for a moment. Because the urge to reach out and grab that soft, silvery hair in his hand, to pull until she followed his touch and bared her throat to him, to watch the flexing movements of his dark inked fingers against her untainted skin, it made him *ache*.

This isn't The Ranch.

And he was worse for it. Because he hadn't felt that kind of burning hot desire for any woman who'd walked into his club in too long. Sure, he'd danced the menage with Caleb and Skylar on occasion, and he pushed Emerson's buttons just to see what Gabriel would do, but there was something carnal and untethered about the way he wanted to see this blonde sprite laid out on his bed and thoroughly, completely ravished. He was supposed to be getting his head on straight, not thinking about the number of times he could make her come all over his fingers and mouth and cock, but he'd been watching her out of the corner of his eye all day, and if Dante knew anything about anything, it was that men were only so strong.

You invited the lamb into the lion's den.

As if the universe liked its trouble in pairs, his phone buzzed in his pocket.

Heard you hired a new assistant.

Bastion was supposed to be on stage somewhere, *not* harassing the man he called a friend about the very limited social circle he kept these days.

How the fuck do you know that?

I know everything.

Who told you?

Because apparently his hard-broiled, adventure-ready, dominant in the bedroom and in life friends were nothing more than gossipy little shits. Not that they hadn't accused him of much the same when they'd been in shit with their women, but the beautiful little blonde who was settling onto her couch in a very, *very* familiar way was not his woman, and she never would be.

They all did.

Dante sighed and slid his phone back into his pocket. Bastion was halfway across the country, New York or Chicago or Miami, he could never keep up. But Violet was sitting on his couch right now, and he was very certain which of the two he'd rather be focusing on right at that moment.

"What's with the sour puss?" she asked, sitting up on her knees to look at him over the back of the couch, which had Dante thinking of all the other things she could on her knees, her perky little breasts curving just so under that little pink sweater, her glossy lips wrapping...

He coughed.

"Sour puss?" he teased. "Are you a hundred years old?"

Violet gave him a sad smile. "It was something my grandmother used to say," she said quietly. "I guess I picked up a few of her phrases over the years."

"Well, as long as you don't start offering me licorice from your purse..."

She pulled her shoulders up around her ears.

"Why, young man, would you like a sweetie? Watch out for the cat hair..."

The words were barely out of her mouth before Violet was falling back on the couch in a fit of self-inflicted giggles. Dante couldn't help but laugh with her. She was infectious in that lightness, as if she'd forgotten all of the shit—and there had undoubtedly been shit—that had gotten her to Duchess, to the bar, to his shop. It was like she was putting the weight of the world down and he was the only one around to see her do it.

"Who are you calling young man?" he asked, when she finally came up for air.

"Would you rather I called you old?" she shot back with a smirk. "I'm going to say forty-two..."

"Forty-two, you little shit." He turned so she couldn't see the look on his face, undoubtedly equal parts arousal and amusement. If she was his, the way his cock was clearly aching for, she'd been flat on her back and begging for mercy for the cheek. And he wouldn't give it, not for a long, long time.

"Dante..." Her voice, so full of humor the moment before, dropped low and soft, as if she was reverting back, turning into the woman he'd seen at the bar, the one who'd called to his baser self to save, to protect, to care for. "Thank you."

He knew she wasn't thanking him for the job, or even the spare room, not really. When the world had felt too big and too scary and too alone, logistics had been logistics, a matter of *if* and *how*. But a safe place, a listening ear, room to put the burden down, that had been all he'd ever wanted. Beau Sinclair had given him that, and the other Sinclair Seven, as they'd been called that summer. He'd found respite, when he'd thought he'd been so incredible alone.

So instead of offering her platitude, instead of writing off the words the way instinct told him to do, he turned and held her bright blue eyes, so full of hope, so full of peace, for the moment, at least.

"It's good to hear you laugh," he said.

Chapter Six

She was getting too comfortable. Saint knew that. She'd told Dante one month and she had meant it with every fiber of her being. New York was still her final destination, and she was still far too close to Seattle to feel like she could stop looking over her shoulder. Around him, though, she could put her guard down, and that was altogether a stupid thing to think. She couldn't put her guard down until she got across the country. Maybe she'd never be able to.

But after just a few days of the routine, sharing a cup of coffee over his kitchen island, then walking down to the studio together, Saint could already breathe again. He still knew nothing about her, not what she was running from, not even her real name, but somehow it felt as though they'd been friends for years. Dante looked gruff and intense, with the piercings he swapped out every morning, the same way he swapped the shades of flannel he wore over his ripped jeans and cuffed up over the rivers of ink that covered every inch of his exposed skin, but he was easy to be around, funny and kind. Maisie hadn't been wrong when she'd said Saint could trust him.

Her concern was that she was starting to do more than trust him. She was starting to like spending time with him, to look forward to the moments after they closed the shop, when they shared dinner on the couch and talked about his work and the clients that had come in that day. He could cook, genuine, delicious Italian food, not that she could be all that surprised, and they shared a love of action movies and terrible television that made Saint's heart ache a little. In another life, she'd have dreamed of a man like him.

A much different, less colorful, less intense version of him.

Because he had his moments of intensity. The way he walked carefully around her past, around what had brought her to Duchess, it spoke of personal experience and understanding, and when his guard dropped there was a shadow in his eyes that made her so incredibly sad. A man with a heart as generous as his should never have to suffer, even if it was likely the suffering had made him, in part, so willing to take in a roughened-up stray like her.

And that wasn't the only kind of intensity either. Lust wasn't something Saint had all too much experience with—*try no experience*—but sometimes, when he thought she wasn't looking, he would watch her the way a lion watched its prey, like he wanted to devour her, to *consume* her. The weight of his gaze would make her belly go hot and chest tighten, and she'd find it difficult to concentrate on whatever she was saying to a client at her desk.

Thankfully, there was plenty to distract her at the studio, including the arrival of new clients, a blond-haired man and a sporty-looking woman, with her long brunette hair braided down her back.

"Reservation name?" she asked, standing from the chair behind the desk.

"They have a standing reservation," Dante said, coming up behind her. He was too close for comfort, close enough that she could smell that familiar artist scent, ink and metal, charcoal. Dante. The warmth of his arm pressing against hers as he clicked on the day's schedule was nearly enough to make her lose focus.

"Violet, this is Reece and Morgan. My new receptionist."

Reece gave her a long, appraising look, then turned back to Dante.

"Well, I was going to ask why you hadn't been up to The Ranch in a few days, but now I'm not wondering anymore." He stuck his hand out to her. "Great to meet you. I hope you're not letting him boss you around too much."

Beside him, Morgan let out a low laugh, and Dante stiffened at Saint's side.

"He is my boss," she managed to say. "For now."

"This town has a way of capturing people's hearts," Morgan said, extending her hand to shake Saint's, as well. "I was quite the adventurer before I ran into this one."

"Some might say you're still very adventurous, Little Storm," Reece whispered low, and Saint had to wonder if the words were even meant to reach her.

"He's just mad he can't keep up," Morgan said with a wink. "I reached the summit before him yesterday."

"You two are going to get stuck in a snowstorm and we're going to have to call out the S&R guys," Dante said, finally, blessedly stepping back from Saint's side enough for her to take a breath.

"Lily's husbands have already offered us both jobs at the training camp," Morgan replied. "Who would even be rescuing who?"

"I'm sorry, did you say husbands?" Saint asked, before she could stop herself. She was from Seattle, and she *had* spent a semester at art school, so the nuances of human relationships weren't entirely lost on her, even if she didn't quite know them firsthand. But the idea of those kind of dynamics being so openly accepted in such a small town was unexpected, to say the least.

Morgan cracked a grin. "She's not the only one..." she whispered conspiratorially. "Her sister runs an inn out in Wolf Creek, and she has two husbands, too, and the sheriff and the fire captain are also in a relationship with their high school sweetheart, *and* Skylar's best friend from back in D.C. is dating *two* FBI agents. She's also an FBI agent, I just thought that made it sound interesting."

Saint laughed. "It did. What is this town...?"

Morgan cocked her head, and turned to Dante, but the question was entirely for Saint when she asked, "You don't know about The Ranch?"

"What about The Ranch?" Saint asked, feeling all of a sudden very naïve. She wasn't a princess trapped in a castle, with no understanding of the world of pleasure or intimacy, but life hadn't exactly worked out the way she had been expecting, and more than a few important things had gotten pushed to the back, back burner.

"The Ranch is the lodge I help run," Dante said, before Morgan could continue. "We spent a summer up there when we were teens, and they called us the Sinclair Seven after the old man who owned it. When he died, he left it to us."

Saint turned to Reece. "One of the Seven, then?" she asked.

He nodded. "One of the Seven. Caleb, Dante, Van and I are the ones in town most of the year. Gabriel's here more now with the foundation, and Bastion and Rafe are our restless wanderers."

"Not too long ago you were a restless wanderer," Dante pointed out.

Reece shrugged. "Love makes you do funny things, man. Speaking of, can I get my girl's name tattooed on my ass?"

"No."

"Fine, fine, here's what I'm actually thinking…"

When they walked away, Morgan leaned over the counter. "I hope we didn't make you feel uncomfortable with all that talk," she said. "I just assumed… Well, it's no matter. If you're a friend of Dante's, you're a friend of ours."

"I was just a little surprised," Saint said. "I guess I assumed a town this small would be a little more buttoned up."

"Duchess has its secrets," Morgan said. "If you ask him, he'll tell you."

"I don't think that's such a good idea," Saint admitted. "I'm only here for a little while, it's best I don't get too comfortable."

Morgan looked at her then, and Saint got the impression that she saw a little too much, like she could edge out secret Saint had never mean to share.

"That's too bad," she said, and it sounded as though she actually meant it. "You might be just what he needs."

* * * *

She had been staring at the ceiling above her bed for two hours when Saint finally sat up and reached for the laptop Dante had lent her. She'd insisted it was too much, and that he had no reason to trust she wouldn't just leave with it and sell it for cash, but he'd been direct and clear when he said if she was that desperate, it was better in, or out, of her hands.

She flipped the light on, then immediately turned it off, because what she was about to do was sneaky in the extreme, and she didn't need any extra light to examine herself in.

The Ranch. Duchess, Montana.

Searching for a ranch in Montana was like searching for a hipster café in Seattle. She might as well have been trying to find a fish in the ocean.

Secret ranch in Duchess Montana…

That just brought up some romance novel about secret cowboy babies.

Morgan had been…alluding to something, something Dante had clearly stopped her from talking about, and that had spiked Saint's curiosity enough that she was now furiously searching for secrets in the middle of the night. She took a deep breath and entered in a phrase she'd never, ever would have thought about before.

The Ranch, Montana. Sex club.

And there it was. The page was discreet, of course. Knowing what she did of Dante's style and artistic skill, it would have surprised her if the page had been gaudy or over the top, but it wasn't, just classic western motifs and innuendo. There were links she didn't dare to click, the club waiver, how to apply for an invitation, rules and regulations. Acceptable practices.

Acceptable practices.

Was that a list, then? Would she find a manual of all the…desires of the people at the club?

Did Dante have those desires?

Maybe Master isn't quite the right phrase. At least, not for that.

He was a contradiction of a man, she knew, dark ink and bright humor, intensity and intense kindness. That he'd opened his doors to her with such generosity told her a million things. Maybe one of the things she didn't yet know was that he had a secret, intense type of desire, one that demanded more than the average.

Not that she knew what the average demanded.

She closed the browser and shut the laptop so quickly she nearly startled herself. This was ridiculous. She was in Montana out of desperation, working in the studio for enough money to get herself across the country. She didn't need to be thinking about her boss'…predilections, whatever they might be. If he ran some sort of secret club in the mountains, well it was no business of hers, just like it was no business of his what she had or hadn't done in her private life.

Except, she hadn't thought much of that non-existent private life in so, so long, and in just a few days in his presence, it was *all* she could think about. It was like some dormant part of her had finally come out of hiding, and Saint found herself battling a demon of curiosity and desire she hadn't ever thought she'd possessed. Maybe it was being on her own, the adrenaline of being on the run, the survival instinct manifesting in some Freudian way.

Or maybe it was just him.

It didn't matter. She would be gone in just over three weeks, and Dante and his club, whatever secrets he might be hiding there, would be well in her rearview mirror.

She would do well to remember it.

Chapter Seven

"How much would a small tattoo cost?" Saint asked over a beer the following week. She had the habit of sitting in the receptionist chair in about every formation except the way the chair was meant to be used, and the current position, with one knee bent and her arm draped over the side gave the impression of casual indifference.

Dante knew better.

He hated that he knew better, but in the two weeks since she had arrived, he'd become innately tuned into her tone and tenor. He could tell when she was genuine, like when she sat down with first timers and walked them through the process, and he could tell when she was putting on a brave face, like when she sat in his studio looking up at him with those crystalline eyes, pretending indifference.

"I'm not going to charge you, Vi," he murmured, flipping through the schedule she'd uploaded to his phone, because sometimes looking at her was physically painful. In more ways than one.

"I want to pay."

"*Mmm*, and I want a Ferrari Testa Rossa in red," he replied, finally looking down at her. "But we can't always get what we want, can we?"

"We can if we beg," she replied, and for the briefest, most fleeting second, Dante had to wonder if she knew more than she was letting on. He hadn't wanted Morgan and Reece to share the particulars of The Ranch, not because he didn't want to bring his pretty little receptionist up the mountain — perhaps again, and again, and again — but because part of him had always worried he was too harsh for pretty things, too stained and dirtied by the world to play with the princess, and Violet was every bit the story princess — his damsel in distress. He couldn't picture her in a place like The Ranch. Or rather, he could picture it all too easily, but he couldn't imagine how a girl like her would react to his world.

And it didn't matter, anyway. She was his receptionist. He was her boss. She was just edging over twenty and he was more than just edging over thirty. Even if she'd looked at him with those bright blue eyes and begged for decadent, indecent things, Dante had to hold firm.

But, of course, his big head and his little head didn't always communicate.

"What are you begging for?" he asked, wondering all at once if maybe he had actually been a masochist the whole time. There was no other reason for putting himself in such a situation.

"For a tattoo," she said, as if it were the most obvious thing in the world. "And to pay for it."

"Vi," he sighed. "I'm not letting you pay for it."

"Why not?" she asked. "Artists deserve recognition for their work. And you're an incredible artist, Dante. I don't want to take advantage of that."

He smiled at her fierceness, at her easy compliment. *Though she be but little…*

"Spoken like a fellow artist," he replied. "And while I happen to agree, it's my gift to give my friends."

"We're friends," she said, as if tasting the word on her tongue for the very first time, as if it were unfamiliar and not to be entirely trusted.

"We binged a whole series of *Fated to the Prince* in an afternoon and ate two boxes of Oreos," he replied. "I think that officially makes us friends." Even if he wanted so, so much more from her than trash TV and junk food.

"I'd like that," she said quietly. "I didn't have too many friends back home."

"Why not?" That got his attention enough that Dante had to put his phone down. "I've seen how you are with the clients. Anyone would want to be your friend." And if he was revealing too much of himself there, well, so be it.

"You're kind," she said quietly, as if still surprised that kindness existed in her world. "And they make it easy. I like helping people. But…"

She paused and took a long, shuddering breath, and not for the first time, Dante wanted to reach for her, to hold her, to make this woman feel the peace and belonging she deserved, but had so clearly been denied.

"My grandmother got sick," she said quietly. "Dementia and all the stuff that comes with it." Her voice was so soft then, so quiet, and it was the first time he had seen her with such a naked type of grief and loneliness. The first night at the bar, she'd been ready to flee or fight, and in the weeks since, he'd become aware of a sense of control and self-reliance he could only attribute to survival. But this woman didn't do quiet, and she didn't do the soft kind of sadness that made his heart break off in chunks, and he didn't like it.

Even if he understood it a little too well.

"You took care of her," he guessed, wishing there was something he could do to erase the sadness in her voice. "Probably all by yourself."

"Her next-door neighbor helped," Violet replied. "Mrs. Lansing. She watched Gram when I went to work."

"Which I'm assuming was most of the time," Dante said. "Medical bills pile up."

"They do. They did." Violet leaned her head on the side of the spinning office chair, and the look made her appear so incredibly innocent, so sweet and loving and without fault. So entirely unlike him. "I haven't had much time for anything else in a long time."

"When was the last time you did something for yourself?" Dante asked. The brightness she brought to the studio every morning, the joy with which she settled into bad television and nights spent on the couch, that was incredibly hard won, and whatever she was running from, it was probably the first time she could relax without waiting for the other shoe to drop, without the guilt of taking time away from her responsibilities. That was something he did understand.

Violet gave him a self-deprecating smile and shook her head, her lips twisting up and down like she was trying to keep herself from crying, and it wrenched at that same sore spot in his chest that made it so difficult for Dante to maintain his distance. He wanted to see those bright eyes smiling up at him again, and he was halfway willing to risk his own peace of mind to do it.

"Okay," he said. "I'll give you your tattoo and you can pay me."

She brightened.

"But not in money."

Chapter Eight

Saint shot him a look. "I thought you said it wasn't that kind of job," she said. God, it felt good to joke. Felt better, still, to tell someone about Gram, about the guilty, private thoughts she'd had about having to sacrifice so much. She'd told no one else about that, and the shame had festered for years now. She loved Gram, loved her fiercely, and would be forever grateful for the life she had been given. But Saint was twenty-three, and it felt like she was just entering the world for the very first time.

Dante just rolled his eyes. "Low-hanging fruit," he replied. "No. To pay for your tattoo we're going to do everything you want to do tonight."

That caught her off-guard.

"What?"

"You haven't done anything for yourself in the years since your grandmother got sick, am I right?"

Saint shook her head. Then she thought about it. Then she nodded.

"Okay then," he continued. "Tonight, we're going to do all the things you want to do. We'll make a list. And if we do all of them, consider that payment."

"Dante." She thought she was past the watery, loose feeling that put her on this side of confessing all her sins, but this act of kindness, this absolute freedom, no guilt, just pure generosity and kindness, it was way, way too much.

"Or you could take the tattoo for free," he said. "Your choice."

"A list it is," Saint said on an incredulous laugh. "Starting with a tattoo."

"Then what?" Dante handed her the notepad they always kept near the phone. "I require at least ten things accomplished."

"Ten is a lot."

"Nine." He looked so fierce on the face, all tattoos and piercings, all dark, beautiful hair. But when he gave her that soft, laughing smile, it made Saint forget, all the hardness, all the reasons she was stuck in this tiny mountain town running for her life.

And tonight, she was going to forget.

"Eight. Final offer," she replied. "Okay, definitely a tattoo," she said, "even if you make me wait until the end for it. And I want to see the stars in the mountains."

He cocked his head to the side. "Consider it done. What's next?"

"I want to take a tequila shot," she said without thinking. The guys in the back of the restaurant would usually end the night with shots—or more—but she always had to end a long shift by caring for her grandmother when she got home, and she'd never indulged with them.

"Scandalous," he teased. "Keep going."

Four, five, and six were buying lotto tickets, going for ice cream, and picking out a new journal, respectively.

"I want to ride on your bike," she said. "For number seven."

"How do you know about the bike?" he asked. "Have you been spying on me?"

"Not even a little bit," she replied. Of course, she had been. It was difficult to stop watching a man like Dante. "I saw your helmet."

"Liar," he said. "You just need one more."

"I'll think," she said. "But right now I want to get started."

He offered her his hand and she took it, loving the way his dark ink contrasted against her pale skin, loving the way his much larger, artist's hand made her feel so small, so feminine.

"Let's start the night with a ride."

In the next ten minutes, Saint was loaded down with a heavy leather jacket and Dante's spare bike helmet, and staring down the barrel of a vintage Moto Guzzi bike. It was deep earth tones, black and brown leather, with ghost illustrations in lighter shades of black along the body and fenders. No doubt Dante's design. He gave her the quick safety run down, instructions for how to communicate when they were on the road, and how to fall off or crash safely.

And then she was climbing on behind him, feeling the plush leather seat accepting their shared weight, as his much larger frame settled in front of her. He was so big, so in her space and completely impossible to ignore, and for a moment, Saint hesitated to lock her arms around his body. This was already too much, already leaps and bounds beyond the acceptable levels of intimacy that would still allow her to leave this town with her heart in one piece, but she didn't care, not tonight, not when there was Dante and the full moon and a motorcycle to ride through mountain roads.

So, she locked her arms around his toned stomach, suddenly far, far too aware of the way he felt under her, the way his body shifted and moved at her touch. It was fire they were playing with here, and she knew only enough to know that burns were unavoidable.

But even the hard swell of his muscles under her fingers wasn't enough to distract Saint from the complete and total rush she felt when the bike revved and then Dante took off, slowly at first and then gaining speed, pushing harder, faster, turning on the hairpin roads through the mountains with absolute finesse, moving into her body as if he could anticipate her every movement. He pushed the bike higher and higher, until they were cresting the nearest mountain peak, until they cleared the trees and all she could see above were a million stars, bright and sparking, the kind of blanketed night sky that made a girl believe in reinvention, in new beginnings, in possible things.

He didn't speak when he pulled the bike to a calm at the summit top, just let her sit there with the Montana sky and the quiet peace. And when Saint finally felt like she'd gotten her fill, she tapped him on the shoulder and wrapped her arms around his waist once again and they took back off down the mountains toward town.

Dante let her pay for the ice cream but not the journal, and when she won ten dollars on her lotto ticket, she split the earnings with him, before swiping a bite of his mint chip and fudge sundae. In return, he took a spoonful of whipped cream and slid it down her cheek and across the tip of her nose, and ice cream turned into a whipped cream and cherry food fight that ended with them both sticky and agreeing it was time to go home, to complete the rest of the list.

"What are we tattooing?" Dante asked her when they finally got back to the studio and got cleaned up. "Did you have something in mind?"

"Something for my Gram," Saint said quietly. "Her name—" She took a deep breath, grappling with the lie she'd told for her own safety. "Her name was Violet."

Dante looked down at her like he saw her, the naked, revealed, all-together unsure version of her, the Saint she'd never shown to anyone, ironic in that he didn't even know her real name.

"Give me a minute," he said, and disappeared to his desk beside the tattoo bench. He returned a few moments later with a small stencil of a delicate, light purple violet with a curving stem and deep green leaves. "For behind your ear," he said.

It was soft and feminine, delicate in its construction, but with a strong enough story to honor the woman who had raised and loved her with all her might.

"It's completely perfect," Saint said on a breath. "Dante, it's perfect."

Like you.

The phrase from one of her Gram's favorite old shows popped into Saint's head in the same instant.

Danger, Will Robinson.

Chapter Nine

Touching Violet's hair was a bad idea. All of the night had been a bad idea, an excuse to get closer to her, to get to know her, to convince her to stick around beyond the time they'd agreed on. But gently moving her long blonde hair off her neck as she lay on his work bench in her tight little leggings and the cropped sweater that was, at this very moment, riding up from her waist, exposing her beautiful pale skin, that was the worst of them all.

Because that same dark instinct seized him again, to gather all that beautiful blonde hair in his hand and pull. Hard. To make her whimper and beg in a position not too different from this one.

Be a professional.

He'd tattooed beautiful women before, in much more delicate places and positions than this. Some of them he'd slept with and some of them he hadn't, and not a single one had called to his baser nature like this one.

"This might sting," he said, trying desperately to remember his training, his craft, the thing he prided himself on above all other things. Except maybe one. "But the location is pretty forgiving, so it shouldn't hurt too much."

"I trust you, Dante."

Those fucking words, they were enough to slay a stronger man. He couldn't take advantage of her. This thing between them had to end, and Dante knew without a shadow of a doubt that the buck was going to have to stop with him.

If I can.

That much was still left to be determined.

"You can talk to me while I work," he said, instead of responding to that devastating promise. "Tell me about your grandmother."

The smile was evident in Violet's voice when she started to share about her grandmother. The elder Violet had raised her from the time she was two years old. She had been a schoolteacher for decades, and spent Violet's childhood taking her to museums, showing her documentaries and classic movies, instilling a love of books and learning, but at the same time highlighting the importance of self-reliance, of humbleness, and gratitude.

"She sounds amazing," Dante said honestly. After all this time, the visions of his own mother were starting to fade, and he found himself wishing he could lock them in a box and keep them from getting exposed to the sun. "But then again, look at you."

He actually did look at her then, at the way his art looked on her skin, the soft petals of the violet flowing with the beautiful curves of her ear, and it took everything in him to keep from leaning over and biting her there. He wanted to stake his claim on this woman with everything in his blood and marrow, and for that reason, he wasn't going to.

"What about you?" she asked, instead of responding to the compliment. Over the last few weeks, he had come to realize she was awful at accepting compliments, which of course made him want to give them all the more.

"What about me?" he asked, sliding some excess ink from her skin.

"What were your parents like?"

"I didn't know my dad," he said. "Not really. My mom ran away when I was pretty young, and we were better off for it, started all over again with two boys and broken English in a country that wasn't her own." That was barely the version of the story that overlapped the truth, but there were some skeletons best left buried.

"She was from Italy," Violet surmised.

"Firenze," he replied. "She died without ever going back."

"Oh, Dante." Violet's voice was so low he could barely hear her from the work bench, but he could feel the rumble of her body below him, and all at once he wanted to cry and wrap her in his arms.

"It was a long time ago," he said, instead of doing either. "My brother raised me after that."

"And where is he?"

That was a question that shouldn't have taken him off guard. Most people knew where their brothers were. They knew because they called each other, often, or spent time drinking beer and watching sports, shooting the shit, moving in and out of each other's circles like they belonged there.

Most brothers.

Not them. Not the Castiglione boys.

"I'm not sure about that," Dante said.

She seemed to read that confession for what it was and reached her arm out to him, squeezing when she found his leg. Which, of course, was the least appropriate thing to add to that moment's inner turmoil. And somehow exactly what he needed.

"You're all done, Vi," he said. "Take a look."

He helped her sit up slowly, unable to ignore the note of flush on her cheeks or the soft muss of her hair from where he'd pinned it away from her ear. She hadn't made a sound the entire time he'd been tattooing her, and yet Dante could recognize that expression for what it was, that kind of heat for the delicious burn that accompanied it. And knowing that Violet like a touch of the darkness with her light was more information that promised to devastate him in a very serious, lasting way.

"Dante." Her eyes filled with tears as she looked into the handheld mirror, and for half a second, he wondered if his hard-earned skills had finally failed him. But then she wrapped her arms around his neck and squeezed tight. Way too tight. "It's absolutely perfect." She traced the tattoo in the air, careful not to touch the healing skin. "Thank you."

"Of course," he murmured against her hair, unable to keep from smelling the sweet vanilla, rich and indulgent. Like Violet, herself.

"I figured out what I want the last thing on the list to be," she said, her voice muffled.

"What's that?"

"I want you to kiss me."

Chapter Ten

For a moment, it was as if time stood still, as if there was no whir from tattoo machines, no chilly mountain air beating against windowpanes, just Saint and Dante in the Inferno Tattoo shop or in the middle of the universe, she couldn't be sure. It didn't matter, not when they were wrapped up in each other's arms and she was pulling back to look up at those storm-blue eyes in obvious tumult.

"Violet." It came out gravelly and rough, in dark contrast with itself, and what she wouldn't give for him to say her real name like that...

"I know I'm not the only one feeling this," she whispered into the dark space between them. Somehow, even with the bright work lights blaring, it still felt like a moment of unfettered intimacy, as if they were back under the stars in the mountains, or perhaps caught in webs of constellations. "I know it's not just me."

"This is a bad idea." That wasn't a no. It wasn't a yes, either, but it wasn't a no.

"Dante—" She reached out to him, to stroke his face, to feel that dark bristle under her fingers, but he stayed the motion with a hand around her wrist.

"Vi." He sounded pained, like it was the hardest thing he had ever done.

Then don't do it.

Of course, if she could have willed things into the universe with hope alone, a million things in her life would have been different.

She tried to pull free from his grip, because dammit, she'd seen the stars tonight and she was going after the things she wanted. But then Dante tightened his hand, pressing his palm to the thin line of vein that ran from her wrist, and a spark of incredible, white heat burst in her lower belly. It was the kind of heat that made her seek out his lips, made her bite her own in an attempt to stave off the dark groan that escaped without her permission. She knew the logistics, the facts about intimacy, but the nuances and the firsthand experiences eluded her, and not one of the books or movies or lessons she'd had in her life had prepared Saint for the way it felt to have his hand staying her movement, the intense loss of power that somehow felt like the most powerful thing in the world.

The groan slipped out, despite her best effort, and in the same moment, Dante's eyes darkened from storm blue to nearly black, like some kind of creature of the night, like there was a hot wire between them and everything she felt she passed through her fingertips to him.

All at once she remembered the secrets his friend Morgan has shared, the club that he ran in the mountains. The place where he probably did so much more than shock innocent girls with simple touches of the hand. This was so much more than a simple touch.

"Dante," she tried again. "I want to know."

And in that moment, Saint found it was true. She did want to know. She wanted to know *everything* this man had to offer her. And she wasn't afraid. Not anymore.

"Wash the tattoo with this" — he handed her a bottle — "and moisturize it before you go to bed tonight."

And then that delicious heat between them was broken and Dante was gone, the dark specter he so looked like disappearing in the night that a moment ago had given them so much intimacy, and now left her colder than she had ever been.

Chapter Eleven

The water was fucking freezing.

It probably would have been cold even if he had turned it all the way up, because it was Montana in November and the water never really got warm, but he'd done it to himself, which kind of made it worse.

It was a last-ditch effort to tamp down some of the incessant arousal he'd been battling for the last two weeks. All fucking night.

For the woman currently asleep down the hall.

Dante, I want to know.

She'd said that after he'd squeezed her wrist and pinned her in place, which meant that Violet knew at least something about the life he lived when she wasn't at the studio. Something that intrigued her.

The angel and devil on his shoulders started boxing. Because if she walked in willingly…that took away so much of his reasoning for keeping her in the dark.

Still.

She was, for the time being at least, his employee. And more than that, Violet was so clearly a woman in trouble. She laughed easily and smiled at every person she met, but behind those beautiful blue eyes he saw a kind of skittishness, like she was constantly watching for signs of danger lurking just around the corner. He'd lived his life that way for long enough to know the toll it took on the mind and body, and he wasn't going to add to whatever unknown stress she was currently under by making his desire her problem.

Though it was definitely, one hundred percent *his* problem, because she insisted on wearing her tight little leggings and crop tank tops and loose cardigans to the studio, and every time the sweater would fall down from her shoulder, which was all the fucking time, he'd have to clench the side of the work bench to keep from kicking out the clients and fucking her right then and there, up against the reception desk.

The worst part, the very worst part of it, was that he could feel her watching him, interest in her eyes and desire written all over the way she bit her bottom lip and hesitated to look away. But fuck, she was so incredibly young and so incredibly naïve about the way his life — and desires — had gone, and he was going to hold the line if it killed him.

It just might.

Especially since she didn't seem all together put off by the allusions Morgan had made when they'd visited the studio a few days earlier to get work done to Reece's sleeve. No, she'd seemed…damn it all to hell…curious.

So, it was Dante and his waning self-control against the world, then.

And there wasn't winter mountain water cold enough to stem that particular tide.

So, he gave in, just as he'd been doing nearly every night since her arrival, and reached for his swollen cock under the spray. The head was already thick, with swirling pre-cum right at the tip, and he slipped his thumb over the crown, shuddering when he brushed the top barbell along his length. He'd been sixteen, the first time he'd pierced his own ears, seventeen when he'd pierced his lip. The line of barbells that ran down the length of his cock had come later in life, when he'd been in full rebel mode, fighting the world and terrified it would take him down with it. Then the hafada double piercing along the seam of his sac, which shot sparks of burning heat along his spine when he thumbed it.

Normally, he'd take his time, tease himself to the edge and hold there for added, heightened pleasure. But he didn't need to do that now, not when the images of Violet were so incredibly fresh in his mind, of her soft shoulder bare from her sweater, the swell of her breasts over the edge of her tank top, the way her tight leggings clung to her curves when she walked up the stairs to the apartment in front of him, how she'd felt squeezing him as they took the mountain roads on his bike. She was sweetness and innocence come to life, and he was the fucker stroking his cock to the very thought of her two doors down the hall.

Two doors down the hall where he suddenly heard the unmistakable sound of movement — and a sob.

Panic caught up with his body before it caught up with his mind, and he was out of the shower and wrapping himself in a towel before he even realized it. With the water off, the repeating, shuddering sobs were louder and more insistent, and he pushed through the bathroom door and down the hall before arriving at the door to Violet's room.

Don't go in there.

The angel and the devil on his shoulders. She was trouble enough, knowing as little as he did about her background, and the more he learned, the more he would undoubtedly become tangled in the web of chaos. Plus, who was even to say if she wanted him barging in, taking over, learning secret private details about her past?

He hesitated just long enough for another muffled sob to escape from behind the door, and then Dante was through it and rushing over to the side of her bed.

Except she wasn't in bed. The lights were on, and Violet was quickly tossing her belongings into her duffle bag and backpack, her hand pressed to her mouth as she did.

I did this.

Dante reached for her hand, and she jumped and nearly screamed at the contact. Her skin was hot to the touch, burning up against whatever memories seemed to be so intensely plaguing her, and he didn't wait another second before reaching for her again.

"Violet, what the fuck?"

She swallowed hard. Her eyes were red-rimmed and puffy, and a hard, intense ache bloomed behind his ribs.

The angel on his shoulder sighed. The devil just laughed.

Because Dante Castiglione had never met a stray he didn't want to save.

The way I wish someone had saved me.

"I have to go." She didn't look at him, just rolled up a sweater and shoved it into her bag. "Please, I have to go."

"Is this because of tonight?" he asked, feeling very much like he was about to lose control himself. Of course, when Dante lost his control, it was likely to end in a broken mirror and maybe a few broken fingers.

"Dante…" It was all she managed before he had her in his lap, sweater still in her hands, suitcase open behind them. Aware now, she let out a lower, shuddering sob that somehow seemed so much more heartbreaking than whatever had been haunting her before he had barged through the door.

"I've got you, *ciccina. Sono qui per te.*" The words rolled in an old familiar language from his tongue, the soothing words a mother had once spoken to a scared little boy in the middle of the night. Only he wasn't feeling in any way maternal toward the woman in his lap now. All he wanted to do was find out what had scared her to pack in such an incredible panic, and to make sure it never happened again.

"What does that mean?" she asked, her voice muffled against his shoulder. His very, very bare shoulder.

"I'm here for you," he murmured into her hair, suddenly, so incredibly aware of her weight in his arms, of the way her body fit so perfectly against his own. She wore a pair of sleep shorts and a cotton T-shirt, and with all of the panic he'd felt only moments before, Dante knew he should have been thinking about anything other than her lithe, petite body pressing against his nearly naked one, but fuck, a man was only so strong.

"And *ciccina*…?"

"Sweetheart," he replied. "Darling."

"Dante…" She pulled back, and in the moon's pale glow, her eyes shimmered, ocean blue, edged with panic and fear that rioted, somehow, in his own gut.

"Violet, tell me. Are you running away because of tonight? Or is it something else?"

She shook her head, and he knew deep in his gut that he would do whatever it took to clear that misery and self-flagellation from her gaze.

"Ask me," she whispered.

She had said she would answer if he asked, if the time came to find out the truth about who she was and what she was running from.

"I don't want to push," he replied, though a fire burned in his veins to learn exactly what had her running fear into the night, and to do whatever it took to keep her safe.

Like calling Niccolo.

The thought came unbidden and entirely unwelcome, and he pushed it away. That would never happen again, Dante had promised himself once, and he had kept that promise all these years.

"I want to tell you," she said quietly. "But it scares me."

"I know," he replied. "I can help. Let me help, *ciccina.*"

"What if you get hurt?" Another sob escaped her lips. "Dante, what if you get hurt because of me?"

"I won't let that happen," he said, stroking her hair, the soft, silk strands catching the light and shimmering like silver stars. "And I won't let anything happen to you, Violet. I promise."

"Saint," she said, holding his gaze, despite her fear. "My name is Saint."

Chapter Twelve

She shouldn't have told him that. Saint knew that the moment her real name slipped from her lips she had lost the battle, with her secrets, with her past. But the very act felt like breathing for the first time in so long, sharing her pain, letting someone else help, even for a moment.

Because she'd been so incredibly terrified when she'd opened the email on her burner and read a single line of text from an unknown sender.

We know what you saw. You won't get far.

And she'd been so terrified rereading that fucking email, again and again until she was drenched in sweat and crying out into the darkness and packing up her shit so she could hit the road again.

Because she'd spent the night with him, as friends, as something dancing the line of so much more than friends, and she refused to bring the trouble to his door.

She wasn't going to let him get hurt, not after all the freedom he'd given her. Even if it broke her heart to know what it felt like to step out of the darkness, just for a moment. And then back it into, with one fucking email.

Only it hadn't been all darkness, because Dante had come, he'd come and he'd taken her into his arms, and he'd held her until the nightmare faded away, burned at the edges like wisps of paper floating away from a campfire. And she was still in his arms, his incredibly strong, bare arms. And bare chest. And…

"I interrupted your shower," she said, on a gasp. "I'm so sorry." She tried to pull back, but he held her, tight, a little too tightly, like he was terrified she was going to run, and there was something so decadent about this man pinning her in place that Saint could breathe against the ebbing panic without choking. He grounded her, with his hands on her skin, and it shot an intense bolt of awareness through her body. Awareness for him, his bareness, his cooling skin, the thousand stories in ink across his chest she wanted to explore. What would it be like to touch this man in a moment of heat, rather than a moment of fear? What would it be like to be an entirely different woman, whose life had gone in such an opposing direction she had never known, to know this man as anything other than a savior in the dark?

He could be so much more.

No. He couldn't. Not in this lifetime.

"Violet—" He paused. "Saint." Dante cocked his head to the side and for the first time in days, weeks, maybe the years since Gram had first gotten sick, she felt as though she were being seen for her, and only for herself. "It suits you."

"I'm sorry," she whispered. "I didn't know if I could trust you."

"You can trust me," he replied, matching her tone, never stopping the movement of his hand in her hair. "And I'm asking — Saint."

She took a deep breath, because somehow after nearly two weeks, it still didn't feel real. None of this felt like her life, which already had felt so distant and out of her control. But this wasn't her, life on the run, constantly looking over her shoulder. It was little wonder she'd been crying out in her sleep.

"Have you heard of the Barbarone family?" she asked. "Out of Seattle?"

Dante stiffened, and Saint almost walked it back, almost pretended like there was nothing to her past or the dreams that so obviously haunted her. Dante, clearly, was no stranger to the kind of chaos she'd left behind.

"I know them," he said, his voice dark and low, a flint-hard reminder of the man he was. Humor, laughter, flirtation, it could all be used to keep people at arm's length, but there was survival in Dante's blood and bones, and sometimes the outside really did reflect the power and strength within. "How do *you* know them?"

Her mind was already on overload, from the email, from the buzzing panic of telling another person what she had gotten caught up in, from how it felt with Dante wrapping her in his arms, like they knew each other in a way she'd never know anyone. But even in the din and chaos, Saint still had to file the reaction away, like he held his own secrets about the Barbarone family, like their lives had collided somehow before they even knew each other.

"I worked in one of their restaurants," she said quietly, and when Dante's eyes hardened and his lips thinned, she added, "only as a server. I swear it."

"So, you know who they are?" he asked. "You know what they do?"

"Not if I knew what was good for me," she replied. "Not if I wanted to keep my job and…and my life."

"Then why not just leave?" Dante asked. "You didn't have to stay."

"I did," Saint replied quietly. Because somehow, some way, this was the hardest part, the saying out loud part, the grieving part. "My gram was sick. Really sick. I wasn't lying about that. She raised me from the time I was two years old and… I don't have a college degree, Dante. I did one semester of school before she needed me to come home, and waiting tables at a good restaurant, I could make enough money for us. Just enough."

"I understand that," he said, his teeth still gritted, but the words a little softer now. He was a man who knew what survival meant. "But if they knew you'd be discreet, what changed? Why run now?"

He paused and sighed, closing his eyes in self-flagellation.

"She died."

The words were hollow, somehow, like they reflected the way Saint's heart had been carved out of her chest, like they echoed through with the same remarkable loneliness she had been living in, a half-life of the kind of cold that burned, long after you went inside.

"Three months ago."

"*Ciccina*," he murmured, the edges of his words dulled, the blade sheathed in his concern. For now.

When he finds out what kind of trouble I brought to his door, it may be the last kindness he shows.

"It was a long time coming," she said, the words snagging in her throat, "and somehow I still wasn't ready for it."

"There are some things we can never fully prepare for," Dante replied. "No matter how much time we have."

"She would have liked you," Saint said quietly, and meaning it. "Violet was this real firecracker. She had such an attitude, but God could she love."

"Violet." It was probably a terrible thing that she could tell Dante was smiling just from the tone of his voice.

"It felt right," Saint replied. "A way to honor her, I guess. And to keep myself safe until I knew I wasn't being followed."

"Why do you think you're being followed?" Dante asked. "There's more to the story, isn't there?"

Saint swallowed and looked out of the window to where the moon shone bright and cold above. They were in the mountains of Montana, not on the piers of Seattle, and she was safe.

"My grandmother died and the house... The house got repossessed. All my money had been going to her care. Nothing else mattered."

"Did you go to them for a loan?" he asked, the words resigned but somehow understanding, like he knew what that meant and he wouldn't damn her for it.

"I thought about it," Saint admitted. "But I knew enough to think twice. I only went to collect my last paycheck before I left the city. My car was already packed, I was supposed to be in and out of the office, just like every other time."

"Saint." He brought his hand back to her hair and stroked, the touch so incredibly gentle, so soft from a man who had such hardness about him, such strength in every muscle and bone, enough to hold them both up. "What happened?"

She said it like a confession. "He shot a man."

Chapter Thirteen

He shot a man.

Dante's skin had become cool in the night air, the rivulets of the icy shower still rolling down his arms and back, but his entire body blazed to life now, hot, burning hot and racing a wildfire path through his body.

She'd witnessed a killing.

A murder.

This fairy of a woman in his arms, with her bright blue eyes and sunshine hair, this *angel*, her wings snagged on the barbed wire, she had seen one of the most heart wrenching, life-changing moments a person could possibly see. Murder in cold blood. He knew, too well and with far too much clarity, what business could mean to a family like the Barbarones, and to them, business would have to include getting rid of Saint.

Because it wasn't just a murder, which would have been enough to send any regular, feeling person into a tailspin of trauma and grief.

It was a mob murder.

And in his experience, the mob didn't like loose ends.

His very, very personal experience. With the very mob she had been escaping from when their lives had collided in the middle of the night.

"You ran." His voice barely sounded like his own, the words so harsh against the dark room.

She doesn't know.

Because how the fuck could she? How could this strange woman who had ended up on his doorstep have the slightest idea the trouble she'd been bringing, the memories she would be stirring up with her arrival, with the chaos of the things she had seen? It was circumstance, a maddening, impossible coincidence that somehow crossed their wires and burned two edges of the same bridge until they met in the middle, cinder and ash, with only a moment to breathe before they plunged into the river below.

"I shouldn't have stayed," she said, pulling back from his arms. Or trying to, at least. Dante wasn't certain he could let her go for anything short of a safe word. In the span of a second, she had become both the wave crashing against his hull, and the anchor keeping him safely moored. "I'll leave first thing in the morning. I'm so sorry, Dante. I never meant to bring you into this."

"What happened tonight?" he asked. "Something happened."

She hesitated, and he could see the war she fought with herself in his arms.

Then finally, she reached for her phone and showed him the screen.

"I've been using a burner, and a fake email address and I thought I covered my tracks," she said, each word coming out on a sniff. "But I got this."

We know what you saw. You won't get far.

That was all it said, and with those simple words, Dante saw a flood of red-hot anger that made his eyes burns and his fists clench and his own body go tight and taut. He had promised himself he'd keep Violet — Saint — at a distance, but under no circumstances was he going to allow anyone else to hurt her either. *Especially* not the Barbarone family.

If ever a chance for redemption had landed in his lap...

"Stay."

He didn't mean to grip her hip, to touch the thin cotton shorts separating their bodies, didn't mean to insist with his fingers and his words, and the tone he'd never once used outside of a scene. But Saint had clawed her way into his life, and for some reason, a reason that was undoubtedly dangerous in a way he'd never lived through before, he couldn't let her go.

It's the only way.

It wasn't the only way. If the Barbarone family came looking for her, the very fact that she had been in his studio, in his apartments, would bring him right into the center of the chaos. It was too late to send her on her journey, too late to wash his hands of the trouble that had come barreling into his world in the form of a beautiful blonde. But that didn't matter.

I don't want her to go.

It was so much more than wanting to. He *couldn't* let her, couldn't send her on her way to be tracked down by the fiercest hitmen he'd ever known. He'd do whatever the fuck it took to keep this woman safe, even if it meant bringing the war to his doorstep.

Even if it meant doing what he should have done all those years ago.

"No," she said, and for the first time since she'd begun telling the story, her voice began to wobble. "No, I'm not letting you get hurt because of this. I'm not."

"And you think I'll let you just walk out there to your death?" It was harsh. He knew that. But something intense and carnal was taking over, revealing the hard edges Dante had spent so long learning to dull. "That's definitely not going to happen."

"You don't owe me anything," she said, and the words came then with the cry she had been trying to hold back. "I was a stranger two weeks ago, Dante. I'm nobody to you. They won't even know to look here. I can leave tomorrow, and you won't be in any more danger."

"But they will be a danger to *you*," he said. "And I'm not in the habit of letting young women walk into the arms of mafia hitmen."

"Right." She pulled back from his arms, pushing out of the bed, as if to put as much space between them as possible. "I forgot how much you love to save a stray. I can take care of myself. I was doing just fine before we met."

"You were broken down in the middle of nowhere with no money and no options," he pointed out, feeling all the more the villain for saying it. But she needed to see. She needed to know she couldn't go running off without a plan. Without help.

Without my *help.*

"Yes." She threw her hands up in the air, which pulled at the bottom of her T-shirt, exposing the thin line of skin above her shorts. Dante closed his eyes and swallowed. This was so not the time to be thinking about his impossible desire for her. Especially since she was turning into a fucking tornado of trouble. "Yes. I was in a fucking bind. You helped me when I didn't have any options — so let me help you. *Let me keep you safe.*"

He stood, extremely aware of how shitty a towel could be for hiding any kind of secrets. But there were more important things to worry about.

"How can you ask that of me?" he asked, "And not understand why I want the same for you?"

"It's my mess." She wiped at her eyes with her fingers. "It's my mess, Dante. You never asked for this."

That wasn't entirely true, but now wasn't the time to go digging up coffins.

"Neither did you," he said, reaching for her. To his immense relief, she let him pull her close. "You were just in the wrong place at the wrong time. It's no more your fault than it is mine."

"You've been so good to me," she said, "I don't want you to get hurt."

"I won't," he assured her. "I know a thing or two about survival, *ciccina*."

"Why would you do this?" They were so incredibly close, and pressed as their bodies were into the corner of the room, there was no way she could ignore how his cock pushed against the towel, or the intense beating of his heart against her chest. "Why put everything on the line for me? You don't even know me."

He knew the moment she felt his cock brush her thigh, knew the moment her panic ebbed out, clouded with lust and desire, the adrenaline confusing and mixing the two. Her pretty eyes burned heavy with lust, and when she bit her lip, Dante couldn't help but follow the way her teeth sunk into swollen flesh. It would be so incredibly easy, so impossibly easy to lean down and capture her mouth, to turn her around, press her against the wall and take what they had both been clearly craving for so many days, to give them both a respite from the harsh burn of survival. But there were even more reasons to grit his teeth and pull away from her, to keep his distance, to get her help and then get her gone.

"In my experience, everyone is worth saving," he said, holding her incredible gaze, and holding his own fist so tightly that the nails dug deep crevasses into his flesh. She was young, ten years younger than him at least, and so incredibly innocent, caught up in a whirlwind of trouble that was very much about to complicate his life, to dredge up a slew of memories he'd thought dead and gone. The last thing he should be doing was touching her.

So, Dante took a deep breath, a deep, deep breath, and stepped away from her, the air between them cooling immediately. "And you're wrong. I do know you."

Chapter Fourteen

"Come with me," Dante said, pulling on the cowboy hat before locking the front door to the studio. "I'm just bartending, and I don't want to leave you alone down here."

"I don't want to interrupt you at work," Saint replied. They had spent the day in a sort of respectful limbo. The teasing and joking Dante was gone, the Dante that flirted with her — and every other woman who walked through the studio door — was gone. He was so incredibly gracious it was making her want to shake him or slap him or kiss him the way he had so clearly wanted to kiss her the night before. She had admitted many things to him the night before, and she had admitted one thing to herself.

She wanted him.

Not just because he was dark and mysterious, with secrets hidden in those gray-blue eyes and tucked into the rivers of ink that covered his chest and arms. Not just because he had given her a soft place to land, and so much more than a kind ear when she had needed it. It was more than that, the way he put her at ease, the connection they had shared from the very first moment they had met, how comfortable she had been in telling him the truth, how he had asked her to. The way she couldn't stop thinking about his club in the mountains, the club he was insisting he would only go to bartend at the for the night.

Don't be a coward, just ask him.

Ask him what, exactly? Do you secretly run a mountain sex club with your friends? Do you tie women up and torture them with feathers and whips?

Do you want to tie me up?

Saint didn't even know if she would like that. Truth be told, she knew very little about what she might like, only that she would be all too willingly the student if he were the teacher.

Which seemed to be a problem for many reasons, not the least of which being that Dante had clearly put up a wall between them. They had discussed, in the light of day, what to do about the email she had received, how they were going to move forward if the threat got worse, when she would leave—her answer, immediately, his, not until things were resolved—but he hadn't touched her all day, hadn't given her one of those knowing smiles out of the corner of his mouth and the corner of his eye, hadn't been anything more than professional and polite.

And it was making her crazy.

"I'll be fine," she said. "I'll call, okay, if something happens."

"If something happens, you come get me," he replied. "Or Reece or Morgan. They'll be at The Ranch tonight."

It was on the tip of her tongue, to ask to go with him, to ask him for answers, which was completely inappropriate, given what she had revealed about the family she was running from.

"Follow Country Road 15," she said. "I remember."

"Good," he replied. "I'll take the bike, so you can have the truck, if you need it."

He handed her the keys to the truck, and she took them, so incredibly aware of the heat of his body when their fingers brushed, of the dark, olive skin of his large hands contrasting her paler ones.

"How do you say, 'have fun' in Italian?'" she asked him.

Dante cocked his head to the side. "*Divertiti*," he replied quietly.

"And how do you say, 'come home safe'?"

"*Tornari a casa salvo*," he replied. "I will, Saint, I promise." He handed her his cowboy hat and grabbed a helmet from the shelf by the back door. Then she watched him walk outside and climb onto the back of the motorcycle they had shared, before she had told him the truth, before the chasm between them had stretched so far and wide.

I'm moving to New York City.

The mantra that had gotten her as far as Duchess no longer seemed so steady, as she watched Dante offer a quick salute. Then he was pulling out of the driveway, past her little sedan he'd repaired as he'd promised, and onto the road, before disappearing out of sight.

"Rom coms, it is," Saint muttered to herself. She stepped back inside and locked the door, then headed for the apartments. The last few months had been absolute hell, and she deserved a break in the form of classic nineties movies, a pedicure, and snacks.

As it turned out, however, not even Jude Law could keep her attention for long. Not for the first time that night, Saint opened her emails and read the message again.

We know what you saw. You won't get far.

That was it. The sender was hidden. There was no signature, just the same two sentences that had been plaguing her since the night before. Dante had wanted to go to the police, but he'd listened to reason eventually. The Barbarone family was well-connected, very, very well-connected, and alerting the cops would be like shining a bright spotlight on exactly where she had gone and what she knew. It was best that they take things slow, keep the doors locked and watch for any signs that her hiding position had been discovered.

Like she hadn't been watching over her shoulder since that first night at the pier, when her entire life had gone up in flames.

Saint's breath caught in her throat and her knee bounced, then bounced again. The tell-tale signs of anxiety began to creep in around her—difficulty swallowing, a sudden, overwhelming sense of being too hot and too cold at the same time, the need to do *something* with her hands.

Breathe in. Breathe out. Gram Violet's voice in her ear was a small comfort.

"That's it," she said to the quiet apartment. "I need to stay busy."

She stood up from the couch and walked into Dante's kitchen, her mission fueling her, allowing her to focus on something other than the panic and the confusion and the sense of desperation that mounted every time she remembered exactly what she was up against. But her hopes were quickly dashed when she took stock of the ingredients before her, and came up very, very short. Butter, flour, sugar. No apples, no cinnamon, no nutmeg. It was all together clear that Dante was a man who cooked and didn't bake.

Fine. She had his keys and she had her wits about her. He might not have approved of her going to the grocery store alone, but Saint couldn't stay in the apartments by herself panicking for another minute. She'd be in and out of the grocery store in no time, and then she could do something productive. Something good.

She pulled her hair into a ponytail and added a ballcap at the last minute, then grabbed one of the flannels Dante had left on the chair. It was too big by half, falling nearly to her knees, but the nights were getting colder and colder, she didn't have much in the way of winterwear.

It's a good thing I'm not staying here, then, she reminded herself, even with the act of pulling on his cozy jacket all too intimate.

It felt all too intimate to climb into Dante's truck, as well, to catch the scent of him in the comfortable leather of the cabin, to hear his classic rock music come over the radio when she turned the truck on. The seat was too far back, and she adjusted, finding it too easy to settle into his space, to make herself comfortable in a world that really wasn't meant for her.

Not in the long-term, at least.

In the short-term, well, she had a pie to make.

The supermarket was just a few minutes from the studio, and it wasn't long before Saint was pulling into a spot. She checked her mirrors, glanced at the entrance, and pulled her ball cap down over her head, tucking her hair up. It wasn't a secret that Dante had a new receptionist — if she'd learned anything in the two weeks of working at Inferno Tattoos it was that Duchess was a small town with a big gossip mill. But she was still trying to keep a low profile, especially after the email she'd just received.

This is a bad idea.

Maybe she had gotten too complacent, living in a small town in Montana. Maybe she should just turn around and head back to the studio. She had promised Dante that she wouldn't take any unnecessary risks, and it definitely wasn't necessary to go out to buy apples and cinnamon. But for the first time in weeks — hell, in months — Saint finally felt like she was starting to live her own life. She didn't need to squirrel away every dime she made just to survive, and she didn't need to race home to relieve Mrs. Lansing. For the first time in longer than she could remember, Saint only had to worry about herself.

I do have to worry about myself.

Because whether or not she was enjoying her temporary new life in Duchess, threats notwithstanding, it was *temporary*. For a damn good reason. Even if she was drawn into the community, attracted to the stability and comfort of a regular, normal life, attracted more — in a dangerous and damning way — to the unlikely knight who had taken her in when she'd most needed a lifeline, she was on the run for her life. No amount of television marathons or shared afternoon coffees or starry night bike rides with her very, *very* handsome boss was going to change that.

In and out in ten minutes.

Saint repeated the promise to herself again as she walked from the truck to the store's front door.

It felt good to be out of the apartment and out of the studio. In the weeks since she'd been in Duchess, she'd found a small community in the people that spent time in Dante's shop, in Maisie, who brought over lunch and coffee from the diner next door, but more than being a hub for art and inspiration, it was Dante himself that brought the connections together. He could shoot the breeze with the biggest, burliest bikers or put the most nervous first-timer at ease…

That made Saint remember the night they had shared in the studio, and without thinking she reached for the small tattoo behind her ear. It was still a dark and purple mess in the mirror, and she had to wonder if her Gram would have completely approved or disapproved, but she couldn't love it more. It was a marker of the new life she would make for herself, a sign that she wasn't going to live out her days for someone else, jumping at shadows with the hope that she might survive another day, another night.

Of course, right now, she very much *was* jumping at shadows, and with each cart that some passing patron swerved out of the way and each nod a stranger gave her as they walked by, Saint was beginning to feel more and more like she shouldn't have left the relatively safety of Dante's apartment.

I'm already here.

She just needed a few more things and then she could be back in the truck and back in the studio in no time.

Except she didn't want to go to the studio or the empty apartment. She didn't want to be alone with the familiar choke of panic waiting for her next breath. Saint knew anxiety the way a terminally ill man knew the reaper, almost an old friend, but chasms apart in their familiarity. As if the reaper himself were reaching out a hand, her panic felt cold this time, prickling raw in a way that had nothing to do with the frozen section of the grocery store.

I should have gone to The Ranch with him tonight.

She hadn't wanted to admit it to herself, but Saint hadn't been able to go. Dante didn't know what she did about what was truly on offer at The Ranch, and she hadn't wanted to reveal any of that to him when crossing that invisible barrier. She was nearly twenty-four years old and still a virgin, and the man she had found herself dreaming of ran a sex club in the mountains.

No wonder he didn't want to kiss me the other night.

The shame of that memory ran white hot and for a moment chased away the cold of the panic. His friend Morgan had alluded to what went on at the club, and from the information on the website, Saint could draw some decently informed conclusions. Against her better judgment or not, one of those conclusions had to be that Dante would want a more experienced woman, a woman familiar with the kind of things they did at the club, a woman he wouldn't have to teach or walk gently with.

Anyone but me.

And so she'd stayed away from the club that night, even though it would have been safer and so much smarter to head up the mountain, where he had assured her they had security, even though the thought of returning to a dark and empty apartment while Dante spent the night with some faceless, talented beauty made her insides crawl…

Saint reached for the dark brown sugar and watched her own trembling hand like it belonged to someone else. It was November in Montana and the night was cold, but her shaking had nothing to do with the brisk breeze outside or the ice cream melting in her basket.

It wasn't even the panic about feeling a certain way for a man she would soon leave in her rearview mirror and never be able to contact again. Panic about feeling and shame was one thing, but panic about survival...

That was a feeling she was becoming far, far too accustomed to, and one she wished she would never have to experience again. She placed the sugar in the basket and then stepped back in the aisle, as if scanning it for more baking supplies, darting her eyes back and forth for any sign of a stranger who might not be a stranger, any sign of a man who looked out of place in this small Montana town.

Not a week ago, *she* would have felt out of place, but working for Inferno Tattoos and enjoying Maisie's company at the diner had given her a peek into the lives of the people who lived in this wild place, and Saint had to hope that would be enough for her to recognize whatever threat was making the hairs on the back of her neck stand up and her stomach go sour.

There was no one else in the aisle with her, and for a moment she was certain she had been riling herself up, jangling her nerves for no other reason than because she was confused about her growing feelings for Dante.

Except in the next second, she caught sight of movement in the security mirror at the end of the next aisle. The image was convex and distorted, and it was difficult to tell the distance of the shoppers in the reflection, but there was no denying that it was him.

Alberto Del Santo.

Enforcer for the Barbarone family.

Dante would have proven the exception, but there weren't all too many Italian men in the wilds of the

Montana mountains, and at once she caught sight of the familiar dark, weathered skin and jet-black hair. When she had worked as a server, she had learned quickly to keep her head down and her ears shut against whatever else might have been going on in the restaurant, but Alberto Del Santo had been around nearly as much as the Barbarone brothers, Lorenzo and Francesco, and try as Saint might, she couldn't will him away, couldn't blink and pretend she had simply been imagining things.

Because she did blink, trying to clear her vision, and when she opened her eyes, Del Santo was still there, clear as day in the fluorescent overhead lights of the grocery store. Even if she didn't know him as well as she did, the man would have stood out in Duchess. He was tall and thick, broad across the chest and shoulders, with a stance that brooked no arguments and had likely, on more than one occasion, kept the riffraff away from his bosses. He wore a long, floor-length black wool coat, unbuttoned, as if daring the Montana cold to try to test him.

No one who tested Del Santo ever won.

It was something everyone who worked in the vicinity of the Barbarone family knew well, even if none of them — Saint included — ever acknowledged the truth of that out loud. It was something everyone in Seattle knew. There was one family in charge of the city, above the law and the courts and the cops, and there was one man who ensured that control by whatever means necessary.

A man who was now hunting *her*.

Saint's grip on the basket slipped, her hands suddenly sweaty and clammy, and only in the last moment did she catch the handle before the basket went crashing to the ground.

I have to get out of here.

It was an eerily familiar mantra to the night she had watched Lorenzo Barbarone shoot a man through the heart, and then she had only been in the back kitchen, with a clear exit strategy. The email had been proof enough that she hadn't gotten out of the restaurant that night unnoticed, but there was something so incredibly different between knowing logically that she was in danger, and seeing the reflection of the most dangerous man on the western seaboard standing ten yards away.

Deep breathes, little Saint. Take the moment you need to breathe.

Gram Violet was the angel in that moment, the guardian angel who wasn't afraid of smacking her charge upside the head, should the occasion arise.

The occasion had definitely arisen, and Saint heeded her Gram's advice. She took a deep, calming breath, then she glanced back to the man in the long black coat. He was still in the same aisle, moving further toward the middle of the aisle and away from her. Chances were, he didn't know she was in the store, and it was nothing but dumb luck that had brought her to the one grocer in town at the same time he had arrived. She could work with dumb luck.

Especially since dumb luck meant she was closer to the back kitchens. A few feet away, the plastic drapes of the meat and seafood freezer sections fluttered against the blowing cold beyond, and Saint gently sat her basket down on the ground and darted a glance in both directions to catch sight of any employees who might be walking by. She took a deep breath, as if diving in the deep end of a cold lake, then crossed the wide aisle, pushed through the plastic drapes, and stepped into the kitchens beyond.

It was cold in the back, air blowing in from the seafood counter on her right and from the back side of the frozen food sections on the left, and she was suddenly aware of all the smells of the back of a grocery store, crab and cheese and cold plastic and old pickles that turned to the sour press of dumpster smell the closer she got to the loading docks in the back. Her entire body was on high alert, and that brought overwhelming awareness, the whirring of the air conditioning system and ice machines, the gentle hum of the butter freezers, trucks in the back pulling in and out.

It was almost too much, too many senses and too many inputs, her mind overrun with the possibilities of what sounds might be out of place, of where a man like Del Santo might be hiding, and what she might be able to reach to protect herself. The icy grip of her anxiety closed its fingers around her arm and...

"You can't be back here, miss."

It wasn't anxiety. It was a young employee, maybe a year or two older than her, wearing a crisp white shirt and what was clearly a clip-on tie. The tag pinned to his pocket said his name was Todd.

"What?"

Saint didn't recognize her own voice, not above the whirling and buzzing the machines and the whirling and buzzing of panic. They were beginning to sound like one in the same.

"I said you can't be back here, miss." His touch on her arm wasn't very strong. In fact, in another time and another life, she might have praised his manners. No doubt she hadn't heard him the first time he had tried to get her attention. "I can take you back through the store, if you're looking for something."

"No!" The panic in her voice surprised Todd as much as it surprised Saint and he pulled back for a moment, suspicion in his eyes.

Think, little Saint. Think.

"My ex-husband is out there," she said quickly. "I have a restraining order, but he doesn't care..." She lowered her voice as if in confession. "He owns a gun."

Todd's eyes widened and his touch on her arm gentled. "We should call the police," he said.

Saint shook her head. "No police, please. I just... I just need to get to my car. He'll leave if he knows I'm gone."

The split-second in which Todd seemed to make up his mind felt to Saint like a million years, but he finally nodded and guided her through the kitchen, until they got to the door out to the loading docks.

"Are you sure you don't want me to call the police, miss?" he asked, genuine worry in his eyes. She'd repent for the lies later.

"No, it'll only bring more trouble," Saint said. And wasn't that the damn truth. "You've done more than enough. You've saved me."

He swallowed and she forced as much of a smile as she could, before disappearing through the door and down the ramp. Dante's truck was around the side of the building, and she kept alert as she walked quickly across the parking lot, trying not to draw any attention to herself and at the same time trying not to waste a single second of time. She needed to get out of here right *fucking* now.

To her immense relief, there was no sign of Del Santo as she climbed into the truck and turned over the engine. She pulled out of the grocery store parking lot before even putting on her seat belt, then turned down several side streets at random just to be sure she wasn't being followed.

Now what?

Now she needed help. Dante had told her to ask for help if she needed it. And right now, she needed it more than she ever had in her entire life. Suddenly, all the reasons she'd had for not wanting to visit him at work, all the shame and fear she had felt, seemed short-sighted and insignificant. There was only one choice.

She had to go to The Ranch.

Chapter Fifteen

Dante hadn't been able to get her off his mind all night. He hadn't wanted to push her to come with him, but a growing part of him wished he had. It didn't feel right leaving her alone at the apartment. The email she had received was most definitely a threat, but there was nothing to indicate if the Barbarone family actually knew anything about where she was beside their word, which should have given him a little peace of mind. It didn't.

The only thing that would have made Dante feel better was to have her in his arms, safe and sound and protected against the world.

Of course, that wasn't an option. For about a million reasons that wasn't an option. Even if she wasn't bringing a shitstorm of trouble to their little mountain town—and Dante had the very distinct impression she was about to bring a shitstorm of trouble to their little mountain time—Saint had her entire life ahead of her. She was young and capable, a hard worker with plenty of adventures still to have, adventures that didn't have to include running for her life. She was ten years younger than him, for fuck's sake, and she had no idea what kind of double life he lived, a double life that would no doubt have had her hightailing it for the hills.

Which had been another reason he hadn't pushed her to come tonight. Because he had been planning on working the front desk at their ranch side of the business, with cabin rentals and mountain dining, which would have kept him far enough away from everything else The Ranch had to offer. But still too close. Still far too close to the secrets he held that he wasn't ready to stain her with. He would never be ready to stain her with those secrets.

Or the secrets he had locked down the moment he decided not to tell her about his past. About his family.

As luck had it, they'd needed him to bartend at The Barn, the exclusive club hidden behind the layers of respectability offered by the rest of the business. And so part of him had been a little relieved that Saint hadn't come with him, because that would have led to a night of more questions than answers, and more confessions than he was willing to admit to himself.

I heard you left a pretty girl back at your studio.

Don't you have a job?

Caleb, who was very happily playing poker at the far table with one hand, his other up his wife's skirt, had been a professional athlete before his shoulder had given out. Reece, who had stolen a bottle of whiskey from behind the bar and carried it and a giggling Morgan down the hall to his private suite, had lived through a terrorist attack, and then gone on to fall in love with the biggest adrenaline junkie Dante had ever met. Van had survived three tours in the Middle East and an arguably more dangerous feud with Caleb's little sister Rhylee. And Bastion was the hardboiled rock and roll star with sleeves of ink and a fuck-you-very-much attitude. But the four of them — Dante was certain it would be five if Gabriel and Em were in town — were acting like fucking church ladies gossiping about the new pastor's wife.

Miss me?

He did, of course. He always missed Bastion when he was on tour, but even that dull feeling of loss did little to stop the rising nerves clawing at his neck. For a million reasons, he should be glad that Saint wasn't here. But he had one very important reason he wished she was.

Before Dante could spiral any further, a leggy blonde wearing a leather bustier and a pair of knee-high boots walked up to the bar and leaned over the hard wood separating them.

"Monica," he said with a nod. "Drink?"

"I'd like a tall drink of water, if you don't mind, baby," she said on a laugh. "Our mutual friend said I should try to cheer you up."

Bastion has spies everywhere...

"He's far too concerned with my life," Dante said, filling a glass with soda water and pushing it toward her. The club had a very specific drink policy, and Dante was drop dead serious about keeping his patrons safe, just as he was about protecting his sub, when the time came.

"Oh, come now," she said, "we had fun once upon a time, didn't we?"

"We did, Mon," he said. "But I'm working."

Of course, he didn't have to be working. He could tap out with any of his brothers and they'd be fucking overjoyed for it. But there was no way Dante was about to let himself get lost in the distraction of a pretty face for the night. Not when Saint was home alone, and he only had an hour left before he could go back down the mountain and keep her safe.

Sure, that's the only reason you're not playing.

Monica was a good partner. She was brattier than his preferred subs, but their kinks suited, and she hadn't been wrong that they enjoyed each other's company on occasion. But now, in this den of iniquity he'd been so proud to build, surrounded by beautiful half-naked women, Dante couldn't keep him mind from wandering to thoughts of Saint.

"I'll work you over," Monica said, reaching out with one delicate finger and running her nail along the underside of his chin.

It was at that exact moment that the doors to the barn opened, and Saint burst inside.

Chapter Sixteen

"I couldn't stop her, boss, I'm sorry." This from one of their trainee Doms who worked security, a kid named Miles who came running up a few moments behind her. All noise in the room dulled, the lounge coming to a complete and deadly silence.

"It's not your fault, Miles," Dante said, not even bothering to look at the kid. "Go help Caleb." Miles disappeared and a moment later, the sound resumed in the grand room, play and laughter and music. Dante was certain that was true, but all he could focus on was Saint.

"What's wrong?"

She was tucked into his big flannel, which shouldn't have sparked such a sense of intense propriety in him, especially not now, but Dante filed it away for later, because fuck she was just about the cutest thing he'd ever seen.

Except she was here. At his club. Not just the campus, but the dark, depraved club he swore he'd never introduce her to, and that meant something was very, very wrong.

"He's here." The words came out on a whisper, scraped raw and nearly too quiet to hear. "I saw him at the grocery store."

"Come here." He pulled her in tight, not giving a shit about the curious looks of the other patrons, just needing to feel her, alive, well, with a strong beating heart, still so incredibly warm against him. She let out a dark, shuddering sob, and Dante squeezed harder, needing her to know, without words, that he was here. She wasn't alone.

"Who did you see, *ciccina*?" For a second, he wanted to ask why she was at the grocery store. And he then very, very much wanted to punish her for going to the grocery store when she should have been safe and sound at home, but there were more pressing matters to attend to.

"Alberto Del Santo."

Ten minutes later, they were gathered in the kitchen with Caleb and Skylar, Morgan and Reece, and Van. From the middle of the club, and Dante wasn't entirely certain it was safe to know where, Rhylee Cash had emerged and joined them. It was starting to become a common occurrence, this group holing up in the back room of the club to catch bad guys and save lives. It hadn't been all that long along when they'd saved Morgan from the hands of a corrupt, drug-smuggling senator, and the thought that Reece might have had to live without the woman who had turned out to be the love of life soured Dante's stomach.

Not nearly as much as the expression on Saint's face right now, though. He wasn't sick with worry, not like he had been waiting for word that she was okay. No, the only emotion Dante could find, pulsing hard and red hot through his veins, was fury. It was making it difficult to think, let alone offer the comfort she needed in that moment, and the panic and fear in Saint's eyes were the only thing keeping him from rushing out into the night in a blind rage.

"You know Morgan and Reece," Dante said, placing his hand at the small of her back to steady her. From somewhere behind them, one of his friends produced a chair, and he guided her to sit. Her entire body was shaking, and Dante placed his hand on the chair for something to squeeze with all the strength in his body. "Skylar and Caleb" — he indicated to his friend — "Caleb's sister Rhylee, and Van. This is…" He hesitated just for a moment, but she nodded.

"You can tell them," she whispered. "It doesn't really matter now."

"This is Saint," he said, watching as Morgan and Reece exchanged looks. He'd introduced them to her as Violet just a few days before, after all.

"I'm sorry I lied," she said quietly. "I was trying to stay safe, to keep Dante safe, after he helped me so much. I was supposed to be gone before they ever found me."

"Who exactly found you?" Van asked. Ever the strategist. In this moment, Dante couldn't be more grateful for it.

"Alberto Del Santo," she said, and her voice was strong and steady when she repeated his name for the second time that night. Pride swelled in Dante's chest pushing out the bad, if only for a moment. "He works for the Barbarone family in Seattle."

"Works for is the polite way to put it," Dante said. "Berto is the worst kind of enforcer. He's cruel, ruthless, and very efficient. He never leaves a trace, and they've never been able to pin him."

Saint grimaced, and Dante moved his hand, ever so slightly, to stroke her shoulder. If he touched her too much now, he might just turn into the feral beast that was simmering far too close to the surface. He'd been that man once, and it wasn't a version of himself he had any interest into sharing with this pure and beautiful woman.

"Why is he here?" This from Caleb, who had wrapped one arm around Skylar's shoulder, exactly the way Dante ached to do to Saint. Only Caleb could call Sky his own. Dante would never have that luxury.

"I shouldn't be dragging your friends into this." Saint turned to him. "This is my fight."

"We take care of our own here," Reece said, and it was all too easy to remember how he and Morgan had shown up after their fight at the compound, shot, bloodied and bruised. It was as if Dante's own brother had appeared looking for mercy.

Of course, Dante's own brother never did look for mercy.

"If you're Dante's, you're one of ours too."

If you're Dante's, you're one of ours too.

"I'm not... We're not..." She faltered, and he squeezed her shoulder.

"You work for me, *ciccina*, and I promised I would help you. That means they're here to help too."

"Okay..." Saint let out a low breath. "I saw something I shouldn't have, when I worked in their restaurant. The Barbarone family doesn't like loose ends. So, I ran."

"Hence the fake name," Morgan asked.

"My grandmother's name," Saint replied. "I wasn't planning on staying anywhere, but I ran out of cash and Dante offered to help and... I was in the grocery store. I don't think he saw me, but I escaped out the back and I came right here. It's only a matter of time before they find me."

"Dante." Caleb clapped him on the shoulder, and it was like Dante could read his mind, could guess what he was going to say well before he was going to say it. Because it was the same thing Dante had been thinking for days, the same thing that had been keeping him up at night. He had hoped it wasn't going to come to this, but to keep Saint safe, he would do whatever it took. "You know what you have to do, right?"

"What's that?" Saint asked, turning to face him. Her bright, ice-blue eyes sparkled with fear and pain and unshed tears, and that was all it took for Dante to step over the edge. "What do you have to do?"

"I have to call my brother."

Chapter Seventeen

A cup of tea and one of the banana nut muffins Rhylee Cash had offered her later, and Saint was finally beginning to feel like herself. After running halfway across the country, she was becoming all too familiar with adrenaline rushes, and the come down didn't seem to get any better. But she was safe, for now, in the highly fortified and protected Sinclair Ranch compound, and Dante was working on a plan.

A plan, as far as Saint could tell, that involved reaching out to his estranged brother after more than a decade. A plan that had his friends exchanging furtive, knowing looks. But she was tired, so incredibly tired from getting herself out of yet another life and death situation, and it was becoming more and more difficult to pay attention to anything around her.

All she wanted to do was lay her head down and sleep for about a hundred years. With him by her side. Because in the moments of panic, in the ebb and flow of fear and adrenaline that had gotten her out of the grocery store and up the mountain, the only thing that had been able to keep her calm was the thought of Dante. And when she was so entirely sure she was about to lose her shit, he had wrapped himself around her and given her the comfort and support she had needed most.

"We're going to figure this out," Morgan said, sitting down beside her on the couch in the back room. It was comforting and welcoming, and she could see Dante's touch all over it, in the tiny, framed illustrations on the wall and the dark, elegant colors. "You should know that these guys saved my life a little while back too. We'll come up with something."

"Were you in trouble with a major crime family?" Saint asked, unable to keep the bite of self-recrimination out of her voice.

"Corrupt senator selling drugs across the border," she replied. "And illegally dumping pharmaceutical waste in the mountains." She rolled up her sleeve and exposed a patch of spider-webbed skin. "I actually got shot at the compound, which is how Reece dragged me here."

"That's not exactly how I remember it," Reece said, pulling up a chair and leaning forward on his knees. "Little miss adventurer over here never met a threat she didn't want to face head on. And I get the impression that you're just as fearless, Saint."

She'd been holding it together by the skin of her damned teeth since the moment she'd caught sight of Del Santo in the grocery store. She'd been holding it together with white knuckles and adrenaline pumping through her veins and eyes on the fucking horizon, but now, safe in this place with these people she barely knew but were willing to risk everything for her, with kindness she couldn't deserve but couldn't give back for the world —

She lost it.

The tears burned hot and heavy, and then Reece and Morgan became watery refractions, bursting into silvery cold light in the split second before Saint buried her head in hands. Morgan was there, and then Skylar on her other side, and they just stroked her back and whispered soothing, comforting words, and through the haze of panic and adrenaline and fear and grief and guilt, the maelstrom of all the thick, heavy emotions she'd been feeling in the weeks since she'd left, in the months since she'd said goodbye to Violet, in the years since Violet had gotten sick, swirled a twisted cyclone around her, and she cried until she wasn't certain she'd ever be able to cry again, until she'd wrung herself dry and the tell-tale pulse of a headache formed low at her temples, unless the room slowly came back into view, three lovely strangers staring at her with nothing but kindness in their eyes and sympathy on their lips.

"Hell of a first impression," Saint managed to whisper, grateful for the glass of water Rhylee handed her. Reece, Caleb and Van had made themselves scarce, and Dante was still nowhere to be found, likely making that very secret call. But she had enough of an audience as it was, and in that moment, her head throbbing and her heart still beating a million miles a minute, the only thing Saint could think about was that she couldn't remember the last time she'd been surrounded by friends.

"We don't do things by half-measure here," Skylar replied. "When my Callie was in her teenage phase, I bought tissues in bulk, so you're almost making me nostalgic."

Saint grinned despite herself. "How old is she now?" she asked.

"She's in college now," Skylar replied, as if she couldn't believe it herself. "And she does know all about what goes on here—the abridged version, anyway…"

That was a distraction Saint could *definitely* use right now. Because in all of the emergency panic that had driven her up the hill and into the arms of these welcoming strangers, she'd caught sight of something she'd wished she hadn't seen—a striking blonde woman leaning over the bar and stroking Dante's chin. Like she had some kind of ownership over him like she knew what she wanted and she wasn't afraid to go after it.

I don't even know what I like.

Because she'd never had the chance to find out…

"What exactly…does go on around here?" she asked tentatively. They'd been so kind with her breaking down and all the offers of help, and she couldn't help but think they would be kind about this too.

"I *knew* he was keeping it from you," Morgan said with a wicked grin. "That day in the shop he was being all weird about."

"Why wouldn't he want me to know?" Saint voiced the question that had been weighing on her mind since Morgan had first made passing mention of The Ranch, and she'd gone ahead and started searching.

"The Ranch isn't for the faint of heart," Skylar said with a shrug. "You need an invitation to even learn about it, so everyone is vetted before they walk through the door. My guess is that he just didn't want to scare you off…"

"Would it have?" Rhylee asked, fishing around in her backpack and handing Saint a sports drink, which she accepted gratefully. "Scared you off?"

She took a long drink, and it dulled some of the insistent throbbing at the back of her head.

"I don't know," she admitted quietly, suddenly feeling so young and inexperienced amongst these beautiful women who knew exactly what they wanted. How could she know what she wanted if she'd never tried anything... "I've never..." The final words got choked in the back of her throat, and she had to blame the crying fit and not the hot wash of shame that came with them.

"Never played?" Morgan prompted gently, "or never..."

"Never..." With her pale skin and light features, it had always been impossible to hide a blush, and the heat stole over her cheeks like she'd spent the afternoon frying in the sun. "It's not that I didn't want to, I just..." Fuck it—*sorry, Gram. You don't need to be here for this.* "My grandmother got sick just after I started college. After a while, it became a full-time thing to take care of her and so that's what I did. She took care of me, and I took care of her."

"You're like our Skylar here," Rhylee said, nudging her sister-in-law, "selfless and loving... Makes the rest of us look bad."

Skylar rolled her eyes, but her cheeks pinked. "Nothing wrong with a later start," she said, and there was definitely a maternal tone to her voice. "If I'd gotten a later start, I wouldn't have been sixteen and pregnant..."

Morgan barked out a laugh, but took a swig of her own water to cover it up.

"The Ranch is a safe place," Rhylee continued. "They work hard to make sure it stays that way. But you don't need to know anything more if you don't want to."

"That's the thing," Saint confessed, saying the words out loud for the first time. "I think I *do* want to know more."

"Well..." Rhylee had all the twinkle of a younger sister's mischief in her eyes when she said, "Then I think you know exactly who you have to ask."

As if the words had summoned him, Dante and the others walked back into the kitchen. His normally humorous experience was gone, and his lips were drawn into a tight line. It made his cheekbones and jaw more pronounced, and it made him look dangerous as hell. It didn't scare Saint nearly as much as it should have to see him so darkly handsome. Dante Castiglione was just the man she wanted on her team when the shit hit the fan, even if guilt surged in her gut at being the one to make his pretty blue eyes darken to near black.

He caught and held her gaze, and for a moment, for a beat of her heart, Saint swore she saw desire there, not just for intimacy, but a desire to keep her safe, a desire to protect her no matter what came next. And that scared her more than anything else.

"Let's get ready to," he said, his tone brooking no argument. "They're on the way."

Chapter Eighteen

The road ahead was dark.

Dante had lived in the mountains his whole life, and the winter chill that lingered at the edge of November always brought shadows and darkness, but it wasn't the starless night that made everything seem so lifeless and barren. Not now.

Saint was asleep in the passenger seat, her head resting on his bundled flannel and her lips parted ever so slightly. It was an unforgiving sleep, that much was clear. Dante knew all about unforgiving sleeps. But no doubt the adrenaline that had driven her from the shop up to The Ranch had worn off and left her dropping, and he wasn't surprised she was exhausted. She'd been quite literally running for her life and he…

I should have been there. I should have stayed with her — kept her from going to the store by herself.

He wasn't prone to self-flagellation. He'd seen grown men flay themselves bare at that altar of recrimination and guilt, and it never seemed to help.

But something about Saint, about the fear and panic in her eyes when she'd come running into the room, about the aching, almost painful instinct he felt to protect her, it had Dante suddenly understanding in abject clarity why men had gone to battle in the name of…

In the name of nothing.

His feelings for her were protective, nothing else. She was on the run for her life, and he wanted to keep her safe, which was why he was currently driving halfway across the state in the middle of the night, surrounded by the Princes Motorcycle Club.

The club like the kind he'd sworn he'd never ride with again.

Led by the brother he hadn't seen in more than ten years.

Beside him, Saint stirred and slowly came back to life. She stretched as much as she was able in the cab of the truck, and finally looked over at him. Even with his eyes on the road, Dante could feel the full weight of her gaze, and he had to fight not to squirm under her scrutiny. Saint was small, petite and angelic, with her light hair and glacial blue eyes, and she still made him want to confess his sins.

Power, Dante knew, came in many forms. He was fairly certain Saint didn't even know the type of power she held, or exactly how brave and capable she was. There was strength in that too.

"Where are we?" she asked, looking out of the window into the stretching mountain darkness, which looked just the same as all the rest of Montana's stretching mountain darkness.

"Still in Montana," he said. "Heading west."

"And where are we going?"

"A safe house."

A safe house, because she was being hunted by one of the most dangerous men in the Barbarone collective. Because she had almost been kidnapped — or worse — just a few hours before, and because instead of telling her to hit the road and take her danger with her, Dante had committed to doing everything in his power to keep her safe — for reasons he still wasn't entirely sure of himself.

Well, he knew *some* of the reasons.

Because this wasn't his first run-in with the Barbarone family. It was the reason he had made the call and, ultimately, it was the reason Nicco had come.

"Dante…" Her voice was very nearly pleading, as if she knew he was grappling with something and holding on by the very skin of his teeth. At the thought, he stretched his fingers against the steering wheel, aware of just how tightly he'd been gripping the leather. "Please."

He could ask her exactly what it was she wanted to know, but why bother? He already knew, and eventually, likely within the next hundred miles, she'd find out the truth. Better she find out from him.

"Nicco's my brother."

She knew that. He'd told her as much before making the call all those hours ago. It was to their luck that the club had been in Montana for a job, close enough that they could give them an escort, even as the darkest, worst parts of him hoped the number wouldn't work and the shaky plan he'd concocted in his head would end before it even began.

"The brother who raised you," she asked quietly, likely knowing the answer all too well. In the time he'd come to know Saint, he'd realized she was quietly brilliant, collecting information to be stored away for later. Perhaps it was the survival instincts at play, and perhaps it was simply her.

"The brother who raised me," he said. Unbidden came the memories, as they always did when thinking of Nicco, two boys in a tiny kitchen learning how to make red sauce and grow basil plants, two boys sitting around a red checkered table tasting their mama's espresso and making twin faces of disgust at the bitter flavor.

Later, two boys learning how to ride bicycles in the street, learning how to fight the kids who were bigger than them, how to steal bread and peanut butter so they would have enough money for the rent on the small little house. Nicco had taught him how to draw, how to work on the truck he'd used to get to school when he had still gone, how to hustle at pool, and how to pick up girls. It was all the normal things an older brother had been supposed to teach, but by then, it was too late for normalcy in their lives.

"He ran with a club to pay the bills," Dante said quietly. "The Midnight MC. I wanted to pledge."

He didn't miss the soft gasp that escaped Saint's parted lips, and the sound echoed like a shot in the dark, frozen night. For some reason, it mattered to him what she thought, in a twisting, painful way. It was a story he needed to tell, at least in part, in order to keep her safe, but it wasn't one where any of them came out looking like a hero.

"We didn't have much," he felt compelled to explain. "I was still in high school and Nicco was barely twenty. My mom hadn't had any money to spare." Because she had been in hiding, because she had run for her life. The parallels of his mother's story and Saint's own were too stark, bright and glaring like the full moon against a black sky. It was no question why he felt so compelled to save her, to give her the chance his own mama had never been given. A chance stolen from her for nearly the same reasons it was stolen from Saint. "Nicco did what he had to in order for us to survive."

"I can certainly understand that," Saint said quietly, the words full of emotion and pain, and Dante had to wonder just how much more pain he would be the cause of before they parted ways. "And you wanted to be just like your big brother." At that, he heard the smallest touch of humor in her voice, a whisper of that melodic tone he'd come to know so well in the weeks since she had arrived. He hadn't realized how much he had missed it until a shadow of that familiar joy ebbed into the corner of his vision.

"I did," he admitted. "Nicco was everything to me. And I wanted to help, to do my part for our family, small as it was."

"But he didn't want that, did he?" she asked. The words were too knowing, too aware of the end of the story, and the companionship Dante hadn't realized he'd needed in that moment was so overwhelming that it made his eyes get hot and the road ahead blur in shades of indigo and onyx.

"No," he replied. "He didn't want that."

"What did he say to you?" Saint reached over and placed her hand over his on the gear shift, lending that remarkable strength to him, when he should have been the one lending it to her. Italian men had been taught one version of manhood. Nicco hadn't abided by that so much, but he'd had his brotherhood of part-time outlaws and full-time rough riders, and it had been difficult not to take some of their values to heart. And while Dante had grown as much with the friends he'd made that summer at the Sinclair Ranch, part of him had always felt that draw to be the strong one, the one people could rely on, the one who never cried.

With Saint's hand on his, he could admit, at least to himself, that it could be awfully lonely holding the world up without help.

"How do you know he said something?" he asked, chancing a look over at her. She was sleepy and mussed, her hair falling loose from her braid and her makeup smudged under her eyes. She was the most beautiful woman he'd ever seen in his entire life, and despite the seriousness of the current situation, despite the fact that he was currently riding with a motorcycle club to get away from a hired hitman, that scared him more than anything.

"Like it or not, I know you," she said. "You've been battling this rejection and loneliness for a long time, haven't you?"

Dante bit his lip. "I wanted to be like him," he said again. "And the one thing Nicco wanted was for me to be anything but."

"He was protecting you," she said quietly.

"And what a hell of a way I repaid him for that, cutting him out of my life."

They fell quiet in the cab of the truck, and it was only the whistling mountain winds and sound of the tires on the road that cut through the nearly unbearable silence. Saint, clearly sensing that Dante needed a breath of fresh air, finally broke through the quiet.

"So, you called his club for protection," she asked. "That's why they're here, right?"

He nodded. "It's a new club," he explained. "Nicco went out on his own after a time. They do protection work for people in need of help."

"People like me," she said quietly, bowing her head and looking down at her lap. She looked so small then, deflated and exhausted, like the weight of her mad dash to freedom was finally catching up to her, and it was all he could do to keep from pulling over to the side of the road and hauling her into his arms.

Instead, he brushed his thumb over her palm, enjoying too much the way she tried not to shudder at the touch.

"People like us."

Chapter Nineteen

The safe house was a small cabin at the edge of a lake. They had climbed several mountain paths, the last a single lane that was more trail than road, and Saint had to assume it was to limit the number of ways a person could get to the safe house. The number of ways a person could be ambushed.

Or killed.

Because it was all real now, wasn't it? She wasn't running from the unnamed threat, forever hoping in the back of her mind that she hadn't been seen or heard that night at the pier. No, they knew she had seen what she had seen, and now she was quite literally fighting for her life. Alberto Del Santo was a monster. She had always known that, but seeing him in the grocery store a thousand miles from the restaurant and the city he ran with blood and fist had been like plunging into a frozen lake. No more theory or paranoia. She was very much being hunted.

And very much being protected.

As they neared the small house, she became even more aware of the roar of motorcycles around her. It should have been intimidating. All she knew of bikers was what she had seen on television, and it seemed very much from the stories Dante had begrudgingly shared that there was a level of outlaw to even the most kind-hearted among them. But right now, all she could feel was grateful.

Grateful for the protection.

Grateful for the man beside her, who had looked his past in the face and called in what had to be the most terrifying favor of his life.

Because of her.

Despite the panic and adrenaline and fear pumping through her veins, Saint stumbled over that one thought. Because she couldn't deny the pull she felt toward him, the need to be comforted and cared for, the inexplicable desire to give herself to him without holding back.

Unbidden came the snapshots of the night before, of when she'd come bursting through the doors to The Ranch, only to see Dante in the well-manicured fingers of a beautiful blonde woman wearing very, very little clothing. It *absolutely* wasn't the most important thing going on in her life right at that moment, but she couldn't help feeling a sense of loss. What would a man like him want with a novice like her? It was clear, from the very little she had seen at The Ranch and the innuendos of his friends, that Dante had predilections of a more devious sort. Surely that had been the reason he hadn't been willing to kiss her the night in the studio. She would never be the right woman for a man like him.

Which is fine. I'm leaving as soon as I can.

Gram had had a dream, and Saint was going to see it through. She was going to make it to New York City and build her new life. Maybe she'd even go to an art class and pick up on the lessons she'd once given up on for good. Her whole life would start again once she was no longer running, and she would be able to leave Montana and Dante Castiglione in her rearview mirror for good. That had always been the plan.

Of course, all her plans had gone out the window about a dozen times in the weeks since she had left Seattle. But for now, it would do her good to remember that she couldn't stay, not after all the horror she'd foisted upon Dante and his friends. If she remembered that, well, she'd be able to protect her heart and soul when all this was said and done.

"We're here, *ciccina*," he said, the low rumble to his voice belying a night of no sleep and an onslaught of memories, and guilt seized at her gut again, a reminder that she wasn't leaving Montana in the same state she had found it.

"It's beautiful." And it was. The night was just ebbing away, turning deep indigo to lilac and lavender, stars sparkling like silver trim, languid fingers of sunshine stretching over the far mountains and making the chilly lake ripple and shine in its reflection. She had only ever lived in the city, and while Seattle was surrounded by nature and water, there was nothing so wild as the mountains of Montana. It was easy to see why so many had headed west and made their homes in the land of big sky.

And I won't be one of them.

She couldn't be. It wasn't an option.

Dante parked the truck and took a deep sigh, then gave a nod Saint was sure was more for himself than her, and opened the door. No doubt communication between him and his brother had been limited in their haste to leave Duchess, but it seemed Dante knew that the time for a reckoning of sorts was coming.

So Saint grabbed his flannel, the one she'd first worn to the store, and then slept in on the drive to the middle of nowhere. It was becoming a sort of security blanket, and it would help to keep away some of the bitter cold of the early dawn. She pulled it on, took a deep breath of her own, and stepped out of the truck.

There were half a dozen bikers with them. Dante had explained that his brother's crew had been working a job in Montana, and that they had been lucky the crew was so close. Normally, they were based out of Colorado, which was more than a half day's drive away, and normally they'd ride with more members, but she was grateful for what they had and the safe house they had been able to provide.

She was grateful, too, that it was a smaller group, because even the few members there cut an intimidating sight. The bikes had been loud from the truck's cab while they were on the open road, but the last one pulling up the path now felt like the roar of thunder in faraway hills. The men wore leather jackets and black face covers to keep away the chill, and she could barely imagine how cold that chill was in the dark of November in the mountains.

"We need to talk."

It was like peering into the looking glass, or the distorted reflection in the lake by the cabin. The man before them was lithe, almost slender, with less of the muscled, powerful build she had come to know in these past weeks. He was taller than Dante, too, by at least a few inches, and his hair was pulled back at his neck, so she couldn't tell if it was longer or shorter than his brother's. His face was more angular, cheekbones pronounced above the top of his face cover, but the eyes...

They were Dante's eyes, the same rich purple gray of storms at sea, a color artists had no doubt been trying to capture for millennia, but which got snagged somewhere between wine dark and the eye of the hurricane. They were ringed at the edges with shadows more pronounced than Dante's, but no less familiar, and they seemed to look through her, as if somehow understanding her all at once and not caring to learn anything more.

"Niccolo." Dante came to stand at Saint's side, and his presence, full and colorful, bolstered her, and shook away some of the cold she felt looking into the hardened reflection of his brother.

Saint couldn't help herself. She laughed. Because the air was freezing and her panic had ebbed and flowed more in one night than in her entire life, and she didn't know up from down anymore. She laughed, and when she tried to bite the laugh back, because this was a very serious situation, the laughter bubbled out in an entirely undignified way, until finally, finally, she could take a few gasping breaths...

"Your mother named you Dante and Niccolo," she said, trying and failing to collect herself. It felt like instead of looking through the glass, she had fallen into Wonderland and was peering at herself through the wrong end of a telescope. "Like, Dante Alighieri and Niccolo Machiavelli."

"Wait until he tells you the name of his crew," Dante replied, his tone dry but the edges of his mouth peeking up at the corners.

Saint turned to his brother expectantly. "Let me guess — The Princes..."

Niccolo didn't respond, just turned to Dante. "You named your shop Inferno Tattoos."

Dante's humor faded a touch. "How did you know that?" he asked, and it was as if she could see the small boy in his brother's footsteps, desperate for approval, for acknowledgment, for love. No doubt the elder Castiglione brother had done what he had to do, but some lessons were lost on lonely children who just wanted a warm place to put their hearts.

"I know a lot," Niccolo replied. "Which is why we need to talk. Inside."

He led them up the path into the small cabin, disarming a high-tech security system by the front door and rearming it the moment they were inside. The cabin was comfortable and well-furnished, with a large rug covering most of the hard wood in the living room and two leather couches angled cattycorner to face a fireplace. The living room connected to the kitchen, which was small but functional and open, with an island in the middle and windows looking out to the mountains and lake beyond. Down a small hallway, she caught sight of a few closed doors, likely bedrooms and a bathroom.

It wasn't Dante's stylish and well-appointed apartments, but it was more comfortable than she could have expected from a safe house in the middle of nowhere, and not a few weeks before she had been sleeping in her car at rest stops during the afternoon, so Saint was in no position to say a word.

She hovered right at the edge of the living room, unsure of what role to play in this strange, life-threatening family reunion. But the truth was she was nearly dead on her feet, even with the snatches of sleep she'd been able to grab on the ride over, and when Dante urged her to sit, she settled into the surprisingly comfortable couch with relief. She startled only when the side door opened and another biker walked through, hitting something on his phone that turned the alarm off, before shutting the door behind him.

"This is Ash," Nicco said, finally sitting down on the couch across from them and leaning forward on his knees. "My sergeant at arms. He wires the security for all our safe houses. Ash—" Nicco's movements were sardonic, somehow, as if sarcasm could be conveyed with the flip of a hand—a hand as tattooed as Dante's. "My little brother."

Ash didn't seem to notice the tone in Nicco's movement, or if he did, he chose to ignore it, instead reaching out and shaking first Dante's hand and then Saint's.

"Saint," she said quietly. He was an intimidating man for reasons that went beyond the physical, though he had to be at least as tall as Dante, and nearly as broad. It was the discerning green gaze that swept over her, not in an appreciative, male kind of a way, but assessing and strategic, as if trying to determine exactly what kind of trouble she was in or threat she might pose.

"Are you telling me or asking me?" he said, and the lightness of his tone immediately put her at ease, despite the seriousness of the moment, and she couldn't help but smile.

"My name," she replied, "Saint."

He nodded. "I know. Nic told me everything. You'll have to forgive his unwelcoming attitude. This is a rough reunion of sorts."

"Ash." No doubt that tone had felled bigger men, but Ash didn't seem cowed by Nicco's warning. Instead, he just grinned at her and settled beside his captain on the couch.

"My brother tells me you saw Alberto Del Santo in the grocery store," Nicco began without preamble, "are you certain?"

And that was how the morning went. She told them the same story she had told Dante days before, about Seattle and the Barbarone family, about watching a man die in cold blood and taking off without a glance in the rearview mirror. She told them about going to the grocery store and catching sight of the man who had as much reason to be in Duchess, Montana as a nun did a brothel, and after what felt like hours of recounting and sharing, but surely only took as long as it needed for the sun to rise over the tips of the mountains, she finally brought them up to the moment Dante had made the call.

Her throat was getting scratchy and raw, and her eyes were starting to burn from the effort of keeping them open when Dante finally put his hand on her thigh.

"Niccolo," he said, his own voice sounding just as frayed as hers, "she needs to rest."

Nicco stood and gave her an appraising look. "We have all we need," he said. "I'm sorry this is happening to you, Saint. We'll make sure you don't get hurt."

It was the kindest thing he'd said to her since their first meeting, and Saint had to swallow hard to keep the emotion from bubbling to the surface, and there were so many emotions that wanted to bubble and spill over. But she'd have time for that later, when she wasn't surrounded by the very incarnations of masculine power and strength, when she could feel weak and sad all on her own without anyone else watching.

Instead, she rose too, barely skimming the height of Nicco Castiglione's shoulder, and held his gaze. "Thank you," she said, before making eye contact with Ash. "Thank you both."

"It's what we do," Nicco said, and then he walked toward the door without another word.

It was Dante who spoke next. "I'm going to get Saint settled," he said. "Don't leave yet."

Nicco nodded and then he and Ash stepped outside, leaving her alone with Dante in the startling bright morning light. She didn't know how to talk to him now, not when the evidence of his sacrifice was glaring her in the face, not when it was so clear that he hadn't had to do all that he had for her.

"I don't deserve all this," Saint said quietly, and why was it so much easier to look the broody biker in the eye than the caring artist who had done everything in his power to keep her safe, despite have only known her a few weeks? "This thing with you and your brother, I never meant to… I'm sorry, Dante."

He placed his hand on her chin, the touch still starting and sizzling, despite all that her mind and body had gone through in the past days. It was impossible to deny how he made her feel, as much as Saint wanted to, as much as he deserved better than the complicated and quite literally life-threatening mess she had brought into his life.

"Nicco and I needed a reckoning," he said, holding her gaze, holding her chin with just a little too much force, to keep her from looking away. "This just gave us a reason to have it. And he's right. The Princes may look mean as hell, but they're dedicated to protecting people, *ciccina*. This is what they do."

"You didn't have to come with," she said. "I would have been fine."

He shook his head. "I know it feels impossible for you to believe, but you're not in this alone anymore." This. This life. This journey she had been on for so long, where it felt like the weight of the world, her grandmother's illness, the mortgage, food on the table, it had all been on her shoulders. She'd been the one making the decisions and cutting out on her own, and he was right that she didn't trust what that meant.

"I'm just a stranger to you," she said, "you never signed up for this mess."

"I did," he replied, those stormy purple eyes so similar to his brother's, and yet so incredibly different, full of brightness and life and possibility. What would it be like to be the possibility in Dante's life? "And you're not a stranger anymore, Saint."

"But..."

"No." His tone was firm and intense, and Saint could admit only to herself that it sparked a sudden and not entirely unwelcome heat low in her belly. "Don't argue with me about this. I'm not going anywhere so just say thank you."

She swallowed. "Thank you."

"Good," he said. "Now you look like you're about to fall over. Go get some rest. There will be plenty of time to talk later."

She wanted to argue, because the headstrong, independent woman she was wasn't used to being told what to do, but the truth was that her muscles ached and her eyes felt like sandpaper after staying awake through most of the night. Before she could do anything else, she needed to rest.

"Just...promise me you'll protect yourself," she said, and she knew he understood her meaning, that he needed to keep himself safe when he finally confronted his past, that the time had come, as he had said, for a reckoning, and she had no interest in watching him burn alive.

"I promise, *ciccina*," he said. "You don't need to worry about me."

Saint smiled at him, maybe a little sad and a little watery, but a smile, nonetheless. But as she grabbed her bag and headed for the first bedroom she could find in the safehouse cabin, she knew the truth. Despite all she was up against, despite the threat that loomed like stormy shadows over the mountains, the very actual threat to her life, she very much had to worry about Dante. In fact, he was the thing that scared her the most.

Chapter Twenty

Niccolo was sitting on a bench at the edge of the small pond when Dante walked outside. He had no doubt that some of the other Princes were hidden around the property, or likely further down the hill where the private road began, but he only passed two bikes. Likely Ash had made himself scarce without leaving his king to fend for himself. In the short time Dante had been part of the club with his brother, before Beau Sinclair had knocked some sense into him, Dante had learned exactly how the clubs could operate like royal courts. The man at the top was revered. There would always be good kings and bad kings through history.

So which is my brother now?

It was the question that he hadn't had time to ponder since the late-night call he hadn't hesitated to make. Surely there was a lesson to be learned about how quickly he looked his past in the eye when Saint was in trouble, but he had a large enough emotional minefield to cross at that moment, and he didn't need his feelings for her to add any to the rough terrain.

Still, he had come to the end of the line.

"*Puoi sederti, fratello piccolo...*" Niccolo said quietly from the bench. "Sit."

Because they'd known each other better in the mother tongue, because there was something more raw and vulnerable about speaking in the language they had shared as boys.

"*Grazie per l'auitare*, Niccolo," Dante murmured. "*Per tutto...*"

"Like I told your friend," Nicco replied without turning around. "It's what we do."

"You didn't have to do it for me," Dante said, voicing the words that cut at his very heart and soul. He wouldn't have been the man he was if it hadn't been for his brother — for better and for worse.

"You still don't understand, *fratello piccolo*. I always have to do it for you."

The words sat heavy in the too-bright morning light. It was cold, and the water before them rippled with the light breeze that passed through the mountains. Nicco didn't so much as shiver, though he barely had any bulk on his thin and wiry frame. He was so much thinner than Dante remembered seeing him last, so much older.

So am I.

"I heard Beau Sinclair sorted you out all right," Nicco said. "I'm glad for that."

"You told him to take me in, didn't you?" Dante asked. "You told him I had nowhere else to go."

They'd all been on their own journeys that summer. Reece had sought respite from a dad quick to anger, Gabriel had run from one too many foster homes, and

Rafe had been a wild young princeling who had needed sorting. Dante hadn't had any type of home to go to at all. Not after Nicco had hit the road.

"I did," Nicco replied. "He was a good man."

"The best." That was a subject that Dante would never tire of. Beau had saved all their lives that one summer he'd given them work. He'd saved them all again when he had tied the Sinclair Seven together with the land he had left them. Nicco had his brothers. Dante had his. "He left us the land and the ranch."

"I know." Nicco's words were almost sad. Maybe it was only that Dante knew him well enough to read between the lines of rough pain and loneliness. Even now.

"You kept tabs on me," Dante said, remembering how his brother had known the name of the shop he'd worked so hard to build. "Why?"

"You already know the answer to that," Nicco replied. "It's the same reason you have my number stored in your phone."

Love. Of course. After all these years, after the pumping, swelling pain in his heart had subsided to something livable, though it still brought a special type of agony with deep breath, Dante still loved his brother. Nicco had given everything to keep him safe, to protect him, to raise him right. That didn't change, no matter how shit things had been when they'd parted ways.

"Saint says you did it to protect me," he said quietly. "Kicking me out. Pushing me away."

"She's smart." Nicco looked at him then, appraising, and for the quickest of seconds, Dante could see the old version of his brother, quick to humor and play. "Pretty, too."

Dante knew it was bait, but he couldn't help rising to it, despite his smarter self. Estranged or not, there was something about brothers that could bring out the very worst in a man.

"Don't you fucking dare…"

Nicco snorted out a laugh, and if laughs could sound dusty and ill-used, it would have.

"Yeah, I knew it."

"You don't know anything."

When his brother leaned back against the bench and stretched his arms wide, it showed just how thin he had become. The same eyes Dante saw in the mirror every day looked back at him, but from a ghostly, skeletal face — gaunt, even. It made his stomach clench and his heart ache.

"I know you don't walk over hot coals for a woman unless you feel something for her," he said with a little too much self-awareness, and Dante had to wonder if that was the reason for the grim look about his brother. "And I know she looks at you like you hang the fucking moon."

She shouldn't. She shouldn't look at me for anything. Not a woman like her.

"Which brings me to my most important question," Niccolo continued. "Does she know?"

For the second time, Dante considered playing dumb. But for the second time, he had to concede it wouldn't get him very far. He knew what Nicco was asking.

"No," he said. "She doesn't know about Mom."

"That's a hell of a secret to keep," Nicco said. There was no judgment in his voice, just a frank statement of fact that was so much worse. Because it *was* a hell of a secret to keep, and no doubt it would break Saint's heart to learn the truth. He had no intention of breaking Saint's heart.

"You're one to talk," Dante said, instead of any of that. "You look like shit. What's going on?"

"I can take care of my own, *fratello piccolo*," Nicco said, rising. "I'm the older brother. It's my job to worry. Not the other way around."

Which answered none of the concerns he'd had about where his brother had been for more than a decade, and left Dante with the burning feeling of guilt again. He could have reached out. He could have called for something other than an emergency. And he hadn't.

"It doesn't have to be that way," he replied. "I'm here now. I can help."

Nicco shook his head. "You need to stay focused on that girl in there. I'll manage the rest."

He walked up the path toward his bike, the distance between them suddenly growing cold and altogether too bright.

"Your pretty friend is right," he said, the words whipping around on the frozen mountain air. "I was trying to keep you safe."

And before Dante could catch the meaning, before he could ask Nicco to just, please stop, to listen, to talk, to *something* after all this time apart, Nicco had pulled on his helmet and started up his bike, the sound like thunder in the stark morning. Ash seemed to appear from nowhere and quickly joined him, and then, like a distant memory Dante could still see after all these years, he watched his brother drive away. Again.

Chapter Twenty-One

When Saint finally woke, the room was edging into darkness again. In the weeks since she'd been living in Montana, she'd come to understand the early nights and sudden drops in temperature, and likely it seemed later than it really was. Her internal clock was entirely messed up, anyway, what with the driving through the night and falling asleep after dawn, and the only thing she was truly aware of was that she was suddenly and completely starving.

And in the same moment, she realized there was a very tempting smell coming from the kitchen, one that shook the last vestiges of sleep from the corners of her eyes and had her nearly jumping from the surprisingly comfortable bed in search of food.

Dante stood at the counter in a white tee and a pair of low-slung black jeans. His hair was still wet from a shower, with one errant curl falling down around his face. He had the old radio in the corner of the kitchen turned on and was dancing along to the music, clearly not aware that she had joined him in the kitchen. She stole the moment to watch, to watch the movement of his hips and the powerful muscles of his waist bunch and pull as the shirt rode up. She'd seen that definition only once in the dark, and as much as she craved the food on the stovetop, Saint felt herself craving something even more.

I want him.

Such a dangerous desire. Dante was her savior in this moment of weakness, and it would be a poor repayment to throw herself upon him. Hell, she'd tried once already, the night he'd give her the tattoo, when she'd asked him to kiss her, and he'd sent her packing to her room. He hadn't even known her real name then, or the type of trouble she would bring to his door, and he'd still turned her away.

Now. Now he knew everything, and no doubt that was enough to terrify even the strongest man.

Well, not everything.

He didn't know that she'd never been with a man, and knowing the little she did of his club and the kind of games he liked to play, that was sure to be a dealbreaker. Hell, the woman who had been flirting with him at the bar when she'd unceremoniously burst in after her run in with Del Santo had been dressed in leather and studs, with bands around her neck and wrists. Saint had no idea how she could stand up to that kind of lifestyle, when she knew so very little about her own desire.

But I can look…

And for a moment, that was all she did, watching him dance as he cooked at the stove, a relaxed, happy version of the man she'd come to know. He had disappeared after the call to his brother, but Dante, for all he promised dark secrets and dark desires, wanted to be happy, he craved a kind of creation and sunshine, even with the dark bands of ink that ran the length of his arms and covered his neck and fingers. He was an artist, and he saw beauty in the world, and the moment she got the chance, Saint was going to leave him to enjoy that beauty without the mess she had brought to his doorstep to screw it all up.

"I know you're watching me, *ciccina*," he said. "If you're in the kitchen, you have to dance."

"I'd prefer to see you dance," she said, not able to hold back a grin. "Do those macho cowboy friends of yours know you like to dance the salsa?"

"*Salsa non è Italiano. Questo è La Veneziana.*"

He stepped forward and took her hand, then spun her around quite of out beat to the music, before kicking one foot forward and then the other. She quickly caught onto the dance, laughing with each new step, taking the chance to spin him, before stepping back again. They were both laughing by the time Dante spun her again and caught her in his arms, too close, far too close for the dance moves, too close for safety, for comfort. They were alone in a cabin in the mountains, and she was running out of reasons why this was a bad idea.

There are plenty of reasons. You just don't care.

With his strong, muscled chest at her back and his arms wrapping too tightly around her, Saint could admit, if only to herself, that she really, really didn't care. He had asked her once when was the last time she had done something for herself...

Maybe it was the night for doing what she wanted for a change.

"Saint..." He groaned, their bodies so close she could feel the reverberation through her, echoing her own flagging self-control...

Before he could continue, however, a timer on the oven dinged, and he took the chance to step away from her, leaving Saint feeling utterly and completely cold.

"What are you making?" she asked, her voice rough and ragged to her own ears.

"Porcini risotto," he said, quickly stirring something on the stovetop. "It was one of my favorites growing up."

Each time he mentioned those years of his childhood, she got closer to understanding him, to understanding all the things that had made him into the man he was, the connection he had with family, the loss he had undoubtedly felt at his estrangement with his brother. No doubt, seeing Niccolo again had brought back many memories of their time as boys.

"It smells amazing," she admitted. "You have many talents."

Dante laughed. "I'm a temperamental artist who needs an outlet," he said. "Cooking helps me focus on something else, so I can do my best work."

She understood that too well.

"I wanted to be an artist."

She wasn't certain where that confession had come from, but it took Dante by surprise, and he paused in his movements at the stove. Saint stepped forward, watching out of the kitchen window as the last vestiges of sun dipped below the far mountains, because that one was hell of a metaphor for her life, wasn't it. "I did a semester of school, before Gram got sick."

"You went to art school," he said, an emotion she didn't quite recognize coloring the edges of his tone. She wanted to look at him, but in that moment, Saint knew it would be her undoing. No doubt she would see pity in those stormy dark eyes, a sadness for all the opportunities that had been swept away in the tumultuous seas of her short life, and she wouldn't be able to handle that. Not from him.

"I did." Thankfully her voice was steady. "I was a painter." And the light outside the window now, casting golden glows along the edges of the mountain range, made her want to be a painter once more.

"You still are," he said. "You don't stop being an artist."

"I'm not so sure of that," Saint finally said, stepping away from the window because she didn't have her paints or her canvas, and she couldn't miss one more opportunity to capture a beautiful thing. "It's been years since I've picked up a brush."

"When we get back to Duchess," he replied, "I have plenty of supplies for you to use. I prefer pen and ink."

Of course he did. Dante's story was told in pen and ink, in the ink that adorned every bare inch of his rich brown skin. She'd seen only the snatches of illustrations on his bare chest, but his knuckles and neck were covered in those slashing lines, like dance set to the surface of the skin.

"One day I'd like to see all of your tattoos," she said, and while the words were a line she shouldn't have been crossing, Saint realized she truly and completely meant them as one artist to another. She wanted to see his work, even if he himself was the canvas.

"Be careful what you wish for, *ciccina*," Dante said. "There are some secrets best kept."

Saint let out a sad little laugh. "I don't wish for much," she replied. "For so long, I wished for Gram to get better, then I wished for her to remember my face. Then I stopped wishing altogether."

She accepted a plate from him, and they settled at the small kitchen table. The smell of the dish before her was overwhelming in its comfort, rich and earthy, and infused with the touch of a dozen generations of home cooking. She missed her own grandmother in that moment in a way she hadn't allowed herself to since running from the restaurant that fateful night.

"Why did your grandmother raise you?" Dante asked. He poured her a glass of wine and she took a long sip before answering.

"My parents died in a car crash when I was very little," she said finally. "I was in the back seat." Which was why even now, she still needed to count to one hundred and ground herself when the panic threatened to overwhelm.

"You survived." There was an expectation about his voice, like he wasn't surprised by this. It seemed Saint had spent most of her life doing what needed to be done to survive.

"Seems I was born to do that, doesn't it," she replied. The words were starting to get hot and stick in her throat, and she took a bite of the meal before her, savoring the spices and hearty warmth.

"You are a fighter," he said. "And we will get through this. Niccolo will keep us safe, I have no doubt of it."

"You can leave me here with them," she said, repeating her words from earlier in the day, even as they fell on deaf ears. "I'm not afraid to be alone."

Dante's eyes darkened, and for a moment she saw even more of the resemblance to his brother, even more of that darkness simmering below the surface. She'd done what she had to do to survive, but so had he, and they had barely scratched the surface of those early days, or what had happened between him and his brother. She had known the man as kind, caring when she'd needed a safe place to land, but there was most undoubtedly a fighter kept caged and angry, and despite herself, Saint wanted to know the man in his entirety.

"Saint...if you ask me one more time..."

"You'll what?" The food had given her energy, and the wine had made her bold, and they were alone in this safe house cabin in the mountains running for their lives, and she didn't want to die without answers, without at least one answer to the stupid question that had stolen her focus from everything more important. She was nearly twenty-four years old, and she was in charge of her own life, *God damn it*. "You'll punish me like one of those women from your club, Dante? You'll treat me like some kind of child? I'm young but I know how to survive. You said so yourself, and forgive me for wanting to take care of you like you're wanting to take care of me. You deserve it as much as I do."

His eyes flared and it was no longer the threat of the storm at sea, but the storm itself bearing down on her — and Saint didn't look away, not from his intense gaze, not from the harsh, solid way he held himself to keep from reaching out to her. She had no doubt in her mind that he wanted to reach out, but to caress or strangle, she wasn't entirely sure.

"You don't know me," he replied calmly, only his veins pulsing along his forearm belying exactly how hard it was for him to hold onto that calm. "You don't know what I deserve."

"I do." At this, Saint stood up and pushed away from the table. Because this infuriating, impossible man was determined to make himself unlovable, determined to keep the bridge between them locked and closed, and while she knew it was smart, knew it was the best way to keep both of them from losing their hearts, their minds, and maybe even their lives, she didn't care, not anymore. It was time to face this head on, and to take what they had both been denying themselves for too many nights.

"I know that your friends love you, that they'll jump on a grenade for a stranger because you asked. I know that you bring your community together in your shop, and that you give people beautiful art they can admire for the rest of their lives. And I know you've done everything you can to keep me safe, even if it means bringing danger right to your front door. So, whatever it is I don't know, I'm certain it doesn't balance out to that. I want to know the truth, now. I deserve it."

"The truth." It wasn't a question, and from the expression in his eyes and the tightening of his jaw, she knew that her aim had been true. He had been keeping the club from her, this other life he hadn't wanted her to know about, because what, she would shame him? Hate him? "You want to know about The Ranch."

He stood then, and in an instant, Saint went from power and control to the sudden and irrevocable feeling of being hunted. She stepped back from the kitchen, moving toward the living room, as if there was sanctum to be found in the couches and throw pillows. His steps were slow, but with his long stride, it only took the work of a moment before he was backing her against the wall. The bricks were cold beneath her sweater, but Saint's body was on fire, burning from his every look, his every step. It should have scared her, to be this vulnerable, to know so little about the ways of men, the ways of *this* man, but the only fear she felt was the fear that he might stop before she ever learned what she wanted to know.

"I want to know about The Ranch," she whispered, as he got somehow closer, the soft tips of his dark curls brushing her cheek, his gaze so intense she was amazed she didn't burst into cinder and flame right then and there.

"You want to know about the filthy, depraved things we do at my club?" he asked, running one tattooed finger down the length of her neck. "About the pain and pleasure we inflict on willing little subs. Are you sure you want to know, Saint? Once you do, there's no going back."

"You're not going to scare me." Her voice was barely recognizable to her own ears. "I know what you're trying to do and it's not going to work. You can't push me away like this. I won't let you."

"That's just the thing," Dante replied, his mouth hovering just at her ear, his words so hot on her skin she was certain they left a trail of fire in their wake, "my subs don't *let* me do anything. I'm the one in control. I'm the one who decides what happens next."

"So decide," Saint challenged. "Decide if you're going to be an asshole determined to keep me on some kind of" — she struggled with the word, but pushed it through gritted teeth — "*fucked*-up pedestal, or if you're brave enough to give us what we both want."

She paused, a terrible thought entering her head in the heat of the moment. "Unless you don't want me like I want you," she whispered. "Unless you're worried I won't fit into your…lifestyle or whatever it's called. Unless that's why you didn't want to kiss me."

Dante pulled back from her, and she felt the loss of his warmth immediately, an ache building over her to pull him back. The distance between them couldn't have been more than a few inches, but it felt like the biggest chasm, uncrossable and deadly.

"You think I didn't want you that night," he said quietly. "You think it didn't take all the strength I had in me to walk away from you. Turning you away was one of the hardest things I have *ever* done, Saint."

"Then why did you?"

Chapter Twenty-Two

Then why did you?

Why had he turned her away the night they'd crossed off all those things on her bucket list, riding a motorcycle under the stars and getting her first tattoo? He hadn't even known her then, certainly hadn't known what she was up against or exactly what kind of trouble her arrival was sure to bring, but he had known, even then, that she'd pulled him into her current. She was lightness and beauty — her name was literally *Saint* — and he was the poet who had descended to the pits of hell.

"Because you're young," he said. "You're so young and so innocent, and I can't do it. I can't be the one to break you."

"It doesn't seem like breaking," she said quietly. "The other girls, they don't seem broken at all. I think you're looking for an excuse to push me away, Dante. So, answer me this, are you ashamed of your club, of your...your *brothers*, you called them? Is it wrong to want the things you want, as long as no one gets hurt?"

Of course it wasn't. She was right, as he realized Saint often was in the weeks he'd gotten to know her. She was right that they'd worked so incredibly hard to build a place of refuge and safety for their members, for men and women just like them, with specific desires and needs. He had always been proud of that, but he'd also never brought someone into the lifestyle either, had only ever played with people who already knew exactly what they were getting into. The idea of making Saint kneel for him, crawl for him, it was…

Otherworldly.

It was darker, a darker instinct than he was used to be, but he'd been denying his craving for this woman nearly since the day she had walked into the diner next to his shop, and that craving wouldn't be denied any longer. He wanted her with a ferocity that terrified him — and should have terrified her.

"People do get hurt," he replied, because he was losing his ability to reason, losing his grip on all the very good arguments for why they needed to go into their separate bedrooms and lock the doors. "My people get hurt."

"Do they want to get hurt?" she asked.

The twinkle in her eyes would be his undoing, Dante had no doubt of that. She was determined to reason with him when he was already past the edge of operating on his baser instinct, but she was also curious. This debate wasn't simply Saint pushing his buttons until he finally cracked open and gave her what she wanted — and he was likely to do that sooner than later — but it was her looking for answers, about the secrets he had been keeping, about the truths she might find in herself.

And if Dante knew anything, it was that some truths couldn't be denied.

"Yes," he admitted. "They do."

"And do you stop when they ask?" she fumbled, the language clearly unfamiliar on her tongue, but her determination greater than her ignorance. "When you use the word or the signal or whatever it is you do, do you stop?"

"Yes." It was the one absolute in their play, non-negotiable.

"So exactly what darkness are you protecting me from?" she asked. "Because that's what this is, right, some valiant effort to keep me safe from your baser instincts, the reason you didn't kiss me, the reason you don't want me to know about your club? I am not a child, Dante."

That much was clear, young as she was, she was all woman, her fierceness and determination to survive, how hard she worked for the ones she loved, how brave she was when faced with horrors most would never know. She was all woman as she stood in the living room of that safehouse in another one of her fucking sweaters, soft and pale as her skin surely would be, her curves stretching the cotton of soft leggings, her hair collected into a loose ponytail he wanted to pull with his entire being.

"I know that," he murmured. He should leave, should walk into the frozen lake to try to calm his surging libido, but his feet were rooted to the spot, and he couldn't move his eyes from her. "I just couldn't stand if you looked at me differently after knowing," he admitted. "It's not for everyone, Saint. It is dark and filthy and wild, and I don't want to scare you."

"I trust you," she whispered, the words so incredibly loud in the cold mountain night. "I trust you to keep me safe."

And that was his undoing. The tether snapped, the ends catching at his ankles as he free fell into his own submission, no control, no holding back, no reason, not anymore, not when she was pressed against the wall and looking at him like he held all the answers to the universe.

And because he'd been dreaming of it, aching for it for so many fucking days, Dante leaned down and stole the kiss he'd been denying them both. It was harsh and hot, almost burning with anger because he didn't want to want her like this, because he couldn't stop himself, and the mixture of loathing and carnal desire was potent and demanding and he swept his tongue over her lips until she parted to him like a sacrifice. Kissing her was like kissing the sun, like kissing one of the stars far overhead, and for a moment, Saint let herself be taken, claimed, and explored, before she was kissing him back, pushing into the harsh pressure between them, demanding answers of her own with her lips and tongue, until soft moans spilled from her parted, swollen lips, and she leaned back against the bricks, panting hard, her face flush and her eyes glazed.

"It doesn't have to be kink," he said, something he'd never said to anyone else in his entire life, because once he'd realized what he wanted, it had always been kink, always been the relationship between power and domination and submission. He hadn't engaged in normal, regular person sex since he was eighteen, and even that had been tinged at the edges with an intensity he would only later come to understand. But for her, for Saint, he could be different.

"I want you," she whispered, shaking her head. "I want all of you. Show me."

"There's things you need to know," he said, aware enough, at least, that she hadn't signed the papers for their club, that she likely barely knew what she wanted, let alone how to play the games that had becomes as indelible as the ink on his skin, permanent and pulsing through his body.

"A safe word, right?" she asked. She was breathing heavy, and he took masculine pride in the expression on her face, dazed and glassy.

"We use three," he said, "green, yellow, red. Green means go, yellow means slow down, red means stop immediately. You will answer me honestly when I ask you, do you understand? The entire dynamic depends on trust. I have to know I can trust you to tell me the truth."

"Yes," she said. "Green, yellow, red."

"Where are you right now?" he tried, the words falling free like a familiar line on a page, like a comfortable old riding jacket that fit just right. This was who he was meant to be, as much as he had wanted to deny it.

"Green," she said, holding his gaze. "Is this...is this necessary?"

He invaded her space then, getting so close to her they could be sharing the same breath, and took her chin in his hand, loving the image of his dark tattooed fingers around her delicate skin.

"This is everything," he explained. "In my world, you will do exactly as I tell you to. You'll cry, you'll beg for mercy, you'll beg for pleasure, for pain, and you'll play by my rules. It is not a game, Saint. It is not a part I play, it's who I am. If that scares you, if that confuses you, it's not too late to walk away. But you have to know the rules, and you have to follow them."

She swallowed hard, and he was struck with the sudden urge to move his hand from her chin to the slender column of her throat, just to see what she would do, how she would react to such an intimate touch. But she needed slow, for now, and he could wait.

"Now, where are you?"

"Green," she murmured. "Green, Dante."

He believed her.

"When we are in a scene," he explained, "you will call me Sir or Master Dante. Master is reserved for exclusive partnerships. If we ever play with another Dominant, you will refer to them the same."

"You play together," she asked. "How?"

"Curious thing." He bit the lobe of her ear and reveled in the shudder it sent through her entire body. "You want to hear all the sinful things we do, or do you want to experience them for yourself?"

Chapter Twenty-Three

She shuddered, so incredibly aware of this man, the man she had called a friend and savior, who was now, in the most ironic of all ways, guiding her into the depths of sin and depravity. She hadn't been certain she wanted what he was offering until his words were in her ears and his hand was on her chin, and she had known in that moment that there was no Dante without the Master, there would be no having him without having his dark and wicked side.

And so much more important, she *wanted* that dark and wicked side. She wanted to know what was behind the velvet curtain, especially if it continued to make her feel so incredibly *aware*, like she was tethered to his every filthy word and hardened promise by golden threads. Not golden. Silver-purple threads the color of his eyes.

What color will those eyes turn when he's in the throes of pleasure?

It seemed that having firsthand knowledge of intimacy wasn't exactly a prerequisite for understanding her body's reaction to him. And her body was most *definitely* having a reaction to him, to the veins pulsing in his strong forearms, to the muscle at his throat, to the heavy gravel tone of his voice as he dared her to try something new.

"I want to experience them for myself," Saint admitted, and she found it wasn't the confession she thought it would be. Despite Dante's — *Master Dante's* — fears of somehow corrupting her to wickedness, she'd never thought of sex as sinful. She'd also never thought of it as all that important, not when she had so much else on her mind, and to that she hadn't exactly spent time determining exactly what it was she would want when the time came.

It turned out she very much did want his type of terrible pleasure, the kind tinged at the edges with hardness and sin, and she wanted it all with a ferocity she hadn't understood until the moment the feast was laid out before her.

"How much?" he asked, the words the silken promise of a deadly pirate with his blade only temporarily sheathed. "How much do you want to experience, *ciccina*?"

She spoke only the truth, perhaps for the very first time, when she said, "All of it. Sir."

Heat flared, the purple of a flame hotter than hot, the ash of an erupted volcano, deadly to the touch. And Saint knew why. Because the word was somehow brand new and entirely familiar on her tongue, and she understood what he had meant when he said it wasn't a game, wasn't a part he played. That word had *power* and though she understood that she would be the one submitting, understood it in her very marrow, Saint knew that the power was, in the end, all in her hands.

"Say it again." It sounded an awful lot like begging from a man she couldn't picture on his knees. "Saint, again."

"Sir."

It was heady, the wash of delicious heat that word brought, like it was tied to her most sensitive parts, tugging at her nipples and lower, slicking the inside of her thighs with desire she knew so very little about, but understood so completely.

"You're going to be the death of me," he murmured, as if to himself. "The things I have been dreaming of doing to you…"

He pulled back, and then, to her dismay, walked across the small living room, settling into a large chair as far from her as he could be. The way he leaned back, with his dark jeans and his dark gaze, he looked no more or less than the king of the underworld, and Saint knew Persephone had gone below the surface a willing sacrifice.

No. Not a sacrifice. A queen in her own right.

"Come here," he said, his tone direct and undeniable. It made her want to obey, which was something Saint had never before considered for herself. "Come sit on my lap, little angel."

Saint swallowed and took the few steps she needed to cross the small living room before coming to stand before him. Master Dante made space for her, and she settled on his lap, aware, so incredibly aware, of just how masculine he was, the hard press of his muscled arm against her back, the persistent throbbing of his length below her ass. She had nothing to compare it to, but surely that was a larger pressure than most. Surely that would be a tight fit…

He'll find out sooner than later… Best tell him while you can.

Except what if he found out and turned her away, in that lingering, almost pathological need to protect her? What if he stopped all this before it even began, and she was left with more questions than answers?

"Stop moving, Saint," he murmured into her ear, the brush of his stubble rough on her cheek, and brandishing its own burning hot flame that connected straight to her core. She hadn't even realized she was moving until his hand clamped hard on her hip and stilled her movements, interrupting the bright pleasure she had been unknowingly chasing. Not that she minded his hand on her hip. There was a possessiveness to the movement that had her craving all sorts of bruises, and Saint leaned back against him, sagging into his strong grip.

"Your pleasure is mine to give and mine to keep," he continued. "I decide when you ride, when you touch, when you come, and how long you have to keep coming for. And I didn't give you permission to ride my cock, *ciccina*, did I?"

"No," she managed, heat rising up her chest, part shame and part frustration and all need in a way she couldn't articulate. "No, Sir."

He nipped hard at her ear, sending twin shockwaves of pain and pleasure bursting through her, and making Saint want to do exactly what it was he had told her not to…

"Good," he continued, peppering dark kisses along the line of her throat, and it took all the power Saint had inside herself not to buck back against him and chase that dangerous pleasure again. She wasn't unfamiliar with her own desire, not entirely, but need shrouded her, covered her like a veil and made it difficult to think beyond when Master Dante was going to touch her next. "You're a natural, aren't you, just waiting for the right master to tell you want to do. So sweet. So *eager…*"

He slipped the hand on her hip under the top of her leggings and brushed her bare skin and Saint sucked in a quick breath and reached for the arms of the chair to steady herself, because this may have been her first time playing this game, but she was going to follow the rules, damn it, no matter how incredibly difficult he was making it...

"You are eager for me, aren't you, angel," he asked. "What will I find when I move my hand?"

"Sir." It wasn't begging. Not yet. But the soft plea spilled from her lips, languid and hard to recognize, her body reacting so much quicker than her brain.

"Where are you, Saint?" he asked, sliding his hand further down her leggings.

She wracked her brain, desperately trying to remember the important information, and finally found it. "Green, Sir," she managed. "But I need..."

"I know what you need," he said, his voice harsh and demanding. "I know exactly what you need, and I decide when and how to give it to you. Am I clear?"

"Yes, Sir," she murmured, each time the word fell from her lips, it brought with a surge of pleasure that made her belly hot and the space between her thighs clench and ache. It was a strange sensation, the emptiness, like she needed to be filled up. Like she needed to be *claimed*.

And she was claimed, as he slid his fingers further down her thighs, stretching the fabric as he traced every inch of her skin, leaving a trail of fire in his wake. She wouldn't beg. Even if she knew it would lead to the very opposite effect from what she wanted, Saint was also determined to be good, because it *mattered*, more than she could explain. It was innate and deeper inside her than she understood, but true and undeniable.

"I hate these fucking leggings," Master Dante whispered. "Every time you wear them, I want to rip them off with my bare hands..."

"Sir…" This was a question.

"Like you don't know how much I've been wanting for you, *ciccina*," he answered. "In your tight little leggings and those short shorts you wear to bed every night. You've been driving me to the absolute limit of my control." At that, he finally, mercifully, slid his finger along the line of her panties, and Saint nearly burst with the bright pleasure and sensation it wrought. "The night you told me who you were" — he continued stroking, like she could understand a single word he was saying while he touched her like that — "I was in the shower, fisting my cock and trying not to think about how it would feel for you to wrap your mouth around me, Saint. I didn't kiss you that night, because it would have led to me fucking you on the studio floor…"

Images swirled in her mind of exactly how they would look bound together, writhing and pulsing, and her core squeezed hard, her entire body aching for more touch, more pressure, more, more, more…

"Instead," Master Dante continued, moving his fingers way too slow, the touch uneven and unpredictable, so she never knew where it was coming from next, "I get to take my time with you. I get to *savor* you. And I will, Saint, make no mistake of that."

He brushed her clit over the fabric, and she lost the control she had been clinging to, the abject pleasure washing over her with a kind of natural unyielding intensity, bursting through her body until she was a writhing, clawing mess, chasing her release over his fingers again and again, until she wasn't sure where his slick skin started and hers ended.

"And here I thought we were doing so well," Master Dante said. "But it is my fault, I suppose. I should have told you never to come without my permission. *Ah, well, I can be merciful.*"

"Sir," she managed, as he slicked over her swollen clit again.

He just laughed. "I could put you over my knee, but not this time. This time, you're going to come again."

"I...can't." It was an intense feeling, and one that had overwhelmed her entire body, until Saint had lost her sense of reality. "It's too much..."

"It's not nearly enough," he replied. "And you can, and you will or I *will* take you over my knee and spank your pretty ass pink." Her cheeks heated at that, and Master Dante noticed. Saint had no doubt he would notice just about anything. For better or for worse. "So I ask you, will you come again for me, little Saint? All over my fingers. Will you cover me in your pleasure?"

It didn't take long, not with his filthy words in her ear and the brush of his stubble along her skin, and those incredible fingers stroking and stroking and stroking, until the words spilled from Saint's lips that she hadn't even realized she was capable of saying...

"Please, Sir, can I come..."

And he kissed the back of her neck with a darkness that consumed and opened her up all at once.

"Yes, *ciccina*. Come for me."

And she did, because it was too much and not nearly enough, because it felt right to be held like this, his grip on her consuming and demanding, and pushing right to the edge and then over and over and over until she was riding that impossible wave of her pleasure bursting into bright lights again and again. Finally, the intensity of her release began to fade, and she slouched against him, her body already wracked with pleasure. Somehow Saint knew it wouldn't be nearly enough for him.

"Open, angel. Taste yourself on my fingers." He slid his fingers from her pants and pressed them to her parted lips, and she accepted, loving the hot wash of shame and the intense pleasure that followed. It was the combination of her own taste, feminine and earthly, and his masculine, overwhelming one that had her moaning around his fingers, until she felt the brush of his cock against her ass again.

"Do you want another taste?" he asked, and Saint found herself nodding, then slowly pulling back from his fingers, before sliding off his lap and onto the floor before the chair. She couldn't explain the impulse, but the rightness of kneeling before him settled into her bones and kept her head down and, despite herself, made more of that impossible heat brighten in her belly. How could she ache for more when she had already been given so much? How could she take more when she was already wracked and exhausted by the pleasure he'd given her?

But she did. She wanted so much more.

"Look at you down on your knees for me," he said, sitting forward and peering down at her. "Such a pretty picture you make, Saint, like you were made for my submission." How could she deny the words when they felt *right*, when they felt true and real deep in her bones? Submission. His submission.

"I think you deserve a reward for being so incredibly good for me," Master Dante said. "Come, take it."

She sat up and reached for the belt he had unbuckled, pulling it free and tossing it to the floor. A frisson on nerves bloomed in her chest, but it was nothing compared to the frenzy of excitement and desire, to see him, to *taste* him.

There was no fabric below the zipper, Saint realized, as she slowly ticked down each tooth, and in a moment, he sprung free. He was larger than she had even felt when sitting on his lap, thick and long, with a swollen head that glistened and leaked in the low cabin light, and she looked up at him with what she was sure was abject wanton desire.

And it wasn't just the size. At the base of his cock was a glistening ring, and a line of shiny silver barbells ran up the swollen length, pulling against the straining skin. It should have terrified her. But hell, it only made her more curious.

"Ask nicely," he said, and Saint groaned, searching for the unfamiliar words.

"Please, Sir..."

"Please, Sir, *what...*"

"Can I taste you?"

"Beg for my cock, angel. I want the filthy words on your pretty little lips before they're wrapped around me."

"Please, Sir, can I suck...your cock?" It was a vulgar word, but the act suddenly didn't seem vulgar at all. It seemed erotic and sensual and beautiful, and when Dante smirked and nodded, she leaned forward and took an exploring lick. His entire body stiffened, and she did it again, loving the power she held over him, even from her knees, loving how a man as strong and stalwart as he was could be cowed by such a simple touch.

But then simple wasn't enough anymore. She learned forward and took that large head between her lips and sucked hard, following instinct so much more than experience, and responding only to the way Master Dante's body tightened with each microscopic movement. His skin was slick, and she tasted salt and sweat and the hint of metal tinging the edges, and she ran her tongue over one of the barbells, loving how it made him tighten and swell in her mouth. He was holding onto his control, and she found herself desperate to make that control break, so she took more of him, though he was so large in her mouth, it was hard to tell exactly how much, and she sucked and licked until he was nearly shaking, until his hands were in her hair, and she wasn't entirely certain if he was pushing her down or pulling her back.

"*Mmm*, that's enough of that," he said finally, gripping her ponytail and gently guiding her head away. There was something deeply arousing about the way his hand felt in her hair and Saint leaned back into the touch. 'The first time I come I want to be between your legs, filling you up and marking you, angel."

"Sir." The word escaped and he grinned, before tucking his cock back into his pants.

"Up, little one," he said. "Let's get these fucking leggings off before I rip them for good. Then you'll have to walk around wearing only your panties and my cum on your skin…"

She swallowed hard and stood, quickly pulling off her sweater and leggings until she was standing before him in only a tank top and her cotton panties. He walked around her, as if inspecting her, and his intense gaze made her nipples tighten into hard peaks. And then, in an instant, Master Dante was throwing her over his shoulder and carrying her out of the living room. For a moment, the world went upside down, and then it went right side up again, as he dropped her onto the large bed in the other bedroom of the small cabin.

"I have this thing," he admitted, his eyes and then his hands raking over her, "where I like to push my submissive to pleasure. I like to see them so thoroughly debauched they can't think or walk straight. I like it when my little one is shaking in my arms and telling me they can't take another release, only for them to come all over again when I tell them to. And unless you need to use your safe words, *ciccina*, that is exactly what I'm planning on doing to you tonight."

He pushed her down on the bed and spread her legs, moving between them like a predatory cat. She was all of a sudden aware of every silver line and scar on her pale skin, but it was difficult to think that way when Dante leaned down between her legs and began pressing those damning kisses to the soft skin at the inside of her thighs. He very well may have been tormenting her, because he was moving so incredibly slowly she thought she might truly lose her mind, but there was no use in pleading when he'd made it incredibly clear what he would do to her if she did.

"You're so sweet," he whispered against her thigh, "peaches and cream, for my innocent little angel."

"I'm not so innocent," she protested, though it wasn't exactly true, was it? She'd only just had her very first non-self-induced release. "There are things I want."

He bit her and she yelped, but couldn't ignore the flood of heat to her core at the literal bite of pain. It seemed to heighten the pleasure, inexplicably, to make both sensations brighter and more intense, and it made her curious for things she wasn't sure she could ever say out loud.

"And I can't wait to hear about each and every one of them..." he said. "But first, I'm very interested in seeing if you taste how I've been imagining."

Hell, why was it so hot to think about him imagining her, to think about him stroking his cock in the shower because she had wanted a kiss...

"Wait, I..."

He paused at her words, his fingers looped into the edge of her panties, and gave her an expectant look.

"No one's ever..."

There were quite a few ways to finish that sentence, but Master Dante seemed to take the most obvious of them to heart…

"No one's ever tasted you here?" he asked, sliding her panties down her legs. "No one's ever made you come on their tongue?"

Saint shook her head, and caught sight of his grin in the one second before her pulled her panties the rest of the way off and then buried his face between her legs.

The sensation was completely overwhelming. The intense pleasure she had felt with his fingers over the cotton of her underwear was nothing compared to the burning, blasting heat of his tongue between her folds, teasing the swollen tip of her clit, licking like he was a man starved and she was a feast laid out for him. It had been arousing to take him in her mouth, to make him want to lose control, and she wondered if he got harder from kissing between her legs. Then she didn't wonder much of anything between the pleasure that was mounting and intense and stealing her breath as he spread her wide and devoured her, sucking her sensitive clit and stroking her entrance before gently pushing one finger inside her.

She was close, so incredibly, *fucking* close to whatever that wild precipice was, and she was about to tell him as much, about to beg him for the permission she needed to find it, when Master Dante froze, his body going completely still above and inside her.

"Saint." He was very, very serious when he looked her in the eye, and she knew, without a shadow of a doubt, that he'd discovered her last secret. "Are you a virgin?"

Chapter Twenty-Four

Are you a virgin?

For a moment, Dante couldn't breathe. He knew exactly what he should be feeling—abject fucking panic. He'd known she was innocent, had known Saint had lived a sheltered life of responsibility, had known from the very first look at her that she represented goodness and sweetness and light. And from the very first morning she'd woken up in his apartment, he'd wanted to pull her hair and wreck her makeup and introduce her to the kind of depravity he'd fought with all his might to keep her safe from.

He knew, in the midst of this chaos, the trouble that was no doubt brewing outside like a winter storm, the shit he needed to resolve with his brother, the secrets he still kept from her, that he had to hope she would never find out, he should be terrified. It was one thing to introduce someone to the lifestyle, which he'd been hesitant about enough as it was. But to introduce her to sex altogether...

He should have been panicked.

But all he felt was *need*. It was bone deep and aching, like he had to act on it, or he'd be ripped apart from the inside. It was something he'd never put much stock in his whole life of playing, and if someone had asked him before this very moment how he felt about training a virgin, Dante probably would have walked away. Too messy, too complicated, too many ways for things to go wrong.

But not with Saint.

With Saint, he wanted to rear back and howl at the fucking moon like the carnal creature he was. He wanted to burn her scent onto his skin, and his touch into her bones, and he wanted to take away the possibility that she ever, *ever* thought of another man.

He'd figure out why all that was later. Much later. For now...

"Saint." His tone was rough, strangled and dark, and it spoke to a side of himself Dante rarely let out to play. "Tell me the truth."

"Yes." Her voice was so incredibly small, and he wanted to wrap her in his arms and hold her tight, wanted to tie her to the bed with her legs spread and her hands bound and never let her out of his sight. "I'm sorry I didn't tell you."

"Were you going to tell me?" he asked. "Or were you hoping I wasn't going to find out?"

Which would have been impossible. Even sliding one finger into her tight little body was enough to tell him all he had needed to know. When he pressed his cock inside her...

The cock that was now straining hard against his pants, stretching taught around the metal of his piercings and no doubt staining his jeans with pre-cum. Because the very idea of burying himself inside her was enough to make him want to sink to his knees and beg for absolution. This wasn't Dante descending into hell. This was Caravaggio, a wreck of baroque sin and human chiaroscuro, Dante the dark, capturing all of Saint's light, and twisting it for his own pleasure.

"I was." She didn't quite sound like she believed herself. "I just didn't want you to stop."

The thought had occurred to him. That he should. That he should never have started in the first place because she deserved so much more than a dark fuck in a hidden cabin while on the run for her fucking life. The thought had occurred to him that he should stop and then it had promptly burst into flames, because he was more sin and darkness than he'd wanted to believe, and the idea of walking away from this lush, wet, spread woman was one he couldn't entertain without feeling himself spiral into the depths of hell and madness. Because of course, he was all too familiar with the depths of hell and madness.

"I should," he muttered, biting off the words, bitter on his tongue. "I should walk away from you, Saint. *Ciccina.*"

"Why?" Her blue eyes, normally so icy in their lightness, blazed the blue of flame, then of volcanic eruptions and chemical burns. His feisty girl. A survivor. "Why do you want to walk away from me, Dante?"

He couldn't even scold her for the familiarity, not when he was straining at such a tight leash on his own desire he was certain it would snap and cut him right through the heart.

"You deserve better," he managed. A man not wrecked with his past, estranged from his brother, a prince in the underworld of a sex club he'd personally worked so hard to build. "Saint, if I touch you now, I will *ruin* you."

Not like some Regency miss. Not like her honor and dignity were on the line, but like drawing the first line of a tattoo on unbroken skin, like creating an indelible, permanent mark that neither of them would ever be able to walk away from.

"Then ruin me."

The words were gasoline to a blaze, and in the next instant, he was on top of her again, one hand pinning her wrists overhead, the other pressing to the soft skin at the base of her throat. The beast inside him burned at the way he felt her swallow under his muscles, like he controlled every touch, every breath, *everything*.

Like she wanted him to.

"You are not in control here, *ciccina*," he growled into her ear. "Do you understand?"

"Yes," she whispered. "Yes, Sir. I understand."

"Good…" He tilted his head to nip hard at her ear, then her neck, then her chest, because he wanted to mark her, *claim* her with an intensity he barely understood. He was in control of her, that much Dante knew in his bones. As for himself, he wasn't certain it was possible to be in control of that. "So fucking good for me…"

"I want to be," she replied. "I want to be good for you."

He released her hands and throat and slowly moved down her body, to kiss the soft skin of her stomach. How many times had he dreamed of pulling her sweaters off, or better yet, pulling her leggings down and taking her against the studio wall? He may have been all about giving pleasure, but Dante had never pretended to himself that he didn't crave the roughness, the darkness of it all. And marring this beautiful, pale skin wasn't a sin, but an act of fucking beauty. She was a canvas for him to lay claim.

"*Mmm*, then you can start by apologizing for not telling me the truth," he said. "For keeping secrets."

"Yes." She bucked at his touch, so responsive, so needy. No doubt she was operating all on instinct, but he fucking loved her instinct. She'd be so beautiful in full submission. It was enough to drive a stronger man to complete distraction. "Yes, I'm sorry, Sir. I should have told you the truth."

"Pretty words," he murmured against her stomach, before leaning down to kiss the skin at the top of her sex. She squirmed and he stopped, loving the frustrated huff of breath she released against her better judgment. "Pretty words," he repeated, "but not enough. I have rules about telling the truth, *ciccina*, and there are consequences for lying."

"I didn't *lie*, Sir," she choked out, her tone of confidence and defensiveness making his heart glow with a kind of pride it would be far too complicated and dangerous for him to try to understand.

"A lie of omission, then," he said. "Still a lie. And still deserving of punishment."

"What kind of punishment?" she asked, her body going completely still beneath his touch, not out of fear or concern, but as if she were holding her breath in anticipation of what was to come. Good. He wanted her wanting.

"I haven't decided that yet," he replied. "Because as much as I want to turn your *pretty* ass red, I'm not sure you're ready. On the other hand…"

He pulled back and reached for his bag on the floor, taking only a moment to find what he was looking for.

The go-bag he kept at The Ranch wasn't exactly luxe, but it had the essentials — briefs, a toothbrush, a bag of toys for putting subs into their place.

"Sir…"

"On the other hand, I think there can be just as much punishment in too much pleasure as there is in too much pain," he replied. "And I also think you'll look very pretty writhing around on my bed."

"Yes, Sir," she managed, her words ragged, her face flushed, and her nipples hard points. He knelt between her legs again and forced her open, exposing her lush, wet center, and making her gasp at his touch.

"You're already so wet for me, *ciccina*," he murmured. "I can't wait to see how long you last before you're begging for me to fill you up. I'm thinking at least three more times…"

"*Three.*" She bucked up. "Master Dante, Sir, I can't… I've never."

"You will," he replied, selecting a small toy from the bag and sliding it between her slick folds. "Because I said so, because you lied to me, and you need to apologize properly, and because I want you *begging* for my cock before I stretch you wide and take your virginity, do you understand?"

She probably would have said yes. Already her body was soft and relaxed to his touch and the gentle slide of the toy between her legs, but before she got the chance to respond, Dante turned the toy on.

Saint screamed and bucked up against him, and he pinned down one of her hips, pressing a little too hard into the soft flesh, feeling truly beastly at the thought that his touch might bruise her delicate skin.

"Ride the toy," he instructed. "It's so much smaller than my cock, Saint. We need to get your tight little hole ready, so take your pleasure. I want you coating my fingers in your cum."

"It's too much," she whimpered, her tone already pleasure drunk and her hands gripping the headboard. "It's too much, Sir."

"No, *ciccina*, it's not," he replied. "When you're all trained up for me, I'm going to fill your tight little pussy at the same time your ass is plugged with a toy, and when I press the vibrator to your swollen clit, *then* it will be too much. But right now, you have to be so good for me, do you understand? Show me just how sorry you are for lying and come all over this toy."

He edged it from her folds to her swollen clit and increased the level, and in the next second, Saint fell apart, writhing and screaming and riding the toy like it was his cock. It would be. Soon. If he didn't pass out from blood loss. Everything inside Dante was demanding that he take this woman, but he needed to make sure she was ready, he needed to make sure that she could handle him.

"That was one, my good girl," he whispered. "Now" — he pressed the toy just to the entrance of her pussy and she bucked and whimpered — "again." He pulsed the toy there, the smallest flicks of his hand, until, despite herself, Saint roused to the pleasure and leaned into it. She chased her release with a kind of intensity that made his balls ache and his cock twitch, and he knew he would never get tired of pushing her limits of pleasure and pain.

"Sir, more," she managed. "Please, more."

"Ask me to finger your pretty pussy," he replied, loving how her cunt pulsed around his toy, how she seeped slick, hot wetness all over his fingers. "Use your words."

"Please put a finger inside me," she sounded half-wrecked. He wanted her to sound all the way wrecked.

He pulled the toy out and she gasped. "No, please finger my pussy," she begged, the filthy words like fucking ambrosia to his sin-soaked mind. "Please make me come again, Master Dante."

Now how could he deny her when she begged so prettily?

"You're so fucking tight," he whispered, more to himself than her. What would it take for him to control himself when he finally slid inside her? "You take my finger so good…"

"Thank you, Sir," she mumbled. She might have been a virgin, might have known so little when it came to pleasure and deviance, but she took to submission like a fucking natural, like she was made to be told and praised and demanded of, and that would surely wreck him. For now, though, Dante was much, much more interested in wrecking her.

"Another finger?" he asked. She nodded at him through heavy lidded eyes and he pressed his second finger inside her. It was such an incredibly tight fit, and he pulsed gently, aware that she would have to relax, would have to open to him to take his cock. If he was any kind of good Dominant, he would make damn sure she was ready.

"You're going to come all stretched out like this," he murmured, dazed by just how fucking pretty she looked spread and stretched for him. "You're going to come on my two fingers and if you do, I'll tell you all about how Master Caleb and I fucked his pretty sub."

Saint moaned harsh and low, and he knew he'd hit the mark on her voyeuristic edge. It would be a fucking pleasure to find all the things that made her want, and

Dante knew for certain there would be many, many things. She was a woman with a hunger deep inside her, and he would do whatever the fuck it took to satiate and pleasure her until she was limp-boned and mindless, and then he would start all over again.

"It's so good," she whispered. "Can you...can you talk me through, Sir? Like you did before?"

Dante couldn't help himself. He leaned down and kissed her slick inner thigh, loving the taste of her on his lips, loving the way her thighs trembled under his touch. She had so many things to learn, and yet, part of him knew she'd teach him a thing or two, no doubt.

"You want me to tell you how pretty your swollen pussy looks with my fingers stretching you open?" he asked. "How tight you're going to be wrapped around my cock? I shouldn't want to be your first, *ciccina*, but it makes me so fucking hard to think about claiming you, marking you, taking you before any other man ever gets the chance."

She moaned and twisted around his fingers. "I want it to be you, Sir," she managed. "I want you to be the first one inside me."

"You've never fingered your own pussy?" he asked, because all of a sudden that was exactly what Dante needed to see, exactly how he needed to get her to the edge.

"I have," she confessed. "But it never felt like this..."

"Tell me."

"In the bathtub," she whispered. "Sometimes I'd part my legs and cup my breast and..."

"Did you go fast or slow?" he asked. "Be very specific."

"I'd pinch my nipple," she admitted. "I... I liked the pain of it. I know that's wrong, but it just made everything so much better. And then I'd slip my fingers between my legs and stroke my clit and…"

He pulled free from her pussy and stood, then settled at the edge of the bed. "Keep talking, little one," he continued. "I want to see exactly how much pain you like with your pleasure."

Chapter Twenty-Five

Before she could continue, Master Dante had her over his lap, her bared ass in the air, and her pussy on display to the room. It should have been shameful. Perhaps before she was in this moment, when she was first learning about exactly what he did up at his club, it might have been, getting spanked, getting forced to come again and again until she was sure she'd lose her mind for it.

But it wasn't.

All Saint felt was a bone-deep sense of rightness, as though this was where she belonged and what she deserved, and she was going to do her damnedest to continue enjoying every fucking moment of it. Because he made her *curious*, bold, and not afraid of anything. She could trust this man, and because of that, she knew she could give up her inhibitions and simply feel all the incredible things he was offering her without worry or shame.

"What are your safe words?" he asked, and it took a moment for the words to permeate her pleasure-addled brain.

"Green, yellow, red," she murmured, focusing only on the feeling of him stroking her ass, sliding his fingers up and down her thighs until he was right at her center again, teasing and brushing soft touches across her sensitive skin. Far, far too soft for what she really needed. In this position, she was so much more exposed, but it was difficult not to find the eroticism in that, and in the anticipation that she was very much about to be spanked.

Her pussy pulsed at that knowledge, and Saint gave up on the *shouldn't*. Because she wanted to. She wanted Master Dante and she wanted whatever pleasure or punishment he was willing to give her.

"You will use your safe words if you need them," he said. "Otherwise, you will take the punishment I give you."

"Yes, Sir," she whispered. "Thank you, Sir."

"So welcome, sweet girl," he replied, before bringing his hand down hard on her ass. The sensation burst through her, slow and then fast and then all at once a pounding of bright hot pain on her skin and muscle.

Except it wasn't only pain. The pain was white, but the pleasure that followed was bursting yellow, hot and intense at its heels. They mixed and mingled together, until Saint found herself writhing and bucking against Master Dante's thigh in a desperate search for friction, for release...

"So fucking pretty," he said, soothing the sore spot on her skin with a surprisingly gently touch. "You take this punishment so well. You take your pain so well."

Those words were heady and intense, and they made her preen and glow. Because she wanted to be good for him, wanted to do as he told her and continue to win those smiles and dark tones of approval. It was almost innate now, how much she wanted to please Master Dante, like it had always been inside her.

"I think you can take another," he said, as if in deep thought. "This time when I spank you, I want you to chase the pleasure, Saint. I want you to soak my jeans in your release because you just love how it feels to be punished."

He didn't give her a moment to respond, not that she would have had a response for that anyway, he simply brought his hand down on her ass, on soft, fresh skin, and while she hadn't thought it possible to come just from getting spanked, she realized in that moment exactly the hold he had over her.

Because it was as much mental as it was physical, as much emotional as it was the way his hand brushed her skin with such delicate care before coming down hard and fast, a bright and impossible wash of tangled pleasure and pain that caught her breath and made her lose the control she'd been clinging too. Her body was already so heightened with pleasure from all the previous orgasms, but more than that, Master Dante wanted it.

So Saint wanted it too.

And it was that combination of intense desire and that natural, inexplicable and undeniable need to submit, that finally cracked the foundation loose and had her coming all over his jeans, had her bursting free just from the touch of a harsh, punishing hand. Her pussy clenched hard and her nipples throbbed, and it was all Saint could do to hold on as wave after wave of intense, overwhelming pleasure broke over her.

She could dimly hear Master Dante above her, gently stroking her hair and telling her she was doing so good, taking his punishment so well, and each filthy word from this beautiful man made more hot pleasure surge through her, until Saint was nothing more or less than a live wire, dangerous to the touch and liable to cause complete destruction.

"I could watch you come every day for the rest of my life, and I'd die a happy fucking man," Master Dante said, his tone no longer so full of authority, but wrecked by the same intense pleasure that seemed to be overwriting all her senses and good thoughts. "You're so fucking pretty when you lose control."

"I want you to lose control for me, Sir," Saint admitted. She didn't know all the rules yet, didn't know if she was allowed to want those kinds of things, but she didn't care in that moment. All she wanted was to see this powerful, intense, man at the end of his tether.

"You will, sweet girl," he replied. "But we need you all the way ready, first."

"I'm ready."

"I thought we already agreed" — his tone held a note of amusement, but the dangerous kind, a cat toying with its prey — "that your pleasure belongs to me. I decide when you're ready, little one. And you haven't finished apologizing to me for lying yet."

"It's too much," she tried to protest, knowing it wouldn't do her any good. Unless she used the safe words he had given her, he wouldn't stop with the barrage of pleasure. And Saint didn't want him to, she could admit that much to herself, at least.

"It's just right," he replied, stroking a line between her legs, slick and hot with desire. "My cock is much bigger than this toy or my fingers, *ciccina*. It's going to stretch your tight little pussy wide, and I want to make sure you're dripping wet when I fill you up. The only pain you should feel is the pain I decide to give you, do you understand?"

"Yes, Sir," she managed. "Thank you, Sir."

The last word hitched up, as he gently pressed two fingers back inside of her. At this angle, they felt bigger and more intense, and she had to concede that he might be right about preparation. She'd taken his cock in her mouth, and it had been a ferocious thing, hard and demanding, difficult to wrap her lips around. How it would feel pressing into her...

A surge of wetness spilled from her pussy at the thought. She wanted him to push in, to stretch her wide, to fill her up... And no doubt he knew it.

"Mmm, I would pay a lot of money to know what you're thinking about right now," Master Dante said. "But first I believe I made a promise."

He buried his fingers deep and tugged, just enough to make her buck and strain against his touch, just enough to have her squeezing her pussy around his fingers.

"See I think you want to hear about exactly what goes on at The Ranch, don't you, little Saint? You've been curious since the day Morgan mentioned it in the studio. I bet you even looked it up after they left."

"How did you know?" She pressed back against his fingers, but he only pulled her hair harder. Not that it was any kind of deterrent. Sain was realizing very, very fast, that she liked how it felt to stand at the crossroads of pain and pleasure.

"You blushed over breakfast the next morning," he said. "And my devices are synced."

"You knew…"

"I had a sense." He stroked her from the inside. "And it made me so fucking hard to think about you in my room at the club, Saint. I tried to keep myself away from you, but the fantasies I've been having…"

"Tell me…" It might have been begging, she wasn't entirely sure. Pleasure had clouded her judgment and made her single-minded in its focus.

"Tell you?" he chuckled. "Tell you about the toys I have in my private room at The Ranch, little one? Or about the time Master Caleb brought his Skylar to my rooms and I pierced her nipple, before she took us both."

That had Saint losing control, because she could barely imagine the feel of one cock inside her, let alone two…

"See, I'm not sure I really want to share you," Dante went on. "I don't think I want anyone else to see what you look like all spread and stretched and wet for me. But…" He continued to pump his fingers in and out, in and out, each movement making more of that honey pleasure burst through her. "But I have this *persistent* fantasy, *ciccina*. Do you want to hear it?"

Fuck. "Yes, please, Master Dante…"

"*Mmm*, so pretty when you beg. I have this fantasy of you, with your arms tied behind your back with a pretty pink bow, and matching plug in your tight little ass…" he whispered the words like they were ancient script bound to raise the demons of hell. "Have you ever been touched there? Played there?"

Saint shook her head and Dante's voice was positively lethal when he continued.

"I will teach you so many things, little one," he said, and it came out as a demand, a filthy promise. "I'll teach you how to sit on your knees and beg for my cock, how to hold your release until the moment I tell you to come, how to relax your tight little hole so I can push inside you."

He continued to pump his fingers in and out of her, and Saint thought she might be losing her grip, not just on her pleasure, but on all good sense, on her connection to the world, because she wanted it, all of it. She couldn't explain this desire, or desperate, aching need to do as she was told, but she was absolutely completely certain of it.

"Please," she begged, not even recognizing her own voice against the desperate pleading, but knowing, innately and deeply, that she would do it all again if she had to. Would beg to do it all again, if she were honest. "Can you touch me...?"

"*Fuck.*" Master Dante bit out the world. "You know what you're asking for, don't you, little one? I need to be sure."

"Please...touch my ass while you finger me..." Surely that wasn't *her* begging for him to breach her, to touch her in such a deviant and filthy way, but under his touch, she was free now, free to admit what she wanted and to reach for it, to beg for it.

He moved his fingers from her center, and she realized how empty it made her feel for him to pull out of her, how much more she wanted to feel full and stretched by him. But then he was sliding his thumb through her wetness, and *God* had she ever been so wet in her entire life, certainly not in all the times she'd ever brought herself pleasure. His thumb dipped inside her, and it was filthy and erotic, the parting of her most intimate folds in such a lazy, masculine way, and when he pulled out again, she knew he was slicking himself to tease her tight hole, the one she'd never touched but had always been so secretly curious about, the one she'd tossed a book across the room for featuring, only to pick it up again and read under the covers.

The master and submissive dynamic was entirely new to her, though she felt it deep in her bones and belly, like she was meant to do as he bid her. But it also offered a sense of freedom and weightlessness, like she could give him all her desires and they wouldn't be shameful or taboo or off-limits, because she wasn't asking, wasn't pushing the boundaries herself. And there was something so incredibly freeing about that. Since the time had passed when normal women lost their virginity, it had been hanging over her head like some sword of Damocles, something she would have to explain away, to share in a moment of shameful, sheltered weakness, but not with Dante, not if the harsh expression in his eyes was any indication, not if the way he whispered about claiming and taking her was any relief, and she realized that it had all been leading up to this moment, the moment when he had her bent over his lap, his fingers slick with her many, many releases, and his large thumb circling the rim of her tightest hole and...

Fuck...

"*Fuck...*" The curse spilled free, and she wrenched her body backward, forward, overwhelmed by the sensation and need of relief from its intensity at the same moment she craved so much more of that wicked touch. And it *was* wicked, Saint had enough of a mind to know that much in her haze of pleasure, but she didn't care, not in the least, because when he touched her there, especially when he slid his two fingers back inside her pussy at the same time his thumb teased her hole, she would have begged, submitted, surrendered to whatever it was he offered. It was pleasure in its very purest form, and it was wracking her body like she was some kind of sacrifice at the altar to erotic desire and...

"*Shhh, ciccina,*" he whispered, and it should have made her crazy that his voice was so calm, so darkly steady while she wrecked against the waves of pleasure, but she took it as a guiding light, her light head in the storm, "*Shhh*, relax for me... Let me in..."

"Yes, Sir." The words felt automatic and perfect and she took a deep breath, which was difficult against the bursting glow of her need. For him, though, she tried. In, and out, and finally her body began to relax, the intensity of the pleasure and pressure ebbing away just enough for him to press his slick thumb against her tight muscle and...

"Mmm, I wish you could see yourself now," he murmured. "You're so lush and spread for me, taking my fingers so well. It's a fucking dream to spread you like this..."

He continued whispering filthy, depraved things as he pushed his thumb all the way inside her, and that was her undoing, the complete overwhelming of abject pleasure until Saint had lost her grip on the world, her touch on his leg, her awareness of anything but the wave after wave of need and lust and desire pushing her to the very peak and then, as she found herself babbling, begging, asking for permission she didn't fully understand but knew to be innate within them both, and somehow holding on until the very second when he gave her that permission, Saint fucking broke.

Chapter Twenty-Six

Dante had been going to clubs and learning about submission and domination for more than half his life. He loved the play of power, the intensity of surrender, the opportunity to wring pleasure from a submissive partner, and then to care for them in their renewal. But nothing in the world could have prepared him for the sight of Saint dropping over the edge with his fingers in her tight, virgin pussy and his thumb in her ass.

Because this isn't just about sex.

And that was a voice in his head he paid no mind to, as he gently continued to stroke her over the top of her pleasure, moving slowly to help her down the peak, and finally pulling his fingers free to release her. Not that he wanted to release her. No part of him was interested in letting this woman go, and so he pulled her from his lap into his arms and whispered in her ear that she was so good, so good for him, that she made him so proud, and that he couldn't wait to take her, to earn her pleasure.

Finally, she looked up at him with her eyes fading from glassiness to a startling clarity that should have terrified him. If anyone saw him for the man behind the tattoos and the motorcycle and the bartender humor, it was Saint, and that should have been enough for him to put her down, lock the door behind him, and walk away.

But he just wasn't a strong enough man to do that.

"I know what you're going to say," she said. "You're going to say I've had enough and it's time to call it a night."

She might have been right, if he were more capable of denying his inner impulses.

"I should." Against that greater impulse, he slicked one finger across her swollen lips. She parted, as if on instinct, and sucked the finger into her mouth, which made his cock jump and swell in his jeans.

She released him and said, "I don't want you to walk away again. I want this. With you." And then, while holding his gaze with those crystal blue eyes, "Master Dante."

"You make it hard for a man to deny you," he admitted. Confessed. "But it's my responsibility to be sure. Where are you right now, *ciccina*?"

"Green, sir," she said with a smile. "Like, neon green."

"Cheeky... And are you sore?"

"A little," she replied. "I'd like to be more."

"You think you're so funny, don't you?" He couldn't help it. She made him laugh, made him feel at ease in a way few partners had done in recent memory. Made him push all thoughts of those real and terrifying confessions from his mind. There was only one thing he wanted to think about right now.

"I do, actually," she said. "But I'm not exactly in the mood to make you laugh right now, Sir."

"And tell me, *ciccina*," he whispered, laying her down on the bed and coming to hover over her, "what are you in the mood to make me do?"

"Fuck me."

The word sounded a little rusty on her lips, rough and ragged coming from such a soft and feminine mouth, but that only made him hotter, harder, more desperate to claim this woman as his own. Whatever that might mean.

"You know you aren't in charge here," he said, standing to pull off his jeans and tee. Then he was climbing onto the bed and sitting with his back to the headboard. He reached for one of the condoms he'd tossed to his side table and pulled it on, give his cock a hard, long stroke as he did. No matter how they did this, it was going to be a tight fit, and the animal, beastly side of him took over when he thought about how she would look sliding down his cock.

"Come here, Saint," he murmured to her. "Straddle my lap. Rub your pretty wet pussy along my cock."

She whimpered and did as she was told, pressing her swollen clit against his length and sliding back and forth until Dante had to dig his fingernails into the flesh of his hand to keep from giving into his baser instincts.

"Good girl," he said, loving the way her eyes flashed that hot, volcanic blue when he praised her. "Now put the tip of my cock at your entrance, just the tip…"

Which might just be enough to kill him. Because she was *so* tight, even with all the releases she'd had, even with the slickness of her pleasure between her folds and staining the inside of her beautiful pale thighs.

"Permission to speak, Sir?" she managed, her voice so ragged, so incredibly delicious in its wretchedness. She was right at the edge of complete consumption, and he was going to be the one to take her there if it meant descending into the very depths of hell itself.

"Granted," he said, bringing one hand to the apex of their coupling to stroke her clit.

"You feel big," she whispered. "And your piercings are... *Sir*."

He moved in that instant, not up but forward, sliding his cock piercing along her clit and making her lose her grip and nearly her balance.

"For your pleasure, *ciccina*," he murmured. "It'll feel so good inside you, I promise."

"Does it feel good for you?" she asked, the slightest hesitation in her eyes for the very first time.

"You have no idea," he said. "But this is about you. This is about me earning your pleasure, earning your release around my cock."

"I heard women don't always...the first time."

She sounded nervous now, and Dante would have done whatever it took to get rid of that expression on her face, to put her at ease and stem her concerns and her fears.

"It's my job to make sure you do," he said, meaning every fucking word. "Saint, when I'm a master in a scene, your pleasure, your comfort, is my number one priority."

"And what of your pleasure?" she asked. "You must want..."

"I want everything," he answered with a rough honesty, "but that's not what's important right now. What's important right now is that you're going to press down, just an inch, and tell me how it feels."

She took a deep breath, and it was as if it swelled in his chest, because *fuck* this woman wasn't scared of anything. She was a fighter, a survivor, and she went after the things she wanted.

"Where are you?" he asked.

"Yellow," she said. "It's big, but it feels, *oh my God*, it feels so good. I want more."

"I want you to take a breath in for me," he said. "Slow and steady, then breathe out."

He repeated the action himself, because having her tight little channel clenching around the head of his swollen and aching cock was enough to drive a man to absolute madness.

"Better," she said. "Can I…?"

"Go at your own pace," Dante instructed. "Slowly, no rush. You'll take me all the way when the time is right."

And *fuck* but there was nothing, *nothing* like the watching her sink down on his cock one fucking agonizing inch at a time, her soft gasps of discomfort turning into whimpers of pleasure and promise, into gratitude and begging, and more than once Dante found himself counting back from one hundred in his family tongue to keep from losing himself to the pleasure.

Until finally, amazingly, Saint was completely seated on his cock. She was so fucking tight it felt like a vise around him, but it was nothing compared to the expression of pleasure and need etched in her pretty eyes, or the expression he was so quickly coming to recognize that she was about to beg for so much more.

"You'll get it," he preempted her. "But first tell me how you feel sitting on my cock, little one."

"It's so big inside me," she confessed. "I didn't think I could take you but…" He shifted the smallest amount, and she gasped. "Please, I need to move."

"You don't need to do anything except what I tell you," he replied. "Stay right where you are and describe it to me."

Maybe he was the masochist, because was there anything more erotic, more fucking incredible than having this woman wrapped around him confessing?

"It's stretching me," she said, "but I'm so full… It's what I wanted when your fingers were inside me, this…fullness. And I can feel your piercings and it's so…good…"

"You are incredible, Saint," Dante admitted. "Like you were made for me to pleasure and enjoy."

"Please enjoy me…" She was getting that dazed, heady expression on her face again, and it truly was enough to wreck a man. "I've come so many times tonight, I want to give you the same pleasure."

"I get pleasure from watching you find yours," he said. "It's my favorite thing to do…"

"Prove it."

Cheeky thing. He thrust up the smallest amount and she gasped, reaching for the headboard to steady herself against the onslaught of pleasure. So he did it again. By the third thrust, Saint was meeting his movement and beginning to lift up and down on his cock all on her own, and then she was riding him in earnest, a little messy and out of rhythm, as she chased her pleasure and desire, but the most fucking incredible thing he'd ever felt, ever seen. She was relaxed now, her pussy still so incredibly tight around him, but her body no longer bowed so taut, and she was singularly focused on making him lose control.

Which he would do, eventually. First, he had to make sure she had everything she needed.

"Do you want to make me proud, little one?" he asked, knowing how much it would goad her, and the flash of intensity in her wild eyes told him he'd hit his mark.

"Always," she whimpered, the word a slicing, hot arrow through his sensitized body. He ignored the wound.

"I want you to soak my cock with your release," he said. "I want you to come all over me. Can you do that?" He slid his hand up to her swollen clit and stroked until she was confessing and babbling and begging, and then, ever so slightly, he pinched.

She detonated around him, squeezing his cock with a kind of wild fervor that would sear into his body and mind for a million years to come, and hot waves of release spilled over him, drenching his cock, claiming him as he was meant to be claiming her. The thought was so wicked and depraved and carnal that it snapped the last vestiges of his control, and he went barreling down the hill of pleasure right after her, thrusting up with as much care as he could until he lost the battle and spilled hot, thick cum into the condom between them. The last thought he could find, because the pleasure addled his whole fucking head, was that he would claim her properly. Soon.

Chapter Twenty-Seven

Saint was only dimly aware of Dante lifting her up and carrying her to the bathroom. The room smelled of cedar and fresh mountain air, but all she could think about was him, the scent of this man who had given her...

Everything.

Up until that night, she hadn't known what she hadn't known, and so many things in her life had taken precedence over her time and energy. It had made her a little uncomfortable to be as old as she was and to still be a virgin, but Dante hadn't treated her virginity as something to be ashamed of. On the contrary, he'd treated it as a gift, like she was bestowing him with something grand and great, and not in a weird, old-fashioned kind of way either. He'd given her so much time and attention, and any fears she might have had about pain or discomfort had been quickly assuaged in the face of his guidance and firm care.

Care that continued now, because he placed her at the edge of the tub before drawing a bath and searching the cabinets for some soap and towels. To her surprise, the soap was a luscious lavender and vanilla, unexpected for a safe house cabin in the middle of nowhere, but she was grateful for it. She was already so relaxed, so calm and soft and free from the panic and adrenaline that had been chasing here these past days, and she wanted it to last as long as possible.

"Climb in, *ciccina*," Dante said, after testing the temperature of the bath. "The warm water will help with soreness."

"Will you come in with me, Sir?" She didn't want to lose the sense of connection between them, not just yet. She had come to know this man in the past weeks, and Saint was fairly certain he would find some way to feel guilty about corrupting her sooner than later, which she absolutely wouldn't stand for, but she wanted to hold onto the moment they had shared as long as she was able.

"If that's what you want," he said. "But I think we're done with lessons for the night. Your body needs to recover."

As it was, he had strung half a dozen releases from her, and she was overly sensitized and wrecked with the pleasure of it. She just wanted him close, not that she was about to admit as much. They may have been dancing around this burgeoning desire for days, longer, but it was most certainly going to complicate matters between them, and with her future as uncertain as it was, there was no knowing what might come next for her. For them.

If all she had was a few nights with this beautiful man, it would have to be enough.

Dante slid into the tub behind her, sending small waves dancing upon the surface of the water. He was so incredibly *large*, his body muscled and strong and sturdy, taking up space all around her. He was also incredibly large where it seemed to matter in a very specific and intense way, and there was no doubt in her mind she would be feeling specific and intense memories of him come morning.

I want that.

Maybe it was this newly unleashed sex demon inside her, and maybe it was just *him*, this safe place she had come to land, but she wanted that reminder, that feeling of being owned and claimed and taken in a way that mattered. She still understood so little of the world he came from, but she was very much beginning to understand that.

"You have questions," he said, guiding her body back so she lay against his strong, steady chest. For a moment, Saint simply listened for the beat of his heart.

"Is it always like this?" she asked quietly. "Sex, I mean. Is it always so…" She searched for the word, and was grateful for the heat of the bath to cover her flush when she finally found it. "Completing."

Dante stilled, just for a beat, and then let out a slow, steady breath. "No," he admitted. "I don't think it is."

"Is it for you?" She didn't want to know about the women he had been with before, but also, she very, very much did, and a surprising and unwelcome streak of jealousy burst in her belly.

"Fishing, fishing, Saint," he said on a laugh. God, she was beginning to love that laugh, rich and honey sweet. Like him, she decided. He was darkness and sin, as he'd been so quick to confess to that night, but he was pure and sweet at the same time, and it was that balance that made her feel so safe and so comfortable in his arms. "I work hard to make sure my submissives are provided for. It's my responsibility."

"Heavy is the head that wears the crown," she teased. And then sobered. "Have you had many, then?"

"I have," he replied. "None that were all that serious. I should apologize for trying to scare you away from it. Normally I'm quite proud of the safe play community we've created at The Ranch."

"I understand." She didn't want to understand, but she did. "This is complicated."

"I think we passed complicated when a hired mob hitman traveled eight hundred miles to find you," Dante replied, stroking her arm with a gentle, reassuring touch. "But giving you pleasure is the least complicated thing in my life."

She leaned her head back against him, loving the way he circled her arm with one strong finger and then the crease at her hip. Her body responded to those now familiar touches, but she pushed away the subtle demands for more pleasure. She needed a break, as he had said, and she was content to sit in the water simply talking.

"I liked it," she admitted. "Being submissive. I didn't even know I could like something like that."

"There's a whole world of kink and power for you to explore," Dante murmured into her ear, not dominant, not even flirtatious or promising, but intimate all the same. "There are many different types of Dominants and submissives, many different rules for you to learn and practices to try."

"I'd like that," she said. She felt floaty and warm in the cabin tub, with Dante pressed against her and the barriers between them down. He'd been holding himself back from touching her, and now it felt like they could communicate without the fear of what was to come next. Of course, she had no idea what was to come next, but in that moment, Saint didn't actually mind the uncertainty so much. "I'd like to understand it better. All I do know was that it felt right in the moment."

"Some of us are just drawn into," Dante explained. "For some, it's play. They go for a night at the club and then go home and have their regular life for the rest of the week or the month. Some people are in scene most of the time, if they ever leave."

"And you?"

"I don't expect my subs to scene all the time," he said. "But the Dominant is a part of me, Saint. I need to care for my subs, in and out of scene. It's innate— natural. And when it comes to sex, yes, this is what I need."

She didn't know if she needed it. She'd never had any other kind of sex to compare it to, but she had liked it, then wanted it, then *craved* it by the end, and the honorifics had fallen so freely.

"So I couldn't call you Sir at the shop?" she asked. It was difficult not to be curious about this lifestyle, not when it had just about blown her mind six ways to Sunday.

"Well, I *am* your boss," Dante replied. "So perhaps not a perfect example. That decision will vary from person to person, how much they want to expose their dynamic, how much consent they have from the people around them to witness the play. When I take you to The Ranch, I would expect that you call me Sir, even if we're not in a scene. When we're around the other

Dominants of the club, you'll be a reflection of me, and your behavior should be without reproach."

"So I'm allowed into the club now?" she couldn't help it. Dante was too big and dark and scary not to tease every once in a while.

He stroked one large hand through her hair and used it to gently pull her head back. Whatever kind of play they got themselves into the future, she would be extremely interested to explore that apex of pleasure and pain again. *Extremely.*

"If you keep up the cheek, there will be consequences, little Saint," he said. "And I don't mean a soft punishment like tonight. I have a very wicked imagination."

"All the more reason to misbehave," she teased, yelping slightly when he pulled her hair again. "Sir."

"Just you wait," Dante said. "You have to heal, but when you do, I promise you'll see what happens to little subs who don't do as they're told."

"And I look forward to it," Saint murmured, leaning back against him and taking his free hand in her own. She studied the ink on his knuckles, each a small standalone design, a crescent moon and star, a clover, an owl that spread its wings when he parted his fingers.

"Early in my career," Dante explained. "When I was just learning my style."

She turned his hand over, reading a line of script.

E quindi uscimmo a riveder le stelle. She struggled with the pronunciation, but Dante was quiet as she worked her fingers over the ink at his wrist.

"And thence we came forth to see again the stars," he said. "The end of Dante and Virgil's journey, their return from the underworld."

"A reminder," she guessed. Not guessed. She knew him well enough at this stage to know what those words meant to him, and why they were inked along his veins. "That you can eventually escape hell."

"Something like that," he replied. "I did that one a long time ago, but it's still one of my favorites."

"And what's your other favorite?" she asked. He had seen her, in the moments they had shared that night, in the abject pleasure and submission and release, and in this soft, hidden space, protected as they were, she wanted to see him.

Dante shifted her, and Saint followed the movement until she was looking at the upper quadrant of his chest and shoulder. There was an innate and intense power there, in the swell of his bicep and the ripple of muscle, but at that moment, all she could focus on was the art. A large, cutting image of Da Vinci's Virgin of the Rocks took up most of his chest and shoulder, her hair casting over his bicep and wrapping, as if to give the illustration placement in the three-dimensional world. The artist had captured her likeness, the gentle, downward look of her eyes, the softness of her brow, the almost amused look on her lips, the thin line of a halo wrapped around her hair. The image faded toward the bottom and sides, where it would have cut out to the Child and John the Baptist and Uriel the angel, instead highlighting only Mary, in one of the iconic material illustrations of her from history.

"Your mother." Saint didn't have to ask.

Dante nodded, watching her through those dark, heavy eyes. "Maria," he said. "A proper Italian name, of course."

"Mary…" She searched his gaze, and when he nodded, Saint reached out and followed the lines of ink with her finger. The work was exquisite, as was the body below, but the meaning behind it was what set Dante apart in the world. "What happened to her?"

"It's not a happy story," Dante said quietly. "But I'll tell you. If you want."

Saint nodded, reaching for his hand in the water with her other one. "I do."

"She was married off," he explained. "To a man here in the United States from a powerful Italian family with connections to the homeland. She was nineteen when she came over from Florence."

Saint gasped. "That's awful." Nineteen. Younger than she was now.

"My mother was strong." His words were entirely devoid of emotion, as if he'd learned that was the only way to protect himself while telling his mother's story, and Saint's heart broke for him a little bit more. "But she was alone in a new country where she barely understood the language. She didn't have a lot of options available to her. And she couldn't go back home."

"What happened?"

"She married him. Had Niccolo and then me. And then..." He faltered and cursed low under his breath. "She died."

He didn't seem inclined to give her any more information, and Saint didn't want to push, not when the story already seemed so raw, and Dante already seemed so transported to the history he clearly preferred not to remember. "My mother had run away from her husband by then. She'd run halfway across the country and hidden us in a small house in Montana, where she cooked for a local diner. And when she died, Nicco promised he'd keep me safe."

"Your mother was very brave," she said. "And so was your brother."

Dante swallowed. "I know. Niccolo is a good man, and I owe him more than I can say. We were both so young when we saw each other last, and I know a lot more now than I did back then."

"Will you tell him that?" It was a bold question to ask, but they were in the very tall weeds now.

"I don't know," he said this with such a note of honesty in his voice that she couldn't help but believe him. "I don't know if that's a bridge that can be crossed anymore. The things he did for me, I'll never be able to repay them, and I'll never be able to make up for the way we ended things."

"I don't know your brother," Saint said quietly, "but I once said something similar to my grandmother. She took me in and raised a two-year old far after she ever thought she'd have another baby in the house. I said to her that I could never repay her for all she had done, and she took my hand and told me she had never expected repayment. She loved me and would do whatever it was to keep me safe, and that was the end of that."

"You did repay her," Dante pointed out. "You cared for her to the very end."

"Because I loved her and I would do whatever it was to keep her safe," Saint replied. "Even on the hardest days, there was never any question of that."

"Saint—" Dante gathered her up and helped her from the tub. "You are going to make me a good man whether I like it or not."

She leaned forward, loving how the water between their bodies warmed, and how the big, strong, tattooed man easily accepted her touch.

"That's the difference between us," she said, pulling back from warm brown skin. "I already think you're a good man."

Chapter Twenty-Eight

Dante wasn't used to waking with someone in his bed. He always set the rules before a night with a sub, and he sought out the kind of partners who were on the same page as him.

Because you're so afraid of someone running you don't even give them the chance.

Maybe. Seeing Niccolo again had made it hard to pretend that he wasn't still nursing wounds from the way they had left things, that he wasn't still expecting the other shoe to drop with friends and partners, always, in the back of his mind, thinking they'd leave. Keeping the lines clear had been a way to protect himself but...but maybe it had also been a way to hide his heart away from the world, and to make sure no one ever got close enough to hurt him like that again.

So far the only who had gotten that close was Saint.

The night before, he'd broken about a dozen of those rules, introducing someone into the lifestyle who had never scened before, introducing someone to *sex*, and jumping in with both feet, despite neither of them acknowledging the temporary, complicated conditions surrounding them. It was just that Saint undid him, in a way. She made him want to skip past the rules he'd set for himself and see what waited on the other side.

And she definitely made him want to wake up with a warm, lithe body beside his in the soft glow of the dawn. He could sleep easy, knowing The Princes were prowling the safe house and could keep any threats at bay, and so for the moment, Dante could focus on the way Saint felt in his arms, with her soft, smooth body pressed against his increasingly hard one.

She seemed to have a halfway decent idea of what she was doing to him, because she pressed back with the softest, sweetest moan he had ever heard, and it went straight to his cock. She was barely out of the gate and already pushing him to the absolute limits of torture and temptation.

"You're going to have to stop squirming, *ciccina*," he said. "Or your body won't get the chance to heal from last night.

"I don't want to wait," Saint said on a sleepy morning sigh. "You feel good…"

Nothing but the thin layer of her cotton panties separated his leaking cock from her welcoming pussy, and Dante was struck with the sudden and impossible need to fill her up and claim her tight little body with his fingers, cock and cum. But getting her pregnant was absolutely off the table, no matter how much the thought made his balls tighten and his cock pulse.

"You don't know what's best for you," he said, unable to keep from leaning into her soft, silvery hair. She was messed and mussed, and there was something so incredibly intimate about seeing her before the morning, before the chaos, just the loose-limbed, thoroughly pleasured woman writhing in his arms.

"Maybe I do know," she replied, reaching her arm over his shoulder and pulling him closer, "and maybe I just don't care."

"You should." He wrapped his hand in that silky hair and tugged, loving the way she leaned into the sensation, loving how it felt to have her so ready and willing for his touch. "I like what I like, Saint." He held her hair with one hand and reached his other between her legs, finding her wet panties with his thumb.

"Last night I liked what you liked," she said, a soft moan escaping as he stroked her clit. She was so *eager* even after the intense pleasure of the night before, and it made pride swell in his chest, as she followed his touch and begged for more with every whimper and arch. "Sir."

"I know you did," he said, leaning down to bite the strong column of her neck. "I felt your sweet little pussy clenching around my cock while you came." She whimpered and pushed back against him, the friction making him even harder, and her eagerness making him halfway feral. "But that was just a taste, little angel, an introduction."

"So teach me," she whispered. "Sir."

At the honorific, which she'd shared so willingly, so without prompting, Dante's cock swelled and his balls tightened. He pushed her panties to the side and slipped one finger between her folds, nearly losing his fucking mind when he found her so wet and ready for him, her pussy no doubt still sensitive from the night before, but her folds slick with arousal. He slipped one finger inside, loving the way she bowed and arched to his touch, and he tightened the rest of his hand around her thigh to hold her in place.

"Not yet," he teased, with the part of his brain that was still able to think straight against the intense onslaught of pleasure. "Your body is still healing. And while you belong to me, it's my job to take care of you."

Not that she belonged to him, not in any real lasting sense. But his cock didn't seem to care about the complicated nature of their relationship, and the dominant part of him ached to claim her, to care for her, to make her his in the most intense and carnal of ways.

"Will you take care of me now, Sir?" she asked, and that she wasn't abjectly begging was nothing short of a failure on his part.

"I'm tempted to leave you like this," he said, doing just the opposite as he pulsed his finger in and out of her little hole. She was still so incredibly tight and so incredibly responsive, and he wondered if there would ever be a day when he didn't crave this woman's pleasure. "Leave you all wanting and wet and waiting for me. Maybe I'll make you walk around with your pussy empty and slick, so you're stuck wondering when I'm going to push you up against the nearest wall and fill you up."

Saint gasped and then moaned long and low when he pushed his second finger inside.

"Please, Sir," she whimpered, the sound so fucking pure in the lavender light of the soft morning. "Please fill me up."

She was a natural at begging, just as she was a natural at the submission she'd only just begun to understand. There were so many things he could teach her, and each of them made his cock jump and his lower belly glow with heat, but innate submission was a beautiful thing, and he had no doubt in his mind that Saint had been waiting for the right Dominant for longer than she even knew.

I'm that Dominant.

It didn't matter that he had no idea where their relationship would go, or even when they would be safe to return to their lives. The beast inside him, the one that demanded pleasure and submission and care, it saw her as *his*, and the idea of any other Dominant touching her, even one of his best friends, made Dante a little feral. She was, for the moment — if that was all he was going to get — his to touch and pleasure and care for.

"Not nearly good enough, *ciccina*," he said. "If you want my cock inside you, I need to believe it…"

"I want your cock." This on a whisper that tore from her lips. There was nothing so filthy as the good girl begging for him, using the depraved, forbidden words that she'd likely never say in any other world. "I want to be stretched again. Sir."

"So sweet." He pumped his fingers in and out, each movement earning him another gasp, another whimper. She was already so close, because after just one night together, Dante was already starting to understand her body and natural responses all too well. "So good for me, do you want to come on my fingers, *ciccina*?"

She nodded, and he pulled her hair again, just enough to balance the pain and pleasure she seemed to like so much, and Saint let out another soft whimper.

"Please, Sir," she murmured, "can I come on your fingers?"

"Such pretty words from such a filthy mouth," he said. "But you've earned it. Take your pleasure, angel."

It didn't take much for her to rock against his touch, once, twice, once more, and then she was tightening around him, her channel clenching and fluttering and her body wracking with need. It was a heady fucking feeling to bring her to the edge and watch her fucking fly.

Finally, Saint emerged from the ripples of her lust and desire, and peered up at him over her flushed shoulder.

"Sir?" she prompted, and he hated that a sense of hesitancy was back in her voice. If it were up to him, she'd feel emboldened and confident every moment of the day, which most definitely said something about this thing between them that he didn't want to hear.

"I need to let you rest, little one," he replied. "Let me take of you."

"Can I take care of you?" she asked, the genuine curiosity in her voice keeping him from scolding her for talking out of turn. Not that she didn't like a little punishment. Even in their few shared hours together, he'd already learned just how much his little sub liked to toe the line between pain and pleasure, a line he'd worked hard to perfect.

"Master Dante..."

He was going to say no. Her body did need to recover, after all, and there was still so much they needed to discuss about the lifestyle, about the future, about a million important things that could affect their lives forever, but the name on her lips, the *Master Dante* whispered with a pleasured-laden huskiness, made him trip over his self-control until he was agreeing to things he knew he shouldn't.

"What do you want, little one?" he asked. "Be specific."

"I want..." She sighed, clearly still unused to the dangerous words, and all the more enticing for the edges of innocence that still clung to her flushed cheeks and hesitant tongue. He liked to think himself more evolved than all that, but there was something so incredibly damning about being the first man to touch her the way he had the night before, like eating the pomegranate seeds in the underworld, a contract he hadn't even realized he had signed.

"I want to suck your cock," Saint finished, a hint of pride in her voice that made the same emotion swell in his chest. She was most definitely too good for him, this angelic woman, but he was just bad enough that he wasn't about to turn her away when she offered all the things he wanted. "Can I, Sir?"

"How can I resist you?" he murmured, more to himself than to her, and slowly pulled his fingers from her swollen pussy. He couldn't help himself, and brought her sweet release to his lips, loving the way she tasted on his fingers.

"*Fuck.*" She said it so softly, Dante was certain she hadn't meant for him to hear it, but God, he loved that she was so sensitized, so easily turned on and willing to submit to her most depraved desires. Getting subs to submit to their most depraved desires was just about his favorite thing to do—and doing it with Saint was something else entirely.

"Next time I'll lick it straight from the source," he promised, hearing the intense gruffness in his own voice. His cock had been hard and swollen just from waking pressed up against her, and watching her come all over his fingers had nearly been enough to send him over the edge. "But I believe there was something you wanted, angel."

"Yes," she whispered, "can I?"

He pushed himself up the bed until his back was against the headboard, and she watched the movement with fascination, her eyes never straying too far from the swollen head of his cock, which jutted up proudly, the piercings catching the early morning light streaming in.

"Did they hurt?" she asked, kneeling before him in an absolute act of redemption and sin. With her long blonde hair spilling down her back and her soft skin flush with her last release, she looked every part the debauched angel, on her knees and begging for salvation.

Begging for his cock.

"Yes," he admitted, running his fingers along the familiar barbells.

"Did you like it?" He liked when she smiled, when she gave him that secret little grin that meant she knew more than she let on, and that anyone who underestimated her would be more the fool for it.

"I did," he said, because Dominant or not, Dante had never been afraid of the touch of a little pain. His arms and chest and neck were covered in evidence of that. "I like them much more now."

"So do I…" she replied. "Can I touch them, Sir?"

"I'd insist that you do," he said, leaning back against one folded arm and watching her intently. She was inexperienced, but she more than made up for it with her curiosity and eagerness to explore and learn, and she leaned down and ran her tongue up the line of barbells along his shaft.

Dante swallowed hard, squeezing the headboard behind him for support, not that there would ever be enough support to keep him from losing himself to the pleasure she offered. No doubt she'd have him begging and whimpering before too long.

"Keep going," he said, remembering a second too late that he was the one in charge. "Wrap your pretty lips around my cock, *ciccina*. Take what you want."

That seemed to be the permission she needed, and in the next moment, Saint leaned down and took his swollen head into her mouth. Dante swore low and harsh under his breath, because there was nothing like the touch of an angel sucking his pierced cock to make him lose himself, and Saint didn't give him a moment to catch up to the pleasure. She simply lowered herself, taking another inch and then another, until the entirety of his piercing was buried in her mouth. She licked and sucked as she went, hollowing her cheeks to make her mouth somehow tighter around his cock, and Dante began reciting his mother's prayerbook in Italian in the back of his mind to keep from spilling too quickly into her perfect, waiting mouth.

It didn't matter. When she dropped all the way down on him, running her fingers along his other piercings as she did, Dante lost his fucking control. He bucked up into her mouth just once, and then he was spilling and coming hard and fast against her tongue, hitting the back of her throat with every rough buck, and loving how she seemed so eager to take him, so eager to be his good submissive, to give him pleasure like it was her due.

"*So good,*" he murmured, stroking her hair, her swollen lips, her blush-pink shoulder. Her eyes were glassy, in part from choking on his cock and in part because she clearly had found pleasure in the act, and he was just about to tell her to get on her knees and stick her ass in the air so he could reward her for being so good for him, when he heard a noise in the living room.

Dante's entire body went stiff, and Saint immediately transformed from the beautiful, free, pleasure confident woman to a rabbit caught in the lights of an oncoming car. For a moment, for a beautiful moment, they had been able to forget all the shit stirring around them. But good things only lasted so long.

"Get in the bathroom," he growled at her, his heart ramping up its rhythm for an entirely different reason than it had just a moment before. "And lock the door. There's someone in the house."

Chapter Twenty-Nine

Saint wasn't about to let him go out there alone. This was her disaster and she'd brought it to his door, and she was at least going to be there to make sure he didn't suffer for helping her. But she also wasn't about to face down a potential threat to her life in nothing but a pair of soaked panties, and as if on instinct, she climbed from the bed, taking care to move as softly as possible, and reached for Dante's oversized flannel. He was so much taller than her that the shirt fell to her thighs and that would have to be good enough.

"Bathroom," he said again, keeping his voice low, which only made him sound more intense. As if he could sound more intense. The Dante who had been her boss, her friend and confidant at a time when she needed it most, was nowhere to be found. This man was waging some kind of battle, and she was just glad he was on her team.

"No," she whispered back. "I'm coming with you."

He pulled on his jeans, then reached into the side table and swore low under his breath. "No, you're not." When he turned, she saw he held a gun in his hand, and her belly leaped, her nerves a jangle of fear and confusion. He wasn't the kind of man she had ever expected to see with a gun, but Saint couldn't deny that his tattooed fingers wrapped around the base like he was all-too-familiar with its feel, and she had to concede that she might not know him as well as she thought.

He looked as though he was going to argue again, but there was another, louder sound in the living room, and he shook his head, then motioned for her to stay behind him. That much she could do. As much as guns had been the cause of all the most recent and terrible heartache in her life, as much as she never wanted to hold one in her hand as long as she lived, it was better for both their survival that he lead with the weapon.

She followed his low footsteps down the hall, certain that whoever was waiting for them, Del Santo or Lorenzo or whichever other goon had been sent for her head, could hear the frantic beating of her heart echoing as loudly as the toll of a bell. With each step toward the living room, she felt the panic ebbing into the corners of her vision, her palms clammy and her chest tight with fear. Just a few minutes before she had been falling apart to pleasure in Master Dante's arms, and now she was about face death. Again.

Dante turned the corner, finger on the trigger, eyes on the target ahead, and she reared after him, ready to give whatever kind of backup she might be able to give, when they both came up short.

It wasn't Del Santo. It wasn't any of Lorenzo Barbarone's cronies or cousins.

Niccolo and Ash stood at the kitchen counter. Before them were a handful of grocery bags, and Ash was messing with an ancient looking coffee machine.

"I knew you were angry with each other, but that seems a bit extreme," Ash said to Dante, angling his head to the gun. Dante shook, as if coming out of a stupor, and lowered the gun, placing it carefully on the side table.

"Why do you have a gun?" Saint asked. She knew this wasn't the time, but she couldn't stop the words from spilling free. She would accept his help, if for no other reason than because he hadn't given her a choice, but she wasn't going to be the cause of this man's downfall. She refused.

"It's mine," Niccolo said, accepting a cup of coffee from his sergeant and leaning against the far counter. In the soft purples of the morning light, she could see just how tired he looked, dark circles under what would have been eyes nearly as beautiful as his brother's, if they didn't seem so shadowed around the edges. Those circles were not the work of a single night of patrolling, of that much she was certain. "Insurance."

"You knew how to use it," she pointed out, very much talking to Dante and not his brother.

"It's been a long time since I've had any reason to carry one," he replied. "But I can't apologize for knowing how to survive, Saint."

She had to give him that, knowing as she did about doing what it took to survive. And the truth of the matter was she was only safe because they were surrounded by half a dozen motorcycle riders, each of whom, no doubt, was carrying. So she backed down. For the moment.

"Is there any update on Del Santo?" she asked Niccolo and Ash, who seemed entirely too awake for the hour of the morning and the fact they'd just had a gun pointed at their faces.

"We don't know where he's staying," Ash admitted. "They must have some kind of hideout for him close by, but there's no history of credit cards or other way to track him."

Saint sighed. Until they could pinpoint Del Santo and send him back to Seattle, she was going to be stuck in the safehouse in the middle of nowhere.

Not that being alone in a cabin with Dante had proven anything but fruitful, but she couldn't ask him to stay here with her for much longer. He had a business, friends, a life he had to get back to. She had already imposed enough, and whatever shared moments of pleasure and play they had enjoyed the night before and in the cover of soft dawn light weren't going to change the fact that they couldn't stay here in this safehouse cabin forever.

I still have to get to New York City.

It had been the great dream she and Gram had always shared, a life in the glamorous uptown streets of New York. Whenever they'd had a bad day, and toward the end, there had been more bad days than good, they would make plans for life in New York.

When we live in New York City, we'll try a different restaurant every day.

When we live in New York City, we'll go to the Metropolitan and look at the statues for hours.

When we live in New York City…

When I live in New York City…

It had been her mantra for so many days on the road, the one thing that had kept her from her losing her mind to fear and grief. But in the weeks since she'd moved into Dante's apartments and become his receptionist, she'd found herself saying it less and less, so even the thought of the fantasy life she had created for herself had become a little rusty and unused, and panic of a whole new kind swelled in her lower belly. She couldn't stay here, not in this cabin, and not in this state, and she most definitely couldn't stay by Dante's side. That wasn't in the plan, not for either of them.

"We do have some good news, though," Ash said, placing two cups of coffee on the far side of the island for her and Dante. It struck her that he was likely the one making sure Niccolo ate or drank anything, and she had to wonder how much longer the elder Castiglione brother was going to punish himself for doing what he could with the choices that he had.

"We like good news," Saint replied, sitting down on the stool and pouring some of the milk Ash offered her into the coffee. It was exactly what she needed in that moment, soothing and warm, and she took a much-needed deep breath. "What do you know?"

"We know where he's going to be tonight." This from Nicco, who continued to lounge against the side of the counter. "And we know he's meeting with a contact from the family."

"Who?"

"That much we don't know," Ash admitted. "But it verifies that they're here for you, and they're going to do whatever it takes."

Behind her, Dante stiffened, his body going solid and taut, until pure power emanated from his every muscle. Ash must have seen what she only sensed, because he continued, his voice clearly calmer and his words designed to put Dante at ease.

"We won't let that happen, D," he said. "It's our job to keep you both safe. That's what we signed up for. And we're good at it."

"I know." Dante didn't continue, but his muscles relaxed the smallest amount, and after a moment, he settled onto the stool beside her. "What's the plan for tonight?"

"We can discuss that with our team in a bit," Ash said. "They're switching shifts now."

"I'd like to meet them," Saint said without thinking. "To thank them for everything."

Nicco's eyes flared, with pride, maybe, or approval, and Ash nodded.

"We'll make that happen," he said. "They take pride in protecting people." He glanced back at Nicco with an expression Saint couldn't read, and continued. "We all do."

Nicco held his sergeant's gaze until Ash turned back to them. "Anyway, we brought breakfast and a few more groceries. Neither of you should go out until this is sorted."

"I'm going with you tonight," Dante said, his voice harsher and more intense than she had ever heard it in the entire time she had known him. Even in the throes of pleasure and domination, he still maintained a thread of the lighthearted humor and goodness that made her feel so incredibly safe with him. She had to wonder if it was the presence of his brother, the dark shadow, a reminder of a different life, that made him so rough around the edges, or if she was the cause of this intensity.

"You are not." Nicco's tone brooked no argument.

"Nic."

"Don't."

They were communicating in half words and dark expressions, and then Dante muttered something in Italian she couldn't understand, and Nicco bit off a reply that gave away its meaning even in another language.

Across the counter, Ash sighed. He was a big man, and he still wore his large, imposing riding jacket, his hair loose and bright against the black leather. He didn't have quite as many tattoos as Dante or Niccolo, but they stood out against his lighter skin, stories on his hands and climbing up his neck. He was very much the picture of imposing and intense biker, but she got the impression he was softer below the surface, that he cared for the men in their crew, that he took care of their captain when he couldn't seem to do it for himself.

He gave her a rough smile, flashing the gold of a tooth far in the back of his mouth, and offered her a donut from a paper bag. Saint accepted, but she couldn't take her eyes off the two men, the tension between them simmering hot and heavy, and liable to explore at any time. Finally, she reached over and took Dante's hand, loving how he accepted the touch seemingly without meaning to.

"I want you to stay here with me," she said, realizing as she said the words that she meant them. "It would make me feel better to not be alone."

None of them pointed out that any of The Princes could stick around the in the cabin with her while the raid went down. She didn't want a stranger to keep her safe. She wanted Dante.

"If that's what you prefer, *ciccina*," he said, finally tearing his eyes away from his brother.

"It is," she replied. "Please." The word *Sir* was right on the tip of her tongue, and it almost spilled free without thinking. But she still didn't know the rules of how submissives and Dominants engaged, and she wasn't particularly interested in sharing everything with Niccolo and Ash. No doubt they had come to some conclusions, what with her wearing Dante's flannel and only Dante's flannel, but there were too many details she needed to work out first before spilling every secret.

"Then I'll stay," he said.

Chapter Thirty

Staying was harder than he had expected it to be. Of course, there was a great deal to be said about spending time in a warm, cozy cabin with a beautiful woman over freezing his ass off on the back of a bike in the mountains in November while hunting down a killer, but Dante still felt a sense of guilt and shame for not being out on the road with his brother and the other riders.

Okay, so it wasn't only guilt and shame. There was also an anger bubbling up within him that made it a little difficult to see straight. Which, he knew, was part of the reason Nicco hadn't wanted him to come along. Nicco knew a thing or two about vengeance and served-up justice, and even after all this time could undoubtedly see that anger would cloud Dante's vision on a mission. It was far too important a mission for any of them to be walking in without their head on right, and the rational side of his brain could see as much.

But the much less rational side could only picture the panic in Saint's eyes as she had come barreling into his club after seeing the mob enforcer in the grocery store, and all he could think about was tearing the fucker limb from fucking limb.

Which was why he was nowhere near Saint right now, sitting on the porch of the cabin, and letting the cold seep into his bones. She'd stayed the worst of his anger and irrationality by asking him to stick around, but as the day had ticked away, each hour bringing them closer to the time of the raid, he'd become snappier and more intense, like a caged animal liable to bite even its owner, and the one person he refused to snap at was the woman at the center of all of this.

More than once that day she had expressed her apologies for dragging him into the middle of her mess, and had offered him an out, had told him that he didn't have to stick around for all the fallout. But it was too late for any of that, and he'd told her as much. He was in it with her until everything was safe and right again, and she was just going to have to deal with that.

What he didn't tell her was that the idea of someone hurting her made him see red, for reasons neither of them could stand to deal with right now. He'd seen her face when he'd pulled out the gun, and no part of him wanted to expose her to any other violence or danger — even if that violence and danger was his own temper in that moment.

So he'd parked himself on the porch of the small cabin in a coat that definitely wasn't designed for a Montana winter, and set his sights on the stone path to the safe house. He'd watched his brother and the sergeant at arms and several of The Princes take off for the raid more than an hour before, and his gut was clenching and unclenching with nerves that threatened to shake him apart.

His dominant side had always demanded care. He cared for his subs in an innate and determined way. He *needed* to, just as he had needed to take Saint in that very first night he had seen her at the diner. But caring for people was messy. It made him ignore all his responsibilities and realities to run away with a stranger in the middle of the night, just to make sure she was safe. It made him knot his hands with worry waiting for his estranged brother to come back from a fight that wasn't even his. It made him wish a thousand, a million times in his life that he had been there to protect his mother, paying the guilt of that off in grief for no limited number of days to come.

A sound jerked him from his reverie, and he turned so quickly he nearly felt his neck snap, but it was only the whistle of the wind in the trees and the soft ripple of the water on the pond before the cabin. He ran his hand through his hair, realizing just how chilled his fingers had become when the movement was stiff and clunky, and he pushed up from the porch to head back inside. He could keep her safe, even if, in this moment, that meant nothing more than staying the worst of his temper and keeping her out of the line of fire. There was a world of unspoken truths between them, truths that wouldn't get answered that night, at least, but no matter how things went with the raid, Dante refused to scare her. Saint was tough — she had proven as much a dozen times in the few weeks they'd spent together — but he refused to add any more to the burden of her life, refused to be the cause of any unnecessary pain or heartache.

She was curled up on the couch when he walked back inside, her slim legs tucked underneath her, and her hair pulled into a loose braid down her back, and for a moment he thought she was sleeping. When he rounded the other side of the couch, however, he realized she had a large notepad propped on her knee, and she was furiously scribbling away at the fresh page. She was so engrossed in her work that she didn't seem to hear him, and when he took one step closer, to peek at the illustration coming to life on the page, she nearly jumped out of her skin.

"You scared me," she said, her hand on her chest and rising rapidly with her breathing. "Is there any news?"

Dante shook his head. "Nothing yet." For some reason, it felt like a failure of his own doing to have nothing to report back to her, but it would damn them both if he acknowledged how much he wanted to please her, not just in their shared moments of intimacy, but out, how he wanted to make her laugh and to wipe that deepening frown from her face. He reached out to touch her soft skin, realizing only in the last moment that his hands were still frozen, and he flexed them instead.

"Too cold," he murmured. "I don't want to hurt you."

It was the one thing he'd been able to think about this woman since the start. More than not hurting her, he wanted to do whatever was in his power to keep her safe, wanted to protect her from the grit and grime of the world. She was so *pretty*, blush and blonde and the palest blue, and she deserved so much more than the ink and blood of the life he'd walked away from, the life that was never entirely in his past.

"I'll put the kettle on," she said, unfolding her legs and coming to stand, but Dante stayed her with a look, settling into the seat beside her.

"You're drawing." It wasn't a question, but Saint answered him anyway.

"Yes," she said, almost as if in confession. "I needed something to do with my hands, and I kept reading the same three sentences over and over again." She looked down at the paperback murder mystery book on the coffee table. "I found some games and craft supplies in the closet, which I guess is good for if we have to stay here longer."

"We won't," Dante replied. "Niccolo knows what he's doing."

Saint looked up at him with those icy blue eyes and he saw a million emotions reflected back — fear, hope, uncertainty. He would give up his bike, his tattoo shop, and his share of The Ranch if it meant he'd never have to see that look in her eyes again.

"What is he doing, Dante?" she asked. "I don't want your brother to kill a man for me. I don't want to put that on his soul."

Because she was goodness and light, because Saint never wanted to be burden to anyone, because she only ever wanted the best for the people in her life, even if she had only met them the day before.

"It shouldn't come to that," he said honestly, because part of him had worried about the exact same thing. He'd said as much to his brother when the worry had finally become too much to bear, and gotten better answers than he could have hoped for. "Ash's foster sister is the sheriff," he explained, feeling an enormous sense of relief as she visibly relaxed before him. "Unless

Del Santo causes trouble, they should be able to deliver him straight to her."

"He might," Saint said, "cause trouble. He's known for it."

"Hopefully not for much longer," Dante replied. The words were on his tongue, to tell her about his mother, about his own tangled history with the Barbarone family, but she had enough to worry about, they both did, and bringing up the past when it might not serve them would only cause more and unnecessary heartache.

Coward.

Instead, he asked, "Will you show me what you're drawing?"

Saint pressed the sketchpad to her chest, her cheeks turning a soft, dusty pink that made Dante more than a little feral.

"I'm very rusty," she said, "and my medium was always acrylics and gouache, not pencil."

"You have nothing to prove with me, *ciccina*," he said. "And you don't have to share if you don't want to." Not that he wasn't desperately curious to see the kind of art she produced, but he wasn't going to push it. She'd show him when and if she was ready.

If she's not gone by then…

"I do," Saint admitted. "I just… You know what?" She seemed to win some internal battle with herself, and handed him the sketchpad.

It felt like all the air had gone out of the room. She hadn't shown her art to another living soul in years, and everything had felt possible when she was still in school and learning how to hone her craft. But Dante was a true artist, from the large illustrations adorning his shop to the small flower curving over her ear, and it somehow felt more loaded to show him, like his opinion of her work mattered in a real, significant way.

"Saint." His voice was low and heavy, and it was one of the few times she found that she couldn't read him, couldn't get a sense of reaction he'd had to looking at her illustration, the one she most certainly hadn't meant to share, until she'd decided that there was plenty to be afraid of in her life, and she didn't need to be afraid of the man who had done his damnedest to keep her safe and protected against the scariest thing that had ever happened to her. At least she didn't need to be afraid of showing him her pictures.

The picture he held now was one of him and his brother sitting down by the shore of the lake. She had looked out of the kitchen window the day before and caught sight of them, and she'd been so struck by the brotherliness of it all. They looked so different now, though she'd had to assume they had once looked so similar. But Nicco had clearly gotten thin while Dante had filled out, and they hardly bore a resemblance in the dark. It was in their mannerisms, the way they held their shoulders, and the large motions of their hands that Dante had once told her was how all Italian men spoke, that truly made them look like brothers.

She hadn't meant to capture such a personal, intimate moment, but it had been so obvious to her that Dante was hurting from missing Nicco, and as difficult as it had been for him to make the call, part of him had clearly been incredibly relieved to connect again with the person he loved most in the world. The chasms between them were already so much smaller than they had been a day ago.

"I didn't mean to spy," she said, feeling suddenly so self-conscious in the stretching silence. No doubt Dante would think the work amateur and the content too personal, but Saint didn't always plan what she painted before the first brushstroke, sometimes the ideas just came, as this one had. A snapshot memory of an important moment.

But it wasn't her moment.

"I'm sorry, this was overreaching of me." She reached for the sketchpad, but Dante quickly pulled it away.

"Can I have this?" he asked, and it wasn't her imagination that his voice seemed rougher and little more choked than it had just a moment ago. For better or for worse, she was learning how to read this man, and that was how she knew he wasn't putting it on.

"If you want," she said, and despite everything that the night held, despite the fact that they were holed up in a safe house and running for their lives, she felt a strange glow at the center of her chest. He liked her work, this brilliant, talented artist, and for once, for one moment, the dreams she had locked so far away didn't seem impossible anymore.

"I want, Saint," he said, and she could recognize *that* emotion in an instant, in her chest, in her belly, lower.

"The Princes," she whispered, her own voice suddenly raw and intense, as well. "They'll be back soon."

"We have time." It was as if her body was acting separately from her brain, an innate and dangerous understanding of everything this man had to offer, and all the ways she could please him, make him proud. She still knew so little about the lifestyle that she was only just dipping her toes into, but the physical reaction of his dominant voice on her nerves was impossible to deny. "I promise I don't want anyone else seeing what's mine."

Those words spilled hot as lava on her sensitive skin and Saint swallowed, trying to find sense or direction in the haze of pleasure, but it was so difficult to think when he stripped her down to her baser instincts and made her want to *beg*.

Dante reached out and lifted her chin, and his fingers definitely weren't cold then, not as they stroked her skin and held her firm in place, so she had to look up at him or defy his order and look away. She held his gaze.

"You are mine, aren't you, Saint?"

She went to nod, because somehow that felt less like a confession than saying the words aloud, but his grip was too firm, and she knew that was intentional.

"Yes, Sir," she whispered, loving the glint in his eyes when she called him by that unfamiliar and somehow entirely familiar honorific. "I'm yours."

"Show me," he said. He placed the illustration carefully down on the table without breaking eye contact. Even without touching her, Master Dante had an intense, overwhelming effect, like it wasn't just the sex, the impossible pleasure he had shared so many times in such a short number of hours, but it was the power behind the movement, the intense strength with which he held himself back until he was certain she was satisfied. She wondered if it was a game to him, but knew the second after the thought had passed that it wasn't. Master Dante took his lifestyle as seriously as he did the health and safety at the tattoo shop, and nothing about this was a game to him.

She was starting to think it wasn't so much a game to her either, not with the intense way her body reacted faster than her mind, or the desire she felt to do exactly as he told her. She peeled offer her sweater and went to toss it to the ground, but Master Dante reached out his hand and she passed it over to him, instead. The light pink fabric made the dark ink on his skin even more pronounced, and she couldn't stop from biting her lip at the way her feminine clothes looked in his very masculine possession.

It seemed, if for the moment, at least, that everything about her was in his possession.

Which was why she continued her actions, pulling off her socks and tossing those to the side — because she wasn't remotely interested in what he might want with them — and then shimmying out of her leggings until she was left in just her tank top, bra and panties, the soft worn fabric of the couch against the back of her legs.

"Keep going, little angel," he said. "I didn't tell you to stop."

She pulled her tank off and let it fall to the side, then slowly reached around and loosened her bra, before pulling it off, as well.

The room was chilly. Or, at least, it had been a moment before. But now all Saint could feel was the incredible blasting heat of his gaze upon her, the heat of desire ratcheting up in her belly and making it impossible to think about anything but the next direction he might give her.

"Touch your nipples, Saint," Master Dante said, his tone leaving no room for argument. It would have been embarrassing, ridiculous, even, if it was with any other man in any other way. But he made her want to do the things he told her to do, and took away the shame and intensity, leaving only desire and pleasure in their wake. "However you like. Show me."

"Yes, Sir," she whispered, reaching up and carefully stroking the edge of her nipple. Already her nipples were swollen and tight, sensitive to even the lightest touch, and the soft brushing of her fingers was enough to have Saint pulling back and swearing under her breath at the onslaught of desire and hot rush of need.

"More," Master Dante urged. "Show me how you pleasure yourself when you're alone."

As if acting on instinct, Saint reached for her breast and squeezed, the intensity of the movement and pinch of pain that balanced the overwhelming pleasure making it difficult even to remember she wasn't alone in the room. Her breasts weren't overly large, but they had always been very sensitive, and in the moment even the smallest touches were pushing her right to the edge of her pleasure and desire. How did she pleasure herself when she was alone, with a finger on her swollen clit and a handful of her breast and...

"Sir," she whimpered, loving how the word made her pussy clench and her nipples somehow more sensitive. There was so much she didn't know, but in that moment, she knew she wanted to do exactly as Master Dante told her to. "May I touch my pussy?"

He grinned, more feral than comforting, and gave her a sharp nod.

She slipped her hand below the band of her panties and gently swiped her swollen clit. As sensitized as she was, and as completely aware as she was of Dante watching her every move, the tiniest touch was enough to send Saint nearly throttling to the edge. But she knew that wasn't what he wanted, knew he wanted her to put on a show and tell him everything she liked when it came to pleasure and desire, and so she pulled back, lightened her touch, and then moved her fingers slowly downward to slip between her wet folds. It was intense and overwhelming to feel the effect he had on her, even after just a few moments, and when Master Dante didn't stop her, Saint slipped a finger inside her wet channel, gasping at the sensation of fullness.

She was still so sensitive from the night before, but the reminder of his cock inside her, of the way he had claimed her and taken her and given her such freedom with his command and his touch, it only served to make her want him all the more, and she bucked up against her fingers, knowing he was watching, and barely able to think about anything but the increasing feeling of pleasure.

"All the way, *ciccina*," he demanded, his tone firm and tight, like the grip on his control was starting to crack. "Show me how you come all over your fingers. Don't hold back."

She didn't want to hold back, not when he was watching her, commanding her, and so she slipped another finger inside, feeling the incredible stretch, the overwhelming sensation of pleasure and intensity, and Saint couldn't control the whimper that escaped when felt herself nearing that edge. It was new and yet, somehow entirely familiar, and she arched against her hand once, twice, once more before she was no longer chasing the pleasure, the pleasure was chasing her. All at once it was too much, far, far too much, and she reached for the arm of the chair to steady herself against the onslaught of pleasure and release.

Instead of solid wood, it was Master Dante's voice guiding her there, telling her she was so good for him, that she was so pretty when she came, and she followed the incredible sound of his voice as the aftershocks of pleasure wracked through her body, and she took and took and took.

Chapter Thirty-One

"So good for me, *ciccina*," he said quietly, rooted to his position on the chair, unable to tear his eyes from his little submissive. He had given her a directive, and she hadn't stopped, hadn't hesitated, had simply done as he had asked of her until she was coming all over her fingers and soaking her panties through. It made him swell, both behind the denim of his too-tight jeans and with a soft glow of pride in his chest because she had given him such an incredible gift in her submission, and he had no intention of letting it end with her writhing on the couch.

Not that he would ever forget the image in a million years, because watching his innocent, beautiful Saint give into her own pleasure was a sight for the history books. But Dante wanted more. He found that when it came to Saint, he always wanted more.

"Stand up," he said, loving the glassy expression in her eyes, and the pink flush that ran up her chest and throat to her normally pale cheeks. It was impossible for her to hide any signs of her desire, and that just made it all the easier to push her to the limits of pleasure and need.

It took a moment for the words to register, but Saint stood, looking at him with a curious, dazed expression.

"Are your panties wet, *ciccina*?" he asked, though he could see the glistening evidence of her release on her fingers.

"Yes, Sir," she said, ducking her head to avert her gaze. He wasn't going to have any of that.

"Look at me."

She seemed to face some kind of internal struggle, but then she lifted her head and looked into his eyes. "Yes, Sir," she murmured. "My panties are wet."

"Give them to me," he said.

Saint swallowed, the shame and intensity of the moment clearly catching up to her now that the pleasure was cooling. He was going to have to do something about that — the only shame he wanted her feeling was the fun kind, the kind that pushed limits and made his submissives come hard around his fingers and cock. Shame for desire or lust or kink was unacceptable. But that would come with time. And maybe a firm hand.

"Sir."

Dante didn't say a word, simply held her gaze until Saint was pushing her panties down her thighs and stepping out of them. She picked them up with one delicate finger and, with one more second's hesitation, handed them over to him.

Even in his fingers, they smelled like her pleasure, like the ambrosia of release and sin and desire all wrapped up in a pretty little pink and blonde package, and Dante didn't resist the urge to bury his face in the lace and cotton and smell her. When he pulled back, Saint's cheeks were flushed a dark pink, and he had to wonder if that was from more of the embarrassment of their play, or because she liked it. From the way she bit her lip and seemed incapable of taking a deep breath, he had to assume it was the latter.

So, he held her gaze as he pocketed her panties, daring her to say something, then finally pushed off the chair.

"Lean against the back of the couch," he said. "Spread your legs for me."

For a moment, it looked like Saint was going to argue, but then she bit down on her lower lip and stepped around the couch, leaning over and raising her ass in the air. He knew an act of rebellion as well as any Dominant, and Dante had no doubt in his mind that Saint was trying to get a rise out of him, but he had always found that he got more flies with honey.

"You're trying to get in trouble," he said, stroking the line of her back until she shivered, clearly against her own wishes. "Did you like the punishment last night, little Saint?"

She swallowed, before answering honestly. "I did, Sir."

He had to love her guts. She never seemed to back down from a challenge, no matter what kind of challenge it was.

"Well then it's not much of a punishment, is it?" he asked. "Seems like I'm going to have to find another way to keep you from acting out, doesn't it."

He grabbed her leggings from the floor and brought them around her wrists, which were propped against the back of the couch. The fabric was soft and stretchy, and while he wished he had his kit with him, or better yet, all the toys and tools in his suite back at The Ranch, the leggings did just fine, easily tying into a snug knot against her wrists. It was still fairly loose, and she'd have no trouble escaping, if that was what she decided to do, but he was still teaching, and he had plenty of ideas of what to do if she decided she wanted to escape him. Plenty.

"Tell me where you are, Saint," he said, tugging on her bound wrists one more time before letting her fall back over the edge of the couch.

"Green," she said, with such confidence in her tone he knew she was telling the absolute truth. Saint was truly fearless, and with all she had endured, a little kink play was hardly likely to come as a shock. Still, it was his job to make sure that kink play was performed properly, so he slipped two fingers between her skin and the fabric, stretching the tie just a little until he was satisfied with the fit.

Then he leaned over her back, pushing his swollen cock against her upper thigh and loving the soft, whimpering sound she made at the connection. "I thought I told you to spread your legs," he said, bringing one hand down the slope of her back and over the curve of her ass, before possessively cupping her pussy. She was already so wet, from her earlier release, from the way she submitted, from the binds around her wrists. He was already beginning to understand what she wanted and craved from their shared moments, and he knew she wanted so much of this.

"Yes, Sir," she whispered. She widened her legs another few inches, but Dante didn't give her a second to pause before he was down on his knees, spreading her slick, flush pussy wide. There was something so incredibly carnal, so fucking wild about seeing his dark, masculine hands against her softest, most feminine parts, and his cock swelled and pulsed hard in his jeans, desperately trying to get his attention.

But this moment, this night with its darkness and intensity, wasn't about what he wanted. Well, it was a *little* bit about what he wanted, because he wanted her to come all over his fingers and lips and tongue, and so he didn't wait, didn't give her a heads-up, just buried his face between her legs.

Saint let out a scream at his touch, and he knew she likely reached for purchase, but the binds around her wrists kept her mostly pinned in place in her spot against the couch. He used it to his full advantage, taking the new position to explore her, to make her whimper and buck and scream again, until he couldn't wait a second longer to slide his fingers inside, and to pump them in and out of her tight channel. She was still too tight, and most definitely too sore from the night before, and he would be damned if he caused her any pain she hadn't asked for or earned, so he focused exclusively on the pleasure, on overwhelming her senses and pushing her to the limit, and...

"Master Dante..." she whimpered his name, and he realized she had been whimpering for a few moments, but he'd been too wrapped up in licking and sucking every flush, glowing, swollen part of her. In a moment of possessiveness, he leaned down and nipped at the soft, pink flesh of her inner thigh, and Saint yelped, then tightened around his fingers, which Dante filed away for later. "Master Dante, please..."

She was fraying around the edges, and as much as he wanted to push her right over them, he wasn't holding onto his control with an all-too-tight grip either.

So he pulled back, just far enough to watch how his fingers stretched and slid in and out of her. "Please what, little angel?" he asked. "Tell me what you need."

"I need to come," she nearly begged, bucking back against him as much as she was able in her position, and he used his free hand to grip her hip and hold her in place. "Please can I come?"

"Have you earned it?" he asked. "Have you been good for me?"

She had been *so* good for him, so responsive and submissive and sweet in his arms, and he would tell her as much. Eventually.

"Yes, Sir," she bit out. "I've been good."

"And you think you deserve to come? You think you deserve my mouth on this pretty pussy?"

"Yes, Sir," Saint practically moaned. "Please eat my pussy."

"I do so love eating your pussy," he said, nothing but honesty in his words, "but first."

He leaned down between the beautiful curves of her ass and licked across her hole.

Saint bucked against the couch, swearing under her breath and pulsing around the fingers he still had in her pussy. He stroked them in and out as he licked her tight little hole, loving how she shuddered and arched against him, loving how she didn't protest the touch. He would give her everything she wanted, and the idea of her asshole all filled up with a plug was enough to drive a stronger man to distraction, but he was too focused on giving her what she was wanted, on pushing Saint past the limit until she was begging him to come, begging him to let her come on his fingers and lips. Until he finally gave her permission, and she barreled over the edge of her release with a ferocity he'd come to associate everything about this woman with, until she gave into her pleasure with her whole self, coming hard around his fingers and spilling hot release on his skin, shaking and cursing the whole time.

Finally, after what seemed like wave after wave of her releasing pleasure, her body began to calm, and she murmured only her gratitude, soft confessions spilling from swollen lips, and making Dante *ache*.

But tonight wasn't about that. Tonight had been about taking her mind off the danger surrounding her, about giving her pleasure and release and relief, and there was something so incredible about that that he didn't even care if he cock throbbed in his pants and his balls felt swollen and heavy. He'd get his chance. For now, Saint was sated, happy, well-pleasured, and that was all that mattered.

That should have scared him more.

Chapter Thirty-Two

She hadn't needed to have worried about The Princes returning while Master Dante had been on his knees with head buried between her legs. She had time to shower, change, eat and put the final lines to the illustration of Dante and his brother before there was even a sound in the woods beyond the cabin.

It was yet another reason to be grateful to the man who had come to mean so much to her in the past weeks. He had clearly known that sitting around waiting for news was going to slowly drive them both to the edge, and he had found a way to care for her, to distract her and pleasure her in a way that would make the time pass.

And make our connection stronger.

Not that she should be worrying about that. Not now, when everything in her life was coming to a head. Perhaps it had been foolish to let herself jump into bed with him, but Saint couldn't bring herself to regret it. Like all the daring and intense moments they had shared as he'd taught her about a world she didn't know, it had just felt *right* and if she walked away in the morning clean and unattached, she wouldn't have any regrets.

I don't want to walk away.

Unfortunately, that was the voice that seemed to have been growing louder in the hours The Princes were gone, and now that they were driving up the mountain pass, the sound was positively deafening. She wanted the threat of Del Santo and the Barbarone family to be behind her. She wanted to move on with her life. But if they came back with good news, if they came back with an update that Del Santo was no longer a threat, where exactly did that leave her and Dante?

She didn't have time to think about it, as the club descended upon the small cabin in a cloud of dust and noise, and before she could even think to push away the damning thoughts, Nicco and Ash were strolling through the front door, taking only the moment to reset the alarm, before coming to stand before them in the kitchen.

"Well?" Dante asked, and Saint was grateful for it, the nerves having fried her ability to speak or make sense of anything around her.

"It's done," Nicco replied, dropping his riding gloves on the counter. "Del Santo is locked up and headed back to Washington in the morning. He's not a threat to you anymore."

This was directed at her, with that unnerving, Wonderland version of Dante's beautiful purple eyes, and it took a moment for the words to truly sink in.

"It's over?" she asked quietly, hardly daring to believe the truth of it. She had been running from what she had seen for nearly a month and now…

Now it was over? Just like that?

"You should probably stay here a few more days," Ash said, and she noticed his lip was swollen, caked in dried blood around the edges.

This is all my fault.

It wasn't *all* her fault. She hadn't been the one to kill a man in cold blood. She hadn't been the one to chase the only witness across the country to undoubtedly silence her, as well. But Saint had been the one to bring the danger to this small town, she had been the one to allow strangers into her story, strangers who had gotten hurt because of her.

Ash seemed to catch her meaning without her saying a word, and gave her a devilish grin. The split lip almost had him looking like a pirate, and he had a rakishness about him that was somehow old school and timeless.

"You don't need to worry about my pretty face," he said. "This is nothing. I'm just glad we could help."

"I'm sorry you got hurt," she said, wishing she could go back to the day she'd landed on Dante's doorstep. Knowing if she did, she would never have met him or his incredible friends, knowing there would have been no reason for the brothers to reconnect if she hadn't needed help, and if there was anything she could walk away from all this knowing, it was that Dante would have finally gotten closure on one of the most important chapters of his life.

"Don't be," Ash replied, his tone all serious now. "This is what we do. We help people. We know what we're signing up for."

She nodded, but the guilt weighed in her stomach, nonetheless. This could have gone so much worse. They could have been shot at. One of their team members could have been killed. She could have brought Del Santo up to the Ranch and one of Dante's friends could have been killed... The more she thought over the possibilities, the more overwhelming they became, dark black clouds that threatened to overtake and consume her, guilt and loneliness, and the lingering feeling that it felt so incredibly nice not to have to take care of things all on her own.

"*Ciccina.*" Dante's hand was warm on her back, and she resisted the urge to melt into his touch. He was so sturdy, so strong and reliable, and despite the guilt she felt at bringing this trouble to his door, there was something so incredibly relieving about knowing that he was the one who had her back. "You don't need to do it on your own anymore."

He said so much with that one sentence, told her that she had the help of brawny, fearless professionals who were willing to do what it took to keep her safe. He told her that she wasn't the only one paying the bills and running the house and protecting her grandmother. She didn't have to work herself to the bone anymore just to survive, and she didn't have to go running for the hills either.

"Thank you," she murmured, finding it difficult to look at him. Instead, she reached for his large hand and squeezed tight. He didn't let her release. "Thank you all, please tell the others, I couldn't be more grateful."

"They know," Ash said. "But you're welcome. Now, we think it's best if you stick around through the end of the week, just in case something goes wrong in transit, or Del Santo wasn't alone."

"You think we still have to worry." She hated the flint-sharp edge of fear at the back of her words, like her subconscious somehow knew she'd never truly be free of the threat that had been haunting her this past month, like she'd be waking in sweat dreaming of Del Santo and the Barbarone brothers for the rest of her life.

"We think it's smart to be cautious," Ash replied. "We'll keep our ear to the ground and report back on anything we learn."

"The Ranch is well-protected," Dante said. "It's not as fortified as your safe houses, but it'll be easy enough to tell if someone is coming in that isn't wanted."

Across the counter, Niccolo took a deep breath. "You know it best," he said. "Will it keep her safe?"

There seemed to be an unspoken conversation taking place between the two brothers, and when Dante spoke next, she didn't miss a thing. "I will definitely keep her safe," he said.

"Maybe we should come with you," Ash said. "Just for extra security."

"Just the two of you," Dante replied. "You can use my cabin and Saint and I will stay at The Barn. I can let the guys know."

"Dante," she said, finally turning to look at him, seeing a world of emotion in those stormy eyes. "I don't want anyone else to get hurt because of me."

"No one else will get hurt," he said. "And that includes you, Saint. I'll make sure of it."

Chapter Thirty-Three

The last time she had been at The Ranch, Saint had been focused on one thing and one thing only — survival. She'd had enough presence of mind only to see the beautiful blonde woman wrapping herself around Dante, but that had very much been in her pursuit of safe haven. The details, all that might be lurking behind the curtain, were completely unknown to her, and while she had slept fitfully on the way to the safe house, she couldn't find any rest in the drive back.

The good news was that her nerves had nothing to do with the threats against her life this time. It almost felt like a relief to be worried about the logistics and intricate workings of a kinky cowboy sex club, rather than looking over her shoulder every five minutes to make sure that they weren't being followed by a convoy of mafia enforcers.

But even though it wasn't a big deal in the grand scheme of things, it sure as hell felt like a big deal as they took the final exit for the town of Duchess. The town she'd come to call home these past weeks. The town she would most certainly miss when she put Montana in her rearview mirror.

"What's going on, Saint?" Dante asked, glancing over at her from the driver's seat. "I figured you'd be more relieved that Del Santo is out of the picture."

"I am relieved." That was the God's honest truth. "It's not him."

"Then what is it?" She had come to recognize that tone in his voice, and she knew how much he hated to see the people around him hurting. He'd told her that he liked to bring pleasure, lots and lots of pleasure, and she had to wonder if that need to please and care for the people around him was why he had taken her in and done so much to keep her safe. She'd have time to dissect it all later. For the moment…

"Your club," she admitted. "It was one thing to be your…" She chewed on the word before finally spitting it out, "your submissive when we were alone. But now we're going to your club, and I don't want…"

"You don't want what?" he asked.

"I don't want to embarrass you," she admitted. "I don't know much about all this, but I know that however the submissive acts is some reflection of their master, right? What if I do something wrong and don't even know it?"

He reached his hand over from the steering wheel and linked their fingers together.

"You're right that it's a reflection of me," he said, "but that means it's my job to teach you everything you need to know. I'll let you know what you're doing right and what the rules are, and I won't put you in any situation before you're ready."

He glanced away from the road. "You don't have to scene at the club, Saint. You're in charge."

It was funny, that. She had been wondering about the logistics of the lifestyle at his club, if she had to play, if she could call an audible and just hole up in his cabin or suite or the barn, whatever he had mentioned the night before. But the idea of missing out on the opportunity to scene with Master Dante, in his domain, where he felt most powerful, that made her stomach sour a little bit. She wanted this time with him, even if all she was going to walk away with was memories. Especially then.

"I want to," she said, feeling entirely certain about it. "I just want to make sure."

"I don't know how many times I have to tell you," he replied, bringing her hand up to kiss without taking his eyes off the road, "you're not alone, *ciccina*, not anymore."

Except she could believe that all too easily. Except she could get so very used to being supported and cared for and *seen* and it would be that much harder when she left for New York City, and she was all alone again.

* * * *

She had actually expected more leather. The front lodge of The Sinclair Ranch was Wild West and all cowboy, and they stepped inside long enough for Dante to let Caleb know they were there then headed for The Barn. She should have expected that The Barn would be more than horse stables and hay bales. In fact, it was a beautifully decorated building with a huge open entry, featuring a bar, tables, chairs and plenty of hidden corners for disappearing. Rooms wrapped around the edges of the walls, and the second and third floor hallways which she could see by looking up were protected by a classic western wooden banister. There was leather as much as any western lodge, but she should have known that there wouldn't be anything tawdry or scandalous about the club Dante ran. His shop was immaculate and beautiful, and she had known from the very beginning that he had the eye of an artist.

In fact, the whole place had his touch about it, from the color of the wood banisters to the deep leather seats that asked for intimate connection, for secrets whispered between friends sitting too close. He watched her intently as they walked through the empty space, the morning light still streaming into through privacy protected glass, and she understood what he had meant that he would teach her, that she wouldn't have to know everything from the moment that she stepped out on the floor. That she would never have to step out on the floor, if she didn't want to.

"The seven of us have private suites in the building and cabins just the down the path," Dante explained. "Most of the guys just live up here, but I have the shop down in town, so I go back and forth. The rest of the rooms are playrooms or available for reservations, and the hotel rooms are upstairs, along with some guest cabins down the mountain."

It was an amazing enterprise, and she wasn't the least bit surprised that Dante was part of something so well-organized and managed. Running the tattoo shop downtown had to be complicated enough, but he spent most of his free time up there. Or at least he had, before she had shown up.

"Who are the others?" Saint asked, trying to spy a glimpse of what was available in some of the rooms they passed, but most of the doors were closed up tight. "I met Caleb, Reece, and Van the other night, right?"

"You did," he replied, a playful smile on his face. He really was the most handsome man she had ever met, and it struck her that she got to take him home. At least for the night. "Skylar and Caleb are together and Reece and Morgan you heard—bullets flying, corrupt politicians, the whole thing."

"Sounds familiar," she said. "And the others?"

"Van came back after service," Dante explained, his voice tightening. "He hasn't played in a while, but he does a lot to keep the place running. And Gabriel and Emerson are back and forth between here and Washington D.C. They just started a foundation out here."

She stopped in her tracks. "You're not talking about Gabriel North, are you?" she asked. "And Emerson Laurent? That was all over the news a while back. He gave away his billions for a woman—his political *rival*. I thought it was fake for sure."

"You didn't see Gabriel crying into your pillow," Dante teased. "He was a wreck, which is hilarious in its own right because Gabe is usually the one getting us out of trouble. But he found his way to her, and they're fucking nauseating to be around."

She hip-checked him. Or tried, since he was much, much taller than her. "You love seeing your friends happy."

"I do," Dante admitted. "And they all deserve it. We got the name Sinclair Seven because Beau Sinclair ran the Ranch out here and we all worked together that one summer. We also raised pretty much any kind of hell you could imagine."

"Nicco was gone by then."

"The last thing he did for me was reach out to Beau," Dante said. "It was the best gift he could have given me, because these guys are family now."

"He's still your family," she said. "I don't think he's going anywhere, Dante."

His smile was sad, but it was tinged at the edges with a touch of hope. That kind of hope could be dangerous, Saint knew. She also knew that it was that kind of hope that made life worth living.

"I'm glad I got to see him again," was all he said for a long moment, as they continued down a well-furnished hallway. "But I don't see the other guys all that much either, and they're just as important to me, so maybe there's something to that."

"Do they not live around here?" she asked, curiosity piquing. If he was hiding reformed billionaire Gabriel North in his closet, who else was in there?

"Well, Rafe is a crown prince, so..." He turned, clearly waiting for her reaction, and Saint gave him one.

"He's a *what*?" Her words echoed down the hall.

Dante shrugged. "Crown prince. First-in-line, heir apparent, take your pick. It's a small country right next to Austria and Italy, but he's still set to inherit. He spends most of his time in the House of Lords and learning everything he needs to know about leadership. Not much time left for his American sex club."

She would have called him on the tone, but the smile on Dante's lips told he was joking, so she pressed, "Okay, you have billionaire, literal princes — which you might have mentioned when we binged trashy royal soaps by the way—who's left?"

"Guess," he teased, stopped in front of an innocuous-looking door.

Saint bit her lip. "Politician?" she asked.

He blanched. "Ew, try again."

"Movie star?"

"Closer."

"Rock star."

He grinned. "She gets it in three. You ever heard of Bastion Kane…?"

Saint's mouth dropped open, but there was nothing she could do to put her jaw back where it belonged. "You are absolutely shi-*kidding* me."

"Nope," he said. "And if it gives me any star power by approximation, Bastion and I used to give each other messy hand jobs in the actual barn the summer we worked this ranch…"

She could picture it in an instant, a younger Dante, his skin tanned and dark from the summer sun, contrasted with the pale, honey-haired rock star, who wouldn't have had all the facial piercings yet, maybe just an earring or two, two lost boys trying to find themselves in a world that wasn't meant for them, finding each other, instead, with thick, masculine touches, forbidden promises, a pleasure they no doubt didn't understand at the time, but would come to crave and share with others as they grew older. She wondered if Dante had given Bastion Kane any of his tattoos or piercings, and then wondered if anything more had followed, if the kisses had been as dangerous as the ones she shared with him, how two Dominants played when they both needed so badly to be the one in control.

"That gives you... something..." The word came out whispered, and Saint realized that she had been so caught in the fantasy of the two men together she had been holding her breath. It wasn't something she had ever truly considered before, but Dante was so incredibly beautiful, and she'd seen him the throes of pleasure and something about this confession, for that certainly was what it was, made her want—to hold him, to claim him, to make sure that no one else ever got to be the one to put that satiated look on his face.

Of course, that wasn't going to happen, since she was still leaving at the week's end, since she was still headed east, for New York City and big dreams, but she could pretend, for just a moment. For just a few days.

"You picturing it, angel?" he asked, because somehow, he always seemed to know what depraved and desperate thoughts were running through her head. Most of them he'd put there.

"A little," she admitted. "Do you still?"

"Bastion and I are too similar," he said. "He's my best friend, nothing more." The twinkle in his eye told Saint that he knew she was feeling a strange possessiveness, and that he liked it. "Plus, he's on the road most of the year, and that life isn't for me. But he's important to me, like the rest of them."

"You created your own family," Saint said. "Your ride or die."

"A touch of irony there, considering my brother is an actual biker," he said. "But yes, they're family and this is home. Would you like to see it?"

See the inner sanctum where Dante Castiglione put on his Dominant persona and took his submissives to heights of impossible pleasure? In fact, she very much did want to see it. Given enough time, time she did not have, she wanted to see all the secrets he had to offer.

The room was all Dante.

It looked different to the studio, different even to his apartment, the one she'd come to know so well in the past weeks. It was as if his dark side had come out to play in the slashes of geometric art and shaded black décor. The art was backlit with different neon colors, giving the space the appearance of a tattoo shop, and in the corner of the room, she spied a set-up not dissimilar to the ones in Inferno Tattoos, the leather chair and the inks and lights.

Dante followed her gaze. "Some people like to play doctor, and some people like to play tattoo artist," he joked. "I gave Skylar a piercing there last year during a scene with her and Master Caleb."

Saint narrowed her eyes. "Where?"

Dante grinned. "I like it when you get feisty, angel," he said. "Maybe I should call up all the people I've slept with, and you can fight them one by one."

"What makes you think I wouldn't win?" she asked, suddenly feeling very much like she might.

"Oh, *ciccina*." He lifted her chin with one strong finger, the movement so familiar that it made that delicious heat start to glow in her lower belly, and her thighs tingle and quiver. "I most definitely think you would win. My little survivor."

Saint's heart clenched then, and she swallowed hard, desperate not to be the one to avert her gaze. He knew what he was doing, making it difficult for her to walk away, but there had never been any kind of future built into their games, and she had never meant to put her roots down in Duchess. This wasn't the plan, no matter how much she felt like Dante could truly see her, and how she had been aching to be seen for so incredibly long.

Finally, Dante was the one who pulled away, as if he'd come to the same conclusions she had. He reached for a folder he had taken from the front desk and handed it to her.

"We have a little more structure here at The Ranch than we did in our cabin on the lake," he said. "Waivers and information packets. I want you to read through them, okay. Before you decide how you want to spend your time here."

It was all so official and overwhelming, and Saint wondered if she would have been interested in the lifestyle at all if she hadn't been introduced to it by a man like Dante in a cabin in the mountains in the middle of nowhere.

Scratch that, he could introduce me to anything, anywhere.

She took the folder, suddenly feeling its meaning in her hands. "What are you going to do?" she asked.

"I'm going to talk to my brother."

Chapter Thirty-Four

The air was cold, but Dante welcomed it, needing that sense of brightness and bite to keep his wits about him as he navigated down to the small cabin at the mountain's edge. The cabins had been a later addition, but they allowed the staff to stick around for longer stretches of time, which Caleb and Van had done upon returning home, which Reece had done countless times on his many adventures around the world. Dante rarely used his, typically preferring to return to his apartment in town, but the cleaning service they kept was meticulous and discreet, and it had already been prepared by the time Niccolo and Ash had arrived.

Niccolo was here. At his club.

All at once, he was eighteen again, scraping by in his classes just to graduate high school, trying to land an internship at a tattoo parlor, trying to get on the back of a motorcycle and ride toward freedom. He was eighteen again and desperate for his brother's approval, desperate for the love of the man who had been brother, father, mother to him. It didn't matter how old he was or how long he had been successfully running his tattoo shop, or the fact that Niccolo seemed like he was the one more in need of support, some things never changed — like a boy wanting his brother to be proud of him.

"I'm walking the perimeter," Ash said, stepping off the porch just as Dante arrived. "I found your friend Donavan and he said he'd show me around."

"I appreciate it," Dante replied. "He in there?"

Ash nodded, then paused mid-step. "I know he's your older brother, D," he said. "And I know it's been a hell of a long time since you've seen each other. But he's…he's not doing the best right now. Maybe you can talk some sense into him, get him to eat a real meal or something. It's got me worried."

Dante had spent most of the last weeks worrying about Saint, but even in the chaos of seeing Nic for the first time in so long, he'd known something was up. Castiglione men were known for their broad shoulders and strength, and Nic looked like he could float away in a stiff breeze.

"I'll try," he said to his brother's sergeant. He might be absolutely the wrong person for it, but for Nic, he would try. Ash nodded and headed up the trail.

When Dante walked in, Nic was standing at the kitchen counter, looking out over the mountains beyond. They were born and bred Montana boys, but he would never stop finding awe and magnificence in the nature surrounding them.

"How is Saint?" Nic asked, not turning to look at Dante.

"She's settling in," he said. "I wanted to give her some space. To get accustomed."

"Will she be staying with you then? After this week?"

They had agreed that once Del Santo had been officially delivered to the cops in Washington, and Ash's foster sister had guaranteed that there would be no favors called in or deals made, that Ash and Nicco would take off and rejoin their club, and Saint, well, they hadn't gotten that far.

Because you're being a coward.

It was a distinct possibility that he didn't want to bring up the future because he simply didn't want to think about what would happen after she left. The bright, beautiful woman who had been filling his space with sunshine and laughter these last weeks. It was strange to think that he might wake up one day soon and she wouldn't be there.

"I don't know about that," Dante replied. "There's been a lot going on."

"If you want her to stay, you need to tell her the truth," Nic said. "About Mom."

Dante had known on his walk down the mountain to the small cabin that it would come to this. He had known, but still he had hoped that Nic would somehow forget, that the important, dark, terrible secret that had been hanging over his head would somehow just disappear, and leave him to ask Saint to stay, without damning them both.

"It hasn't come to that yet," he replied. "And I don't want to scare her any more than she's already been scared, Niccolo. This has been hell for her."

"I know." Nic wasn't exactly great at expressing his emotions these days. Once upon a time, he would rage and shout and gesture with the best of his Italian ancestors, but now it seemed like he couldn't bring himself to so much as swear under his breath. "This was a good ending."

No doubt Nicco and the others had seen more shit in their work as protectors than Dante ever wanted to know about it.

"It's good work that you're doing," Dante said. "Important work. You saved her life." Niccolo nodded, and Dante had to wonder what had happened to the temper-prone, passionate brother he'd know a lifetime ago.

"Do you want Saint to stay?" Niccolo asked. "Because you're running out of time to ask her."

Dante knew that, knew that the moment he had invited her to work in his shop, she had said she'd stick around for one month and one month only. Then, she'd been doing it to protect herself and to keep him safe. But they had chased down the threat and she hadn't done anything to amend her statement. Of course, he hadn't asked her to stay, but that was neither here nor there.

"What if she needs to go, Nic?" Dante said. "That's...not easy for me."

It was a hell of a confession to make to the brother who had given him the abandonment issues in the first place, but no doubt Niccolo knew that all too well.

"I didn't want you in the life," Niccolo replied, finally turning to face him. "The Midnight was bad fucking news, Dante, and I wanted to keep you safe. Your orientation was coming up and I needed to get you out before you became a full member."

"So, you said the worst possible things you could." It was like he was back to being that same scared, lonely kid, watching the last of his family driving away forever. "So you told me I was a burden and you wanted to be rid of me?" His voice hitched, and he wished he were back in the suite with Saint, back in her light and sunshine presence.

"I needed to get you to stay away," Niccolo said. "You would have gone down a bad path, Dante. Now look at you. You have the shop and this club and the girl."

He most certainly did *not* have the girl, but that felt too complicated to point out.

"You went down that path," Dante replied. "Nic, I wanted to be just like you."

"That was the last thing I wanted for you." Finally, some fucking passion from his brother. "I wanted to keep you as far away as I possibly could from that crew. We needed money to survive, and I was doing what it took, but I refused to sell your soul too, *fratello*."

"You turned out okay," Dante said. "You have your own club now and you're doing something important, something real."

"Consider it my recompense," Niccolo said. "And even if it means a decade of not talking, I don't have any regrets about pushing you away. Your life is better for it."

Dante hated that Nic was right, hated more that his brother had borne the burden of their survival on his shoulders when he'd still been just a kid, himself. Hated that he hadn't had the balls to pick up the phone and call Nic after all these years, when deep down he had always known the truth.

"I wish things had been easier," Dante said, not quite able to find the words he was really looking for. Maybe Niccolo was right. Fine, he was right, and Dante's life was better for it. But some wounds didn't heal with time, and instead became great, gaping chasms that nothing could fill, and like the testaments of old said, there was nothing truly so devastating as the hate of one brother for another. The words Nicco had thrown at him, the vulnerable boy Dante had been, those had been truths, even if there was also a different truth as to why those words had been said.

"I have a lot of regrets in my life," Nicco said. "But keeping you away from that life will never be one of them."

Chapter Thirty-Five

Saint was just starting to spiral when there was a knock on Dante's suite door. She had spent the better part of the hour going over the materials he had provided, and it felt like stepping into another world. The play they had enjoyed at the safe house in the mountains looked like just that, *play*. But here at The Ranch, the lifestyle was that much more serious. She had waivers to sign and limits to set, and while he had promised that he would do everything in his power to teach her what she needed to know, Saint couldn't help but feel that sense of doubt creeping in. Who was she to be playing this dark and sinful game with such a beautiful man?

Not that she didn't want to. Every part of her baser self was asking, *screaming* for more of his touch, for more of those darkly whispered commands that made her heat up from the inside out, but now that her life was no longer under threat, she was finding it difficult to think about anything but the ways this might all go wrong.

The knock came again, and Saint stood from the bed, where the waivers and packets were laid out across the comforter, and went to answer. Morgan and Skylar stood at the door, and twin emotions warred in Saint's belly. These women were old hats at this lifestyle by now, beautiful and self-possessed and not likely to make fools of themselves in front of an audience. But they had also been so incredibly kind and supportive during the worst moments of Saint's life, and if they could give her grace when she was on the run from a mafia enforcer, no doubt they could help guide her now.

"Did Dante send you?" she asked, stepping into the room to make space for them.

"Nah." Morgan grinned. "We just knew you could use some girl time."

It was that easy. For so long, Saint had been alone, caring for Gram, doing whatever it took to pay the medical bills. She hadn't had enough time to maintain old friendships or make new friends, just as she hadn't had enough time to seek out the companionship Dante had introduced her to, and while she'd told herself she had been fine with such absences, they were very much starting to feel like a loss.

"We were newbies here once too," Skylar said, settling into a large armchair. "Totally freaked me out when I first got here, I thought about making a break for it."

"Why didn't you?" Saint asked. Skylar seemed the type to know herself inside and out, and it was almost reassuring that she sometimes had the same kind of doubts Saint found herself facing now.

"I did, for a bit," Skylar said. "Callie got into an accident, and I booked it for California. I'm a mom first, of course. But I'm not going to pretend that I wasn't scared of what this all meant." She looked around, and Saint was reminded that she had once scened in this room with Dante and Caleb. It wasn't hard to be jealous of such a kind and beautiful woman, but for the time being, Saint was the one staying in Dante's private suite.

"What changed your mind?" Saint asked. The pages were spread across the bed as if in glaring neon, kinks and fetishes with sliding scales, three pages of waivers and consent forms. It was all starting to feel so much more clinical than it had the night in the cabin with Master Dante. And yet, she knew that it was important, to make sure the members of the club were safe, to make sure that everyone was protected while they pushed the limits.

"Callie knocked some sense into me," she said on a laugh. "She pretty much told me that I had to get a life and let her live hers, and that your sex drive doesn't need to die when you become a mom. She was more articulate than that, but it worked."

"She sounds great," Saint said, meaning it.

"She is," Skylar said, a soft smile on her lips. "She'll be back out here for Christmas, and I'd love for you to meet her."

Christmas. It was still nearly a month away. By then, Saint would be long gone, hopefully rebuilding her life in New York City, hopefully walking away without leaving her heart bloody and beaten on the floor of this damned suite.

Instead of any of that, she said, "I'd be honored."

Morgan laughed. "You're going to rabbit, aren't you?" she asked. "I know that look. Hell, I usually have that look on my own face when I get antsy. How long are you going to stay?"

Saint answered honestly. "Through the end of the week," she said. "They want to make sure Del Santo gets back to Washington before I go off on my own."

"It's a good idea," Morgan replied. "Dante wouldn't let anything happen to you."

It was a truth she was becoming all too familiar with, and she couldn't ignore the warm glow in her belly at the reminder of all that he had become to her, all that he had given her, not just protection, not just an introduction to their wild and wonderful lifestyle, but a sense of peace, of freedom, the very feeling of being *seen* not for what she could do, but for who she was.

"He's been..." *Wonderful. Amazing. Everything.* Each of the words that sprung to her mind was dangerous in its own way, and Saint had little doubt that these insightful women could see right through her in an instant. It should have made her like them less, but it didn't.

"Dante is a surprise," Skylar put in. "He likes to play the joker, but there's a lot of depth there. Don't let him fool you — he feels."

Saint knew it, knew it in the way his attitude had begun to change the moment Niccolo had come back into his life. Knew it in the way he cared so deeply for the people around him, even if they were strangers bringing bags of trouble to the door. He was complex and brilliant and talented and...

"You are so screwed," Morgan said on a laugh. "Look at that dreamy little smile."

Saint tried to hide it, she really did, but for the first time, she could truly breathe easily, and with no imminent threats hanging over her head, she could actually begin to enjoy her life. Hell, she deserved as much. And she was going to start enjoying it with the help of one very beautiful Italian artist.

She reached for the packet on the bed and held it up in surrender. "Can you guys help?"

Skylar and Morgan exchanged a knowing look, and it wasn't long before the three of them were settled on the enormous bed ticking off boxes and giggling at turns of phrase that would normally have Saint turning the color of a tomato. Perhaps this was what life was really about, shared moments with friends, lightness, simple joys and pleasures. Perhaps she was finally, finally ready to start living for herself.

And she knew exactly where to start.

Chapter Thirty-Six

He had offered for them to stay the night in his suite. It hadn't been a hardship offer—the idea of Saint spread out in his bed made Dante positively feral. He could picture her blonde hair draped across his pillows, her arms and legs spread, and her lips parted and her breaths shallow as he pushed the limits of pleasure and desire. He could picture about a million ways he could please her in the space he'd worked so hard to call his own, and every single one of them made him want to lock her up in that suite and throw away the key.

But she was new to this world, and he had wanted to give her an out, give her a chance to connect to the lifestyle without being in front of the others, and it had almost come as a surprise when she'd told him she wanted to go to the dance club that night. Almost, but not quite. His Saint was brave as all get-out.

His Saint.

It was becoming dangerous how easily that moniker crossed his mind. In the beginning, he could have kept his distance because he was her boss. Because they had been friends. Because he had made it his personal mission to keep her safe. And when they had crossed the line, the line he had known he shouldn't have crossed but hadn't been able to stop himself from stepping over, those reasons had fallen flat, becoming echoes of good intentions. And now, with whatever was in the air between them, she had wormed herself under his skin and made it difficult to think of her as anything but his.

Which was starting to become a problem, what with her planning on leaving by the end of the week. They hadn't said it out loud, but the deadline for Del Santo arriving back in the custody of the Washington state police was another type of deadline, as well, and Dante knew he hadn't given her any reason to stay.

Because you'll need to tell her the truth.

Because if he asked her, he'd have to bare the one last vulnerable part of himself, and he just wasn't ready for that. Not yet. If she left of her own accord, it would hurt less than if she left because she never wanted to see him again.

But no matter what happened next, they could spend the next few days making memories she could bring with her on the next adventure, and ones he could store away for the lifelong lonely days ahead. So he stepped into the dance club.

It was a large room located at the far end of the building, and though the night was fairly early, it was already moving with an intense, carnal rhythm. For many players, starting with dance and the intimacy of a dark, semi-private space was the first step for a night of pleasure, and it was easy to see why. The grinding and motion of hips and thighs made it all-too easy to think about sex, to think about intimacies of a different kind, and if he looked, he knew he was sure to find couples or groups that had gone beyond the dancing to the next natural step.

But while he normally favored a voyeuristic moment or two, he only had one thing on his mind now.

Finding his Saint.

It wasn't hard. Her silver-blonde hair caught the flashing lights and made it look as though she were emanating a light all her own, brighter than the glow of the moon outside, brighter than the sun rising over the mountains in the early morning. She was dancing with Skylar, Morgan and Rhylee, but Dante could only watch her, only watch the simple relief and joy on her face as she moved to the music and danced with new friends, and it was that joy that him pausing in his steps, just for a moment. She deserved the chance to live a normal life, to go out dancing with friends, to put down the weight of the world for a moment and simply live.

It wasn't until another man started to approach her, because who wouldn't want to approach her, that Dante finally moved across the dancefloor. The man was nearly at Saint's side when Dante caught his eyes and told him without words to get lost. The man must have seen the club owner wristband, because he took one more look at Dante and then Saint and then disappeared back into the crowd.

"You're catching quite a lot of attention there, *ciccina*," he said. "Are you trying to make me jealous?"

She grinned at him, and the abject, unfettered happiness there made Dante's chest swell with pride. Saint was just so *pretty*, so *good*, and it made him want to do whatever it took to ensure that smile never left her face.

"Is it working, Sir?" she asked.

"Cheeky, cheeky, little one," he said. "You keep that up and you'll be in all kinds of trouble. Speaking of trouble, what are you wearing?"

She did a little spin, the lights flashing off the slippery silver dress she was wearing. Some might have called it a dress. It more resembled a scrap of wet fabric, looping around her neck and spilling down.

"Rhylee lent it to me," she said. "What do you think?"

"I think Van better not know she has a dress like that," he said, almost without thinking.

"I thought her brother was Caleb," she replied.

Dante just laughed. "He is, angel... I'll tell you all about it later. But for now..."

He took her hand and with a nod to the other women, led Saint away.

"As for your dress" — he pulled her close, until he was able to whisper in her ear as they moved together to the music — "it makes me never want to let you out of my sight. It makes me want to see the chain snap and the fabric tear."

He placed a hand on her hip and slowly moved their bodies together, loving how free she seemed in the moment, loving how she leaned back against him and let their movements connect, until she was no longer just dancing, but fully pressing back against his swelling cock.

"You are asking for a punishment, aren't you?" he said. "Is that why you're wearing a handkerchief?"

"It's not that small," she protested. "Sir."

"It is, Saint," he said. "If you even think about bending over, the whole club will know the color of your panties."

She stiffened the smallest amount, but it was enough to tell Dante everything he needed to know.

"Angel," he growled into her ear, already knowing the answer before the question was even out, "are you wearing panties?"

She let out a low whimper, the sound going straight to his swelling cock. He would never get tired of hearing her whimper or beg.

"Sir—"

"Answer me, Saint," he said. "Or would you prefer I found out for myself?"

She leaned back into his touch, pressing that lush ass against him in pure, delicious torture, and he didn't want to wait for her answer a moment longer. Instead, he slid his hand from her hip, down the beaded chain sides of the dress, to the very, very high hem. It was the work of a second to slip his hand under the tiny dress, and the first touch confirmed what he had already known to be true.

She was completely bare to him.

"Saint." Her name tore from his lips, rough and jagged. "Are you trying to get in trouble?"

"Maybe, Sir," she said, the word not entirely respectful on her lips. "Maybe I just wanted to be ready for you."

After days of denying himself her touch, after days of pushing her to the limit of pleasure and not taking his own, those words were enough to nearly send him over the edge. He wanted her with a dangerous kind of ferocity, the kind that had driven men to battle and the edges of the earth in search of a woman's touch, and

Dante knew that tonight it would be his control that was being tested.

"Are you ready for me, *ciccina*?" he asked, stroking her pussy at the same time. She was so slick and hot, so wanting for the pleasure he could provide, and he'd give it to her. Eventually.

"Yes, Sir," she whispered. It was almost impossible to hear her over the sound of the music, but Dante couldn't pay attention to anything but the words on her already swollen lips. "I'm so ready for you."

"Tell me," he said.

"I'm wet," she nearly choked on the words. "My pussy is aching for your cock, Sir. You haven't...not since..."

"You needed time to heal," he replied, and while it had seemed so important at the time, all he could think about in that moment was filling her up and making sure she was never empty again.

"I'm healed." She sounded frustrated, which he fucking loved, and he slipped a finger into her tight channel. Saint gasped and bucked back into him, grinding against his cock until he still her movements with his other hand on her hip. "Please, Sir, I need you inside me."

"You need to learn patience, angel," he said. "The night is only beginning and you're already begging for my cock."

"I like it," she admitted, lust already overtaking her.

"The begging," he teased, "or my cock?"

Saint whimpered, low and needy. She was so responsive, so ready for the pleasure he would give her, and he would do anything to be worthy of it.

"Both, Sir," she admitted. "I like... I like being good for you."

Even if at that moment she was being very, *very* bad, grinding against his cock and arching her hips to take his finger deeper inside her tight hole. He should stop her, but it was driving him fucking wild to see her chasing her pleasure on his body, like the dance she had been enjoying before, but darker and more intense, wicked and depraved.

"Be good for me now," he said, "take another finger."

She paused her movements long enough for him to slip another finger inside her, letting out a long, deep moan as he filled her. She was still so incredibly tight, and Dante's cock pulsed hard at the very thought of filling her and making her his.

"Don't come yet," he directed, squeezing her hip hard and loving her reaction to the touch. "If you come on my fingers, you don't get another one for the rest of the night."

And he really hoped she wouldn't, because making Saint come had become just about his favorite pastime.

"Yes, Sir," she said. "I'll be good, I promise."

He pulsed his fingers deep inside her, and she reached for his arm, gripping hard to steady herself against the pleasure, murmuring and whimpering as he pushed her closer to the edge.

"Sir—" She wasn't begging, not yet, which meant he wasn't nearly close to doing his job properly.

"Saint," he replied. "What do you need?"

"I need to come."

"Not yet." This was a command, and she seemed to know as much. Her understanding of the lifestyle and the dynamics between them was innate and natural.

"I need your cock inside me," she said. "Please."

"Try again."

"Will you fuck my tight little pussy, Master Dante..." She was near to babbling, and he loved it when she was close to the edge and whimpering, begging, demanding for anything that might get her there. But she wasn't close enough.

"Tell me what you fantasize about when you're alone," he said. "And then I'll decide if you can come all over my fingers. Tell me that dirty, depraved dream you never want to share with anyone else."

"Sir." She bucked hard, her pussy clenching around his fingers. "I can't, it's...it's filthy."

"Good," he replied. "Tell me everything. You said you wanted to be good for me."

"I do. I do. I just...it's..."

"Where are you, *ciccina*?" he asked. "Red, yellow, green."

"Green." She didn't hesitate. "Green, Sir."

"Good." He pulsed his fingers in and out again just to show her how good. "Now tell me what you think about what your touch yourself."

"*Fuck.*" She rarely swore, and the curse was hot and torn from her lips like a woman on the edge. "Sometimes I get on my hands and knees and finger my pussy, and I think about... I think about someone coming in and filling me up from behind..."

"Do you know the person?" he asked, his own words rough and intense.

Saint shook her head. "No, it's dark and he comes up behind him and sinks into me. He pins my arms above my head and keeps my feet spread wide and he pounds into me."

"You like being tied up and bound? You want to have all your control taken away?"

She nodded. "I think I do, Sir."

"So honest." He slipped a third finger into her tight little hole, loving how she gasped, loving how wet and tight she was as she confessed her dark secrets. "What else does he do, Saint? Does he stroke your pussy?"

"Sometimes," she confessed. "And I tell him it's too much, that I can't take all the pleasure, and he doesn't stop."

"Do you want him to?"

"No," she replied softly, her pussy tightening around his fingers. "No, I don't."

"And then what?" He slid his fingers nearly all the way out before pushing back into her waiting channel. "Does he force you to come over and over again?"

"Sometimes," she admitted. "Sometimes he uses my wetness to…" She hesitated, and he paused his movements too, starting up again only when she spoke. "Sometimes he uses my wetness to push his fingers into my other hole."

"Say it."

"Into my asshole," she whispered.

"And."

"And I like it." This was nothing short of a confession. "I know I shouldn't, I know it's wrong and depraved and filthy and all that, but it feels so *good…*" She practically moaned out the last word, and his cock leaked behind his jeans, wetting his briefs. "Sometimes, I even picture what it might be like for him to push a toy in, one of those silvery plugs or…"

"Tell me." Those were about the only words he could get out in the wake of her intense fantasy.

"Sometimes he pushes himself in."

"How does it feel?" he asked. "When you picture it?"

"So good…" Saint pressed back against his cock and Dante swallowed hard, focusing on the way her pussy clenched around his fingers, rather than the overwhelming, desperate need to be inside her. "It's like being full, all stretched out and…it makes me come."

"Do you need to come right now?" he asked.

"More than anything," she whispered. "But I want to come on your cock, Sir."

It was cheeky and another Dominant might have scolded her for the impertinence, but Dante fucking loved that she was going after what she wanted, loved that she didn't hold back or shy away from her darker, more carnal desires.

He slid his fingers free from her tight hole and brought them up to her lips. Saint parted her mouth, as if on instinct, and he slipped his fingers inside, letting her taste her own desire. She sucked his fingertips clean, then took him deeper into her mouth, each stroke of her tongue pushing him a little bit closer and closer still to the edge of his self-control.

"You just can't help yourself, can you, little one?" he asked. "You need something in your mouth, don't you?"

She moaned around his fingers, and he slowly pulled back then guided her from the dancefloor to the small hallway beyond. They weren't far from his suite, but Saint clearly needed to be fucked hard and fast, and the club lights and sounds followed them to one of the small, curtained rooms just off the dance floor. It wasn't big, but there was a chair pushed against the wall, and Dante settled into it, pulling Saint onto his lap. Low lights made it a little easier to see than in the dance club, and he took in the sight of her, silver dress pushed up her thighs, chains pressing into her pale skin, pink flush rising up her cheeks.

"You said you wanted something," he said, holding her gaze. "Ask me nicely."

"Can I please come on your cock, Sir?" she begged. "Please, I need… I need to."

He reached for one of the condoms discreetly hidden in the side table drawer, then slowly unzipped his jeans, using their proximity to stroke Saint's swollen pussy as he moved his fingers. He pushed his jeans out of the way just enough to roll the condom on his swollen cock, and then he caught her gaze.

"Be so good for me, angel," he said.

"Thank you, Master Dante," she replied in the same moment she sank down on his cock. Dante gripped the arms of the chair against the onslaught of pleasure, counting back in his head as she wrapped her lithe body around him, squeezing like a vise. It was far, far too much, and he knew he wouldn't last long with the way she writhed against him, reaching for the head of the chair to anchor herself and slide up and down along his length. His balls pulled tight, and his cock swelled inside her, making Saint gasp, and Dante thrust up hard and fast. She met him thrust for thrust, taking every inch he gave her, begging, babbling, whimpering, promising sweet, depraved things to him, if only he would let her come.

So, he reached between their bodies, finding her swollen clit and stroking once, twice, one more. "Come for me," he whispered. "Coat my cock in your release. Make me proud."

And then he pinched.

She spiraled. The pain seemed to push her throttling over the edge, and she clenched hard and fast around him, pulsing, pulsing, pulsing, until it sent him flying after her, bucking up and filling the condom with hot, thick cum as Saint fell apart in his arms.

Chapter Thirty-Seven

For a moment, all Saint could do was breathe, and listen to the intense thumping of Dante's heart where she had fallen against his chest. He was beginning to soften slightly inside her, and she knew she'd have to move soon to keep there from being an almighty mess, but she wanted to capture the moment, to stay wrapped in his arms and thoroughly satiated forever. Or for as long as he would have her there.

"You did so good, angel," he murmured, stroking her hair and whispering words of encouragement and support. "So good for me."

It sparkled that now-familiar need in her chest to continue to please him, to show the world she could be his good little submissive. She might not understand how the lifestyle worked in its entirety, but she knew that much, and knew that his praise made her want to do whatever it took to keep.

"Thank you, Sir," she murmured, her own voice a little pleasure drunk. "I should…"

"Go slow," he said. "Be gentle with your body." He watched her slowly pull off of his cock, groaning when the head finally popped free, and he stood, disappearing for a moment behind the closed door and returning having disposed of the condom.

"Lean back," he said, indicating to the chaise in the corner of the room. "Let me take care of you."

She did as he instructed, feeling the soft relief of a warm towel on her inner thighs and lower belly, then lower, to the sensitized place between her legs. It should have been a gentle tending, but instead his kind touch made her body hot all over again, made her think about all the different ways he could care for her, and exactly how she would let him.

"Insatiable," Master Dante murmured, leaning over to bite her soft inner thigh. "I'm trying to take care of you, *ciccina*, and you can't help yourself, can you?"

"No, Sir," she whispered. "I think I just like it when you touch me."

"Well, that's no hardship," he replied. "It's just about all I want to do. You look like a feast laid out just for me, all lush and soft and pink." He stroked one finger between her folds. "So pink."

"Sir..." she whimpered. She didn't mean to, but it was impossible not to have a reaction to the way he touched her. It was impossible not to have a reaction to *him*, with his strong fingers and filthy mouth.

"Yes, little Saint?" Like he didn't know exactly what she was going to ask for. Like he didn't know exactly what she needed at all times.

"Will you touch me again?"

"You haven't had enough?" He knew the answer to that too. She would never have enough of him.

Saint shook her head. "No, Sir," she replied. "I want..."

"You want my mouth on your pussy?" he asked.

Saint swallowed hard. "Please can I come again?" she asked. Begged. It was definitely begging.

"Normally I'd say no," he said, "because insatiable subs don't always get what they want. But you've been so good for me tonight, and I love the way you taste on my tongue."

She arched up at that, at the memory of him burying his face between her legs. It was impossible to forget all the pleasure he'd given her, how she'd begged and pleaded for more. She wasn't above begging and pleading for more in this moment.

"Yes Sir," she managed. "Thank you, Sir."

He didn't respond, simply spread her legs wide until Saint felt like she was on display and leaned down and licked. Her pussy was still so sensitive, and he was ferocious, a starving man in the desert, stealing her pleasure and forcing her closer to the edge. He didn't need to force. She went willingly, following his every touch, bringing her hand to his hair to pull him closer. Again. Again. Again.

It didn't take long. Her body was already so sensitized from the display in the dance club, from the way he had just taken her so hard and fast, and Saint shattered at his final touches until she was quaking and arching around his tongue and fingers, whether to get more relief or to escape the relentless pleasure she wasn't sure, but her body rioted like a live wire, pulsing and wracking until she was finally, finally able to breathe around the intensity, and Master Dante slowly pulled back.

"You are addicting. If you were mine, you'd never go to sleep unsatisfied."

Because, of course, she could pretend away the reality of their friendship, pretend away the world outside of The Ranch and this lifestyle, but at the end of the day, Saint had to build her own life, and it wasn't one they were going to build together.

And that makes me surprisingly sad.

It shouldn't have come as a surprise. Master Dante had become so much more than a boss and friend these past weeks, and her life was better for knowing him — not just because he had quite literally saved it, not just because he had given her this gift of the world behind the curtain. Because of him, because of his smile and his support and the kindness below all the ink and storm. But there was no future here, and it was best she enjoy the time they did have.

"I'm yours for now," she said quietly, meaning it, loving it. "Is that enough?"

Master Dante looked at her with such a fierceness in his eyes, and she loved that too, the way he was so quick to passion. Maybe it was the Italian in his blood — he would say as much. But Saint rather thought it was the artist, a little temperamental, a little moody, feeling everything as if it were etched into his very skin.

"It will have to be," he replied. "So, let's make the most of it."

He reached out his hand, gently guiding her up from the chaise, and took the moment to smooth her slip of a dress and pull her hair back off her shoulders. She didn't miss the way he lingered with his hands in her hair, or her body's jolting reaction to his proprietary touch there. She liked when he claimed what was his, and there was something so visceral about the way his dark, tattooed hand looked in her hair.

She followed him out of the small room. In the hallway, they passed a woman pressed against the wall, her mouth occupied by the ferocious kisses of one man, while another kneeled between her legs and lapped at her pussy, and the sight was so erotic that it had a small whimper escaping from her lips before she could stop it. It turned out that waiting as long as she had for any kind of intimacy meant she now craved it all, every touch, every caress. She wanted to dedicate her time and attention to this world like some sort of depraved academic.

"You like watching, little one?" Master Dante asked, as he continued to guide her out of the dance club with one possessive hand on her back. Of course, this was his club, and she shouldn't have been surprised when he took her through a series of private hallways rather than crossing the floor again.

"I think I might," she whispered. "I don't know how I'd feel about sharing, though."

"That's good," he replied, his hand slipping slightly lower, until it was just caressing the curve of her ass. "I wasn't planning on letting anyone else see what's mine."

She thought about pushing him, in part because she wanted more of his delicious punishment, and in part because she liked seeing Master Dante all riled up, but Saint was too curious about what he did have planned for the night ahead. And she was honest with herself that she didn't want to share him, even though it seemed all too common in this kind of play. She wanted Master Dante all to herself while she could still claim him as hers.

A moment later, they came to his private suite, stepping inside not through the front door, but a hidden door that disappeared nearly into the wall the moment it closed. Saint must have made a face, because Master Dante laughed.

"It's for security," he said, "and privacy. Only a few of us know about the doors and there are rules for using them. You don't need to worry."

She could see the logic in that, and was once again impressed by how carefully they had worked to curate this space, to make it safe and well-protected for the people who liked to walk on the wild side.

People like me.

Because she was in with both feet, and Saint had the sneaking suspicion that when she started her new life, she wasn't going to keep herself from seeking out a club just like this one wherever she ended up. Of course, there was always the chance that there wouldn't be a club just like this. Master Dante and his friends had worked especially hard to create such a safe haven, and it was clear in their small touches and care that they would do anything to keep the club safe and well-maintained, and to protect the people who used it.

"Where are you right now, angel?" Master Dante asked, watching her looking around the room, searching for more of those hidden doorways or whatever other secrets the space might reveal.

"Green, Sir," she replied. "Neon green."

"Always with the attitude." But she recognized the humor and appreciation in his voice, and couldn't help but smile. No doubt some of the other masters would be stricter or more intense. Hell, Morgan and Skylar had given their own rundowns of play just that afternoon, but Master Dante was fun and funny, even in his most serious moments, and he clearly liked it when she pushed the limits — to a certain extent, of course. "But I am glad to hear it."

He settled into a large chair in the middle of the room and watched her with that dangerous, discerning gaze. "On your knees, little one," he said, "hands and knees, I want to see what's mine."

Heat flooded her pussy at the dark tone of his voice, and Saint knew she probably made a sight as she dropped to her hands and knees, displaying herself to the room. To him.

"So fucking pretty," he murmured, more to himself than her. "Go over to the chest by the bed, Saint."

She made to stand, but one *tsk* from Master Dante and she knew she had miscalculated.

"Sir?"

"Yes, little angel," he said. "Tell me what you think it is I want you to do."

"Crawl?" She whimpered the last, because it should have been the worst kind of embarrassment, should have made her want to say her safe words, and take off. But it had the opposite effect. Instead, she could feel slick heat coating her thighs, and her nipples pebbled to hot hard points. It didn't matter how many times he had made her come that night, this position, this terrible demand, made her want him all over again.

"So good," he replied, the approval like molten fucking lava to her sensitized skin. "Crawl for me, little one. Go slowly so I can see you bare and dripping."

And in that moment, as she slowly moved across the floor, her breasts barely contained by the slip of a dress she wore, and the soft rug beneath her knees adding a whole new sensation to her skin, Saint was most definitely dripping. In fact, the more she knew he was watching her debase herself, expose herself, the more it made her pussy clench on emptiness and her lower belly ache with unfulfilled need.

After an eternity, she reached the chest at the end of the bed, and at Master Dante's direction, she opened it.

It shouldn't have surprised her that there was an entire chest of toys in Master Dante's private suite, but Saint couldn't help being overwhelmed by the very magnitude of options. There were large and small dildos, vibrators, anal plugs, beads, crops, whips, paddles, handcuffs, a large bar with a cuff at either end. The chest seemed endless, and her body reacted on instinct, warming and pulsing at the very idea of him using even one of those toys on her.

"Does it scare you, Saint?" he asked. "You can be honest."

She shook her head. "No, Sir." She couldn't keep her eyes from the various toys and tools taking up space in that trunk. What would it be like to test them all out, to play with this man for as many days and nights as it took to find her favorites, to find his. "It makes me curious."

"Curious," he replied. "Well, I love to hear that. Which ones are you most curious about? Show me."

She reached for the bar, the metal a light weight in her hands, and sat back on her heels to present it.

"Do you know what that is?" he asked. Saint shook her head.

"It's a spreader bar, angel," he replied. "It keeps your legs parted, keeps you displayed and accessible. I think you might like having your sweet little pussy on full display, wouldn't you?"

Saint couldn't help it, she nodded. Depravity had gone out the window hours before, and now all she wanted was his touch, the pleasure he deigned to share with her, his pride in her progress.

"Yes," she whispered. "I think I would, Sir."

"So sweet in your submission. Now I need you to keep being good for me. Do you see vibrators? Pick one that you like."

She looked through the small basket of vibrators, some large and overwhelming, some the size of a tube of lipstick, and she picked one of the smaller, more discreet ones that reminded her of the only toy she'd ever actually purchased for herself. Saint held it up for his approval, her chest glowing warm and her nipples tightening when she nodded.

"Lastly," he said, his tone very, very serious, "I need you to pick out a plug, little one. Don't be brave, pick one you feel good about." There was a whole stack of boxes to the side of the chest, each one containing a different type of plug, and some Saint passed by immediately, the size intimidating and somewhat terrifying. She would be brave for him in a lot of things, but she would take Master Dante's words to heart about feeling good about her choice. She was certain he was about to play out the fantasy they had shared on the dance floor, and she damn well better enjoy every second of it.

Finally, she came across a small glass plug. It was pink, with a heart at the end, and fairly small, but the idea of him pushing it slowly inside her made Saint's pussy practically weep, and she had to swallow hard to keep from whimpering out loud.

"Perfect choice," Master Dante said, his tone one of pride that made her own chest puff out. "Now climb onto the bed."

Chapter Thirty-Eight

Saint got onto the bed, feeling every step Master Dante took toward her as he crossed the room. She loved the way he could see her wet and swollen pussy under the tiny hem of the dress, loved the way this position put so much power between them. Master Dante was fully in control, and that meant she was free to enjoy every touch, every command, every ounce of pleasure he wrung from her body.

"I wish you could see yourself like this," he said. "You're my fallen angel, Saint, slick and hot and waiting for my cock. Fucking incredible." He slipped his fingers through her wet folds like he couldn't help himself, and they both groaned at the contact.

"Spread your legs wider." He didn't wait for her to obey, simply pushed her legs apart until it sent her falling forward onto the bed, ass high in the air. Dante wrapped the leather loop at one side of the spreader bar around her ankle, and then the other, securing her into place. And she was absolutely secure. The bar kept her pinned, kept her from getting any of the friction she desperately needed, and exposed her to him in an undeniable and erotic way.

"Where are you, *ciccina*?" he asked.

"Green, Sir," she managed, her words barely a whisper against the heat and need thrumming through her body. "This is…" She couldn't find the words for how *right* it felt, to be spread out and at his mercy, but it did, like she was meant to be claimed and taken by him tonight and all nights to come.

"It is," he replied, as if reading her very thoughts. "It's perfect." He stroked the curve of her ass and gave it a sharp smack, the slight bite of pain reverberating through her body and making her pussy clench. In this position, with her legs spread, it offered none of the relief she so desperately needed.

"Tell me," he continued, "in your fantasy, the one where you get thoroughly taken" — the word made Saint's breath hitch and catch in her throat — "is it slow and gentle, or rough and forceful…?"

She sucked in a breath, smelling only Master Dante on the comforter, and all around her. "Sir, I…"

He smacked her ass again, slightly harder this time. "Angel, there is no shame here. You tell me what you want, and I'll give it to you, but you have to be honest."

"Yes, Sir," she managed. "Forceful, rough. He calls me filthy things… I tell him the toys won't fit and he tells me I can take it all, his cock, his plug, his cum…"

"You know your safe words?" Master Dante asked, his voice more serious than she had ever heard before.

"Yes."

"And if you can't speak, hit the mattress three times," he said. "Show me."

She did as she was told.

"I want you to play with yourself," he told her. "Play with yourself like you have no idea I'm here. I'll come in when I decide you're ready."

And with that, and the stroke of his hand along the curve of her back one more time, Master Dante walked away, his steps fading behind her. For a moment, she wondered if he would come back, and the seconds ticked by before Saint finally reached for the vibrator. In this position, with her legs spread as wide as they were, it was easy enough to press the small toy to her clit and turn it on, the vibration sending a jolt of intense, overwhelming pleasure rioting through her body, and she slowed the level so she could breathe and adjust to the touch.

It felt so *good*, with the bar keeping her spread and wide and adding that touch of exposure and exhibitionism, with the position limiting how much she could push her pleasure over the edge, with the knowledge that someone was watching, the unseen man from her fantasies, the same dark, needy thing she'd been wanting for years, but had always been too ashamed to admit. Master Dante made sure she never felt ashamed, never felt wrong for wanting intimacies that pushed the limit, made sure to keep her safe while she asked for the dark side of her desires.

All that had Saint writhing against the vibrator, desperately searching for the friction she needed to come, not sure if she was even allowed to come, but chasing the relief anyway. She was just surrendering to the thought that he could do what he wanted to punish her, when Saint heard footsteps at the foot of the bed.

"Look what we have here," the man from her fantasy said. "Such a sweet and ready little slut, waiting for someone to come by and enjoy her. I'm not about to waste this opportunity."

The man slid his fingers through her folds and Saint bucked and arched against the touch, too much and not nearly enough in the wake of all the pleasure she'd been so close to grasping.

"Keep toying that little cunt," he whispered, pressing his hard body against hers. "My cock is going to stretch you out."

Saint gasped as she felt the thick head of his cock at her entrance, gasped again as he pushed inside, the fit tight and the stretch offering sweet fucking relief from the desperate need she'd been chasing.

"Oh, you are tight, aren't you? I think we're just going to have to break in this pretty little pussy." He thrust hard, pushing several more inches inside her. With the bar around her ankles, Saint couldn't do much but let him in, and she nearly came on the spot when he gripped her hair and pulled tight.

"I bet you like this, don't you?" he said, his voice low and hardly recognizable as the man who had given her so much salvation in the past weeks. But the familiarity at the edges was just enough, just enough to keep her safe, to let Saint know she was in friendly hands. "You like being taken and stretched out like this, don't you?"

She shook her head. "No, please. Please."

"Please what, little slut?" he asked, thrusting hard and deeper into her waiting body. "Please fuck your throat until you're gagging on my cock? Please fuck you bare and come in this tight little cunt. Do you want me to get you pregnant and swollen?"

Images flashed in her mind of Master Dante filling her up until she was pregnant with his child, and she shuddered in erotic frenzy at the thought. It wasn't real, none of this was real, but fuck it all if the fantasy didn't push her right up to the edge.

"No, please don't come inside me," she begged. "Please take your cock out..."

"Oh no, little slut," he murmured, pushing back in again and again, each thrust getting her that much closer to the precipice of her pleasure. "I have to be in one of these tight little holes. Maybe I should fuck your mouth..." He reached around and slipped two fingers between her lips, and Saint sucked on instinct, until the man at her back laughed.

"Such a little cock slut, I bet you'd suck me so well..."

He pulled his fingers free and slid them between her ass cheeks. "Maybe you'd prefer I fucked you right here, instead." He ran his slick fingers over her tight hole and laughed when Saint clenched, the sound dark and promising.

"Have you ever had a cock in this tight hole, little slut? Sluts like to get their assholes fucked, don't they?"

"No," Saint replied. "No, I'm not a slut. I don't want you to touch me there."

"Touch you here?" he asked, pushing inside, and fuck if that single touch, the one finger in her tight hole, was enough to have her seeing stars. It made her so fucking aware of his cock in her pussy, her whole body tightening and shrinking down to the carnal sensations of what he made her feel. "Fill this tight little hole with my cum? Is that what you want, little slut?"

She shook her head, but behind her, he reached for the box with the plug and lube.

"Looks like our little slut is already training herself for a cock in her asshole, isn't she? Tell me you want it."

He thrust rough and hard, pulling her hair at the same time and making Saint spiral into throes of pleasure and pain.

"I don't," she whimpered. "Please, don't…"

"Don't push the plug in?" he asked. "Like this?" The tip was fairly thin, not much bigger than the finger it replaced, but the stranger didn't stop there. "Look at how your tight ass takes that plug, little slut, tell me you love it."

"No," she replied. "It's too big, it's not going to fit."

"It'll fit," he replied, drizzling more cool lube on the toy and the entrance to her hole. "You might just not like it."

Fuck, why did she like this so much, this total surrender of power, this game of consent that felt like it should be wrong, but was making her hotter and more aroused than anything in her life ever had. That was a question for another day, because he pushed the plug in another notch and all rationale and reason fled her mind, thoughts disappearing in a haze of abject pleasure and need.

"It's too big," she repeated. "Don't."

"Too late," he replied, the perfect touch of cruelty to the edges of his voice. "I've decided I need to see this tight little asshole all stretched out before I come. Now take the toy or it's going to be my cock shoved up your ass."

She whimpered against the words, against the heat and intensity and stretch and tightness, and then the toy's base was pressing against her cheeks and Saint realized she had the whole thing buried inside her and it felt…

Full. Amazing. Right. Felt like she should have given over to this intense power play a long time ago. It was too much, far too much sensation and over-pleasure and overwhelm, but she was with a man she trusted, and that was all that mattered.

"I wonder how long you could keep that little plug in your hole," he said. "How long before you start fucking yourself against it, you little slut. Tell me to fuck your ass with the toy."

"No." She didn't sound very confident.

"Tell me to," he said. "Or I won't let you come."

She whimpered and the words tore from her throat, against the darkness of the room and the overwhelming pleasure. "Please fuck my ass with the toy," she murmured. "Please let me come."

"Little sluts can do better than that," he demanded. "Tell me to fill your cunt up with my cum while I fuck your ass...tell me you're a little slut who likes to be penetrated."

"I'm a little slut who likes to be penetrated," she whimpered. "Please fuck my ass and fill my cunt, I'm so close...so close."

It only took the twist of the toy, the final thrust of his cock inside her, the pull of her hair, and Saint lost the bed below her and the room around her. The floor fell out and she fell with it, spiraling into a burst of pleasure so intense it made fireworks explode behind her eyelids and cum spill between her legs and she rode and took and bucked against him until all the pleasure consumed her and the world went black.

Chapter Thirty-Nine

She was perfect. The night they had finally gotten together at the cabin had been nothing short of spectacular, a gift Saint had never needed to give him, and he had never believed he'd earn, but they had been on the run and afraid for their lives and she had slept fitfully, waking through the night.

Now, after several orgasms and a hell of a scene he would never have pushed for if he hadn't thought she was ready for it, Saint slept peacefully in his arms, her leg wrapped around his thigh and her arms on his chest, blonde hair spilling loose in every direction. It had been the work of a moment to release her from her binds and the toys and to pull her into his arms as she slowly faded from pleasure into unconsciousness, and he'd taken the time just to watch her sleep, her world at ease.

Too bad your world isn't at ease.

Because Dante knew that saying goodbye to her was going to be the hardest thing he ever did. And he also knew that in order to ask her to stay, he was going to have to confess something that would somehow be even harder. He was going to have to tell her the truth and hope it didn't push her away even faster, and that scared him even more. It would be one thing if Saint left as they had agreed, as expected. But if he pushed her away, tainted their parting with lies and confessions, he'd never be able to forgive himself for it.

I don't have a choice.

It was true. If he was going to ask more of her, if he was going to continue being the man she trusted, and *fuck* if he wasn't coming to love being the man she trusted, he was going to have to be honest.

Even if it scared the ever-loving shit out of him.

Because even after all this time, Dante still couldn't stand to watch the people he loved walk away from him.

Saint stirred in his arms, soft sounds that went straight to his chest and branded him. He'd give it one more day. Let her be at peace for one more day before it all went to hell.

"How long was I asleep?" she asked, sitting up and pushing the hair from her eyes.

"Just a little while," he replied. "You needed rest after that last scene."

Her eyes twinkled, and he was certain if she had been capable, he would have seen more desire there. It seemed now that she knew all that the world had to offer, she desired with an intense passion that made him want to try to keep up. But they'd had enough for the night.

"Thank you," she said quietly. "It was better than the fantasy."

Dante's heart squeezed. Everything she said, everything she did, they all pushed him up against the same, unyielding wall, a truth that he was going to have to face down sooner or later.

He was falling for her.

She wasn't just his receptionist or house guest, wasn't just a friend or an intimate partner or the submissive who'd rocked his whole fucking world when he'd meant to rock hers. She was sneaking her way under his skin, and despite everything, he didn't want her to leave. And after all he had faced down in his life, that was somehow the scariest thing to admit.

"Thank you for trusting me," he managed, though the words felt like razor blades in his mouth. Because he hadn't trusted her. Not with the whole truth. Because she deserved more than the muck and mess in his past, this beautiful angel in his arms, and telling her the truth on the tip of his tongue might be the very last thing they ever shared.

"That's the easy part," she replied, snuggling back against him and making Dante's heart clench for a whole new reason. "I feel like my whole world has been opened up. I think..." She paused, studying her fingernails in the low light. "I think I'm going to look for a club like this when I get to New York. So, thank you."

He should have been so proud. He should have been fucking overjoyed that he'd been able to welcome her into this world and make her feel so safe that she wanted to keep exploring, even after they parted ways. But all he could think about was that she was going to be thousands of miles away from him, and she was going to be playing with some other Dom, and it wouldn't be him. The thought of her with another master had Dante's stomach squeezing and made it difficult to breathe, but there was nothing for it. If he wanted her to stay, he owed her the truth.

"I'm proud of you, *ciccina*," was all he could say in response. "You deserve to live your own life on your own terms now."

"I like that," Saint replied. "What should I do first?"

"Well, I believe you already started," he said, desperately trying to lighten the mood, to say anything other than *you should stay here in Montana with me...* "You got a tattoo, rode a motorcycle, and took up with a Dominant in a sex club. What's left?"

"I want to go back to art school," she said quietly, the words slipping free like a confession she hadn't meant to share. "I never gave myself the chance and you made me see how much I deserve to live my truth and... I want to try."

It was hard to swallow. His throat was thick and his mouth dry, and Dante felt worked over like the sole survivor of a shipwreck. He'd given her the confidence she needed to try. He had done that, and it made the hope and so many other dangerous emotions bloom near to bursting. But she'd have to go to New York City to follow her dream, and that meant that she was truly planning on walking away.

"You're so fucking incredible, Saint," he managed, around the knot growing larger in his throat. "How is it you came into my life?"

"You saved me," she replied. "A dozen times, you've saved me."

And he'd have to do it one more time, because Dante realized in that moment that in order to love her, he was going to have to let her go. He was going to have to sever the ties and make sure she was never able to turn around and miss what was in the rearview mirror.

And time was running out.

Chapter Forty

Saint woke early, the sun streaming through the curtains to Dante's suite, and she took the chance to study his sleeping form. She had tested the waters earlier that week, talking of New York City. Brave as he'd called her, and she had felt so fucking brave taking on the fantasy, but she couldn't bring herself to ask directly if she could stay. So, she'd pushed.

It wasn't that she didn't want to go to art school. In fact, she'd been thinking about it since they had captured Del Santo, and the veil had begun to lift on her life. But there were schools close by that would give her what she needed. And there was no Dante in New York City.

They'd spent the last few days exploring each other's bodies, and Saint had found that there was so much to learn about her own desires, and the eye-opening world he had invited her into. He hadn't played with her publicly, but she preferred that, preferred sharing their intimacies in such a safe way, with such a safe person, and there had been *plenty* of intimacies to share.

But while she enjoyed every moment at The Ranch, even the ones spent in the comfort of his private suite, when they enjoyed a meal with his friends, or he bartended for the main lodge, the rock in Saint's gut was getting bigger. Because time wasn't on her side to figure out next steps, and the day had finally come when she was going to have to ask him for what she wanted, or she was finally going to have to leave.

And while she'd been brave enough to survive mob enforcers and cross-country escapes, if Dante told her to go, she was fairly certain it would break her heart.

Because there was one thing she was coming to realize in the moments they had shared, not just the ones where he made her clutch the pillow and scream his name, but in the moments of kindness and gentleness, in the moments where he seemed like he'd burn the world to keep her safe, when she caught sight of the man behind the mask of humor, to the dark artist below, Saint had found the truth about herself.

A dangerous truth, to be sure.

She was falling for him.

When she had first hurdled into Dante's life, she could admit he was beautiful. And then she could admit the small crush, perhaps even savior worship, that had formed those early days in his apartment and studio. And when they'd finally given into the impossible heat between them, she had known that lust, desire, and trust were at play. But she could no longer lie to herself, and she could no longer pretend away the truth of what she had been jumping into these past days with him in the club.

It wasn't a schoolgirl crush. It wasn't misplaced friendship or appreciation for the man who had saved her life. Niccolo and Ash had both done their parts to save her life, and Saint felt nothing for them but simple appreciation and gratitude. No, her feelings for Dante were brighter, richer, and growing stronger with every day she spent submitting to him.

Love.

Beside her, Dante stirred, and Saint took a picture with her mind of how he looked in the soft morning light. It would be the last time she woke beside him unless she told him how she was feeling, unless she asked if she could stay.

It was the first time Saint had considered her own future. She had run from Seattle because she hadn't had a choice, had taken care of Gram because she loved her, had dreamed of New York City because they had dreamed of New York City together, but if she asked Dante if he wanted more, if she asked to stay in Montana with him, it would be *her* choice.

And damn if that wasn't terrifying.

And freeing all at the same time. Because it was. Because she finally understood that she deserved to want, she deserved the chance to carve out the life she had dreamed of. She deserved to dream of a life all for herself.

And even if he said no, even if he told her that the last month had been a fling that had meant nothing to him, she would still have that lesson.

Dante tightened his arm around her waist and Saint relaxed her shoulders. He wouldn't say it meant nothing because it clearly meant something to him. He wasn't a cruel man, and he would never be so callous as to say something specifically designed to hurt. But more than that, he had shown her again and again that he cared, in taking her in the very first time, in asking to borrow her trouble, in calling his estranged brother for help. He hadn't tried to hide any of it from her, and that gave Saint a dangerous, fledgling ray of hope.

"*Ciccina.*" Dante pressed against her, his morning hardness a wonderful distraction as it pulsed against her thighs. "What are you thinking about so early?"

All those thoughts had been so important, so worth saying aloud, but it was very difficult to pay attention when his hand was already snaking between her legs and stroking the thin cotton of her panties until she was arching back into him.

"Nothing," she whispered, because in the next moment, as his fingers found her clit and stroked, it was entirely true. Dante had the ability to render her brainless with a few well-placed strokes.

"I can hear your mind buzzing, angel," he said. "Always thinking, always moving. Maybe you need a distraction."

"You can try," she teased, because in the days since stepping into his lifestyle, she had come to realize that she very much liked teasing her Master.

Not my Master.

He'd explained the difference to her, why the honorific mattered, how calling someone Master meant something entirely different than Master Dante or Master Caleb or Master Reece, and it had made so much sense at the time. But with the proprietary way he held her, fingers pinning her hip to the mattress as his other hand explored her swollen, wet folds, her body and mind were on very different pages. She knew the rational, logical truth of it. But she wanted to submit to him in such a full and complete way, wanted to be his and his alone, and wanted him to belong to her.

"Always with the attitude," he murmured against her ear, that morning-rough tone making her shudder against his strong hold. She liked the Dante with the rough edges and the unfinished lines, liked when he took what he wanted, especially when what he wanted was her. "I'd punish you, little one, if I didn't know how much you liked it."

She squirmed in his arms, desperate for more friction on her clit, but Master Dante held firm, pinning her in place with such a strength that it made her pussy slick and achy.

"If I let go, will you be good for me?" he demanded, "or will you try to climb my cock and take your pleasure without permission?"

Saint swallowed. She'd never admitted it to herself, but the filthy talk and the sinful promises turned her on, made her wet and desperate, and she pressed back against him as much as she was able, until she heard the familiar *tsk* at her ear.

"You just can't help yourself," he said, and in a motion so fluid she barely had time to register it, he turned their bodies, pinning her on her belly and pushing her hands to the top of the bed. He moved away and she missed his heat in an instant, her body relaxing the second he returned. Master Dante took both of her wrists in one hand and wrapped a silk ribbon around them, then secured the ribbon to the headboard, tying her in place. He moved down her body, stroking each curve with the kind of attention designed to push her right to the edge, and finally came to her ankles, which he bound together. It was a deeply erotic pose, and Saint loved how much she was at the mercy of his touch, how easily it would be for him to take her however he wanted.

"You look so pretty wearing my binds," he murmured, rising back, and leaving her with only the heat of his gaze on her skin. "I should leave you here all day, just to see how long you could last before you started begging."

"I'll start now, Sir," Saint managed. "If it would please you."

"Now you're on your best behavior," he said teasingly, sliding his strong hand over the curves of her ass and dipping just between her legs, the ghost of a touch designed to tempt and torment. "Because you want something."

"Yes." It came out on a sigh, because this position, his touch, the demanding words, it all made her *want* with a kind of ferocity that should have scared her but instead made Saint feel more free and alive than she had in a very long time. "Please."

Master Dante chuckled without humor, his tone dark and demanding when he said, "You're going to have to do better than that."

Saint tested the bonds, pulling back until she felt the bite of the fabric against her wrists, until she could push up onto her knees, so her ass was in the air.

"Please touch me, Sir," she managed, barely able to think for the wanting, the needing. He didn't even have to touch her, and Saint could start to feel herself barreling toward the unseen edge. "Please make me come."

"How?" he asked. "You know I like when you use the words. My pretty little angel with her mouth all full of sin." He reached from behind her and stroked her bottom lip with his thumb until Saint opened on instinct, sucking his thumb into her mouth and swirling her tongue around the tip. Master Dante released a sharp breath and pulled back, smearing saliva on her lips, and making heat pulse between her thighs.

"I want your cock inside me," she whispered. Whimpered. It was getting difficult to tell. "In my pussy."

"Say cunt, little angel," he said, "say, 'Master Dante, I want your cock in my tight little cunt.'"

"Master Dante." She bucked forward on his name, because that alone was enough to send her spiraling. "I want your cock in my tight little...cunt..." The word was pure filth on her lips, but it sent her body skittering along edges of pleasure, harsh and biting and sure to leave a mark. "Please fill me up."

"So sweet when you beg," he said, bracketing her legs with his knees and lowering to kiss the inside of her thighs. No doubt he could see her desire staining her panties, especially as he kissed and sucked around the edge of her pleasure until Saint was squirming against the binds and chanting his name like an oath. Finally, he pulled at the sides of her panties and tugged them down her thighs, where they pinned her even further into position and opened her to his inspection.

"So fucking wet and I've barely touched you," he said. "You're going to feel so good squeezing my cock." He kissed the inside of one thigh and then the other, up and up and up and Saint bucked and arched, desperately hoping for more of his touch, more of the sweet relief he could give her.

"Yes, Sir," she managed. "I need you inside me."

"You need to respect your Master's orders," he said. "I tied you up for a reason, little one, because I knew you'd try to take your pleasure before you earned it."

"I'm sorry, Sir," Saint said, but it was difficult to think against the onslaught of sensation from his moving touch and the heat of his nearness. "I'll be good, I promise. I'll be so good for you."

"I don't believe you," he said, slipping one finger into her waiting pussy, and Saint clenched hard around him, needing more, needing so much more.

"What can I do, Sir?" she asked, "to earn your trust?"

He slipped a second finger inside her waiting pussy and Saint almost screamed with the near pleasure of it. He knew exactly what he was doing, exactly how to push her to the edge of her need and desire, and he was going to continue punishing her until she lost her mind to the need of it all.

"You can tell me a secret," he said. "I thoroughly enjoyed the last secret you shared."

The secret that had ended with her in a very similar position to this one, a vibrator at her pussy, a plug in her ass, and Master Dante filling her up with his cock until she blacked out. That had been her go-to fantasy, one of power and control and submission, but in the days since submitting to him, another dark desire had begun to take root, and Saint knew she might not get another chance to ask for what she wanted.

"Sir," she said, pressing back against his fingers and desperately needing more… "I don't have any other secrets…"

"Now that's not true, is it?" he asked, pulling his fingers nearly free before Saint clenched around him.

"No, please, I'll tell you," she said, "please I need you inside me… I'll tell you."

He stroked back in, and she sighed with the relief of his touch, until he stilled his fingers and waited for her to continue.

"It's…filthy," she whispered. "My secret, Sir…it's so dirty…"

"My favorite kind," he replied. "Tell me, little angel, and it'll be my dirty secret to carry, not yours…"

Because that was Master Dante, in bed and out. He would carry her burdens for her and take away her fear and her shame. He would make her feel like she could do anything.

"I want…" Saint swallowed, swallowed harder when Master Dante pushed a third finger into her pussy, stretching her, filling her. "I want you to come inside me," she confessed in a single breath.

"*Fuck, Saint…*" The words were torn from his lips, and she knew he wasn't putting on a show. He liked her secret, and that made pride swell in her chest, because she was very much beginning to love how it felt to make him happy.

"You want me to fill this pretty pussy with my cum?" he asked, finger fucking her in full now, no pretense, just the slow, intense push of his fingers in and out of her waiting heat. "Dripping with my release…"

"Yes, Sir," she said, barely able to hold on against the onslaught of pleasure and need. "I want to feel you inside me."

"Who am I to deny you anything," he said, "especially when I want what you want?"

"You do?"

He pulled free and stroked her pussy, leaning down to lick at her swollen, needy entrance. "Do I want to mark you in my cum until it stains your thighs and fills your cunt?" he asked, taking the pause to lick her again. "Yes, little angel. I do."

"Fill me?" she begged, and this time, it had a dangerous, double meaning.

"I have to keep you safe," he said. "We get our screenings for the club, but I don't want to get you pregnant."

In a fleeting, terrible thought, Saint imagined it wouldn't be so awful at all for Master Dante to do just that, but it was the heat of the moment and the intense erotic connection between them that made such dangerous things seem real.

"I take the pill for cramps," she said. "And I've never been with anyone else."

"I know, *ciccina*," he said. "And if you're certain."

"More than anything," she admitted. "I need you."

Chapter Forty-One

Dante swallowed hard. His pretty little sub was all tied up on his bed, ass in the air, sweet, wet pussy on full display, begging for him to come inside her, and he was about to lose all grip on his self-control. He owed Saint a conversation—a confession, more like—and when it came, it would be the last chance he ever got to tell her the truth. That he cared, that he cared so fucking much he'd do whatever it took to keep her safe, even if that meant protecting her dreams and her future, instead of just keeping her alive.

But that meant that he might just very well be touching her for the last time, and he was going to savor every delicious second he could get. He pushed his briefs to the ground and bracketed her thighs with his knees, loving how this position made it so easy for him to bend down and lick and suck and taste, loving how her sweet little cunt and pretty tight asshole were on full display for him. She loved being on display, he knew that, just like he knew she loved confessing dirty secrets, and always got wet when he shared the depraved fantasies of his own. He knew far, far too much about the beautiful blonde sub who had infiltrated his heart and his soul, and Dante knew for a fact that he wasn't going to walk away from this with either still intact.

"You're going to look so pretty wrapped around my cock," he said, instead of any of those things, because he had to keep himself safe, damnit, and because he wasn't a strong enough man to not be affected by the flutter of a pretty little pussy at his sinful commands. "Push back, angel, take the head."

At the first touch of her pussy against the head of his cock, they both gasped. It had been a long damn time since he'd played with anyone without a condom, and the touch of hot skin to hot skin was nearly enough to have him coming then and there. But he was going to give his beautiful little angel exactly what she wanted. Because the idea of filling her up, until she was spilling over her thighs and dripping with his release all day long, it made him harder and hotter than anything ever had. It was a claiming, no doubt, and if it was going to be the only one he got, he was going to fucking treasure it.

"You feel big," she whispered, as she slowly arched back into his touch. Dante pushed forward the smallest amount, just enough, just enough to stretch her welcoming entrance and slide inside.

"*Mmm*, that's your fault, little angel," he said. "I like your pretty secrets."

"I like the way you feel," she replied. "Without the condom, it's…amazing."

It *was* amazing, and Dante had to take a deep breath to hold his position, especially as Saint's pussy fluttered and clenched around him, clearly aching for more. So he pushed in, each inch a beautiful type of pleasurable torture, until after a millennium, he was buried all the way to the hilt inside her.

"Oh fuck, Sir." She twisted against her bonds, breath hitching when she pulled too tight, and he took a light, experimental thrust. Saint whimpered and groaned, leaning back to meet his every touch, until she was bucking into him and taking him more than he was taking her. For a moment, he let her, loving the way this angelic, beautiful, kind woman went after the things she wanted, after the things she *craved*, and then he finally took over, pinning her hips with one hand and wrapping his other hand in her beautiful silken hair and tugging just enough that it made her pussy squeeze, and then he moved.

He fucked hard and fast, loving how she met him, even against the bonds, loving how her body seemed so incredibly eager, so needy for his, loving the way she whimpered his name like a goddamned prayer, and needing so much more.

"You have to come around my cock, little angel," he said. "I need to feel you coating me in your release."

"Yes, Sir," she replied. "Make me come."

He reached out and stroked her swollen clit, once, twice, once more, until she was screaming his name and clawing at the bonds and then bursting apart around him. It was so much more intense without the barrier of latex between them, and he felt the rush of her hot release as she spilled, coming hard and fast around his cock.

"Fuck, Master Dante, it feels so good, feels so fucking good." This from the woman who had only just become comfortable with swearing at all, and she was babbling pure sweet sin from her pretty lips as she came around his cock.

"Like you were made for me," he said, the need behind the words intense and unyielding, and he took the only version of their meaning he could. "You're going to look so pretty filled with my cum, little angel. My fallen angel, marked and claimed."

"Please, I want it," Saint whimpered. He knew she was close to the edge all over again, knew she was nearly ready to split apart, and he would be the one to take her there. "Inside me, Sir, *please*."

The last, torn with such an intense, carnal need from her lips, was finally what sent Dante throttling over the edge. He unraveled, then tore, then burst apart into a thousand splinters of pleasure and white-hot need, thrusting into her with a force she only mirrored, one more time, one more, and then he was spraying hot, sticky strands of cum into her waiting pussy, filling her. Marking her. Claiming her.

Saint gasped for air, feeling almost like she was swimming, diving, jumping from some great height into the depths below. She was somehow at once separate from her body and aware of every single sensation, the tiniest puff of heat from the vent, the single strand of hair catching on her eyelash. Master Dante was still buried inside her, the last pulsing threads making her pussy squeeze and tighten as he filled her with his release, and she wanted to burst into a radiant star explosion of another climax, as if that were somehow possible, and maybe also burst into tears. Because he had claimed her, completely and totally, and it would be his goodbye.

Master Dante kissed her shoulder as he slowly began to pull his cock free. The sensation was nearly as intense as all the rest and she gasped against the feeling, gasped again when he leaned down to whisper, "Tell me how it feels, little angel, to be filled with my cum."

"Perfect."

It wasn't what she had meant to say, but was the entire truth in its naked glory. She felt owned, in all the ways she had come to love since falling into his life, and the erotic intimacy of it left her body burning hot.

"You're perfect," he murmured, slipping his thumb into her swollen pussy and mixing their releases. It should have been depraved to be opened and dripping, to be available for his touch as she leaked his cum all over her thighs, but she fucking loved it, and Saint was ready to own the things she loved now. "You look so pretty covered in my cum, little angel. So fucking wrecked, all for me."

"Yes," she replied. Always. *All for you today and as long as you'll have me.*

"Where are you, Saint?" he asked, pressing his thumb deeper inside her. It made a soft sound, his come pulled back into her body, and that only served to turn her on more.

"Green, Sir," she whispered. "Thank you."

"Thank you," he said. "For giving me all these gifts. I want to give you something in return."

He pulled his wet thumb free and slid it up the curve of her ass, and Saint shuddered. It had been an overwhelming discovery to realize how much she liked to be touched there, and her body reacted before her mind got the chance.

"Sir," she whimpered, realizing what he meant to do, realizing it would all be too much in all the best ways. "I don't think I can..."

"You can," he said. "And you will. Because you like making me proud, don't you little angel?" She nodded.

"It would make me very proud to finger fuck this pretty hole with my cum. So, tell me — do you think you can?"

"*Yes.*" It was barely a word, but she was barely a person now, wrecked with pleasure and chasing even more, somehow.

"Good girl," he murmured, before pressing his thumb into her tight asshole. Saint cursed and bucked against the binds, but she was at his mercy, his slow, agonizing mercy. "You take my thumb so well, little angel. Makes me wonder how you'd take my cock. We'd have to train your little hole, of course. You're so fucking tight."

"Train?"

"Of course," he said, pulsing his thumb and out of her hole while he nonchalantly spoke, as if she was the only one losing her mind. "With the plugs and the toys. You start small, and then take bigger toys, until you're ready for my cock."

The onslaught of images was intense, moments of him pressing toys into her ass, telling her she was doing so good, that she would be ready for him soon. The moment when he could finally push inside and...

"Would you come in my ass, Sir?" she asked, unable to keep a single secret against the impossibly slow onslaught of pleasure.

"Is that what you want?" he asked.

"Yes." In for a fucking penny. "I think it would be... so hot..."

"I agree," he said, twisting his thumb so it sparked a whole new sensation. "My pretty girl, marked with cum in all her holes. What an image you'd make."

"Thank you, Sir," she whimpered, though she wasn't sure if she was thanking him for the fantasy or the intense touch on her tightest hole that was pushing her closer to the edge of absolute devastation.

"Hmm, you might not thank me if I made you wear it all day," he replied, "dripping my cum from all your tight little holes…"

"*Yes.*" She was nearly there, so fucking close to the edge from his thumb in her asshole and his filthy fucking promises. "I'd do whatever you asked of me, Sir."

"So good," he replied, bringing one hand to her swollen, over-sensitized clit. "Then come for me." He pinched, hard, and the pain and the intimacy and the intense pleasure of his touch sent her careering, throttling over the edge of pleasure and bursting into a bright, white light as her body wracked with sensation, spilling, bucking, arching, taking, coming, coming, coming, until she finally, completely, fell apart in his arms.

For the last time.

Chapter Forty-Two

"Del Santo made it to Washington," Niccolo said without preamble when they gathered in the back room of The Ranch with the others later that day. Ash was leaning against the counter typing furiously on his phone, and finally looked up to nod.

"The sheriff is sticking around to make sure that he gets properly charged," he said. Dante didn't miss the way Ash referred to his foster sister. Not by her name. Not even by their relationship. Just *the sheriff*.

Well, who was he to judge when it came to the way siblings or not-so-siblings interacted. Even across the room, he could see the bags under Niccolo's eyes, the gaunt pull of his cheeks, the harsh line of his jaw. It was looking into a funhouse mirror of himself and seeing a familiar and unfamiliar face looking back, and it made his heart *hurt*. But the chasm between him and Nic was already too wide, already stretching miles and years, and Dante honestly didn't know if he was still allowed to be the one to say anything to his brother. Niccolo had his ghosts, and no doubt some of them were Dante's own fault.

It didn't help that he couldn't much concentrate on what his brother was dealing with. Not when Saint was standing beside him in another pair of those ass-squeezing leggings that made him want to haul her back to his suite and never let her leave. He had her tied up that morning—why on earth had he untied her, knowing that it was the last day they were going to spend together?

She looked pretty as a picture, well-rested, hair freshly washed and pulled into some complicated kind of braid at her back, loose sweater falling off her shoulder. But even with the chance to breathe after weeks on the run, she seemed to have some shadows around the edges of her smile too, and Dante knew that those were *definitely* his fault.

Because he hadn't asked her to stay. Because he couldn't ask her, not when she would be giving up so much to stick around. Not when she had her whole life ahead of her, and his life was here, in this small town in Montana. She deserved New York City, and she deserved art school, and she deserved to start fresh. Without him.

Which was why he was going to have to sever this thing between them before it grew heads and started to bite back. Before the claws dug any further into his heart and burst the vessels there that were keeping him alive. In order to love her, he was going to have to let her go.

"Thank you, Ash," Saint said, "Niccolo, *grazie mille per tutto.*"

Dante's world shifted on its axis and righted again, hearing his familiar language on her tongue. It was a little stilted and very American, but the fact that she had learned even the simple sentence for his brother was…something. Too much. Too much for his already battered soul to handle.

"*Prego, carina,*" Niccolo replied, the ghost of a smile etching the corner of his lips. It was the very first one Dante had seen from him in the past days, but Saint had that effect on people. She burst into every room with a lightness and a joy that made people want to smile, made people want to be the best versions of themselves. Made people want to be in love.

"We need to celebrate this," Morgan said, wrapping her arm around Saint's shoulder. Morgan was much taller, especially in the hiking boots she still wore, but it looked right to see them together, even better when Rhylee popped in from the other room with a grin on her face and came to stand on Saint's other side, squeezing between her and Dante the way only an annoying little sister could.

"Did I hear party?" she asked. "I could *so* go for a party right now."

"Don't you have a job?" Van asked from across the room. Dante had money against himself with when Van would finally come to the realization that he wasn't nearly as annoyed with Rhylee as he wanted to believe he was.

Rhylee just stuck her tongue out at him and leaned her head on Saint's shoulder, whispering something into Saint's ear that made the two women giggle and Van scowl more deeply. Despite all the turmoil in head and his heart, Dante couldn't help a chuckle. Rhylee and Van would come to a head one of these days, and it would end spectacularly, one way or another.

"Saint?" Skylar asked, "Do you want a party?"

Saint grinned, but it was all for Dante, and he, greedy and wanting so much more than he was willing to take, soaked it all in. "I'd love one," she said. "But we need to celebrate Dante, Ash and Nicco. They're the ones who saved me. And so did all of you."

Dante's eyes pricked hot and painful, because she was just like that. She was just the grateful, beautiful woman who refused to see how brave she had been through such a horrid ordeal, who would rather thank the people around her than take any credit for her own survival. And he had to love, too, that she was honoring his friends, the people that mattered most to him in the world. Because she knew they did.

"Then I say, what are we waiting for?" Rhylee said, kissing Saint then Morgan on the cheeks with exaggerated movements that made them all laugh. "Let's party."

* * * *

Within the hour, they were congregated in the backyard of Skylar and Caleb's cabin down the hill, Caleb defending his grill to the death and Reece and Morgan setting up a bonfire that was definitely not regulation for the state of Montana. Dante grabbed a beer for himself and one for Saint from the cooler they'd dragged down from the kitchen, and came to stand at the far end of the porch beside her.

"I'm going to miss Montana," she said without preamble. "Washington is amazing, don't get me wrong, but I've been a city girl all my life and we just don't have *that* where I'm from." *That* was the vista of mountains standing sentinel across the entire horizon. They truly were purple mountain's majesty, a granite violet color cut across with streaks of red dirt and peaked snow caps and the golden slanting light of an early December sunset.

It was just there, on the tip of his tongue, to ask her to stay, to ask her to trust him, but he knew she could never stay without him telling her the last truth between them, and he knew she'd never want to once he did. Which was going to make the tie severing easier than he could possibly want.

"Where will you apply for art school?" he asked instead. "Pratt? FIT?"

Saint laughed, and it was everything, squeezing his very heart and soul until Dante wasn't sure he'd ever breathe again. "I don't know yet," she said. "There's a lot I still need to figure out before that."

Like why he was pushing her away, Dante knew.

"Saint, I..."

Music and laughter came spilling out of the cabin and Skylar and Rhylee joined them on the porch in a cacophony of sound and excitement, sweeping Saint into a conversation about clothes or hair or a movie, he couldn't be sure, because all he could think about was that he was going to lose his chance.

But then all he could think about was that she deserved this, this chance to be among friends, to spend her time with people who appreciated her, who wanted her to be happy. He wasn't going to ruin that, not yet.

"You haven't told her yet," Niccolo said. It wasn't an accusation, but a statement of fact.

"I want her to be happy."

"So, you're going to push her away." Another statement of fact. "You don't give her enough credit."

Dante turned to face his brother, struck with a sudden fear he didn't know how to voice. Niccolo must have been able to read the expression on his face, however, because he chuckled around the cigarette he was lighting.

"I'm not in love with your girl," he said, the smoke billowing into the darkening night. "But you are. And you're being a chickenshit about it."

"Since when do you smoke?" Dante asked, instead of responding.

Niccolo didn't answer. "You're going to tell her the truth and break her heart, so she goes off and starts her next big adventure, and then you're going to stay here in absolute misery."

"That's a lot of words for you."

Nic shrugged. "We have a lot to make up for."

And in hearing that, part of Dante's heart began to knot itself back together, because no matter what happened with Saint, no matter what the future held for Dante and the woman who had captured him so thoroughly, Niccolo wasn't running again, and he wasn't pushing Dante away.

"We do," Dante replied. "And I look forward to it."

Nicco clapped him on the back. "You deserve good things," was all he said, before heading down the hill to join Ash and the others by the fire.

"What were you guys talking about?" Saint asked, saddling up beside him, her cheeks flush and her words breathy.

"He called me a coward," Dante said, "actually a chickenshit."

"Because you haven't asked me to stay," she said teasingly. God, if only it were that easy. If only he could be selfish in the minute and keep the truth under lock and key. But not now. Not when so much was on the line.

"Because there's something I haven't told you."

Saint had been nursing a light buzz, but on hearing those words, her body sobered in an instant and her thoughts cleared. The air was fresh and cold, December in the mountains, but it had nothing to do with the chill that was racing down her spine now.

"What?"

Dante, her joyful, creative, possessive Dante, looked still as stone, his dark, intense gaze making her stomach clench for all the wrong reasons.

"I haven't been totally honest with you, *ciccina*," he said.

"Dante, you're scaring me," Saint replied. Was he married? Was he a criminal? What could be so bad about him that it would keep him from asking for more, that it would stop this amazing thing they had in its tracks? Because all of a sudden, she knew that the reason he hadn't asked for more from their time together was because of this thing between them she hadn't known about, and in the same instant, she realized she hated it.

"Let's go inside," he said, but she held her ground.

"Tell me," she said. "What does Niccolo know that you've been keeping from me?"

Dante sighed, as if gathering the strength. No doubt he'd had days, weeks to gather the strength to tell her this secret, whatever it was.

"I didn't want to scare you," he said. "And this should make it pretty easy for you to leave in the morning."

She filed that away for later, because she was too focused on whatever he was hiding from her, whatever chasm lay between them now.

"You asked if I knew the Barbarone family," he said. "That first night when you told the truth about what happened in Seattle. You asked if I knew them."

"I remember," she said, thinking back to the first night when she had been struck with such panic and fear, and had, for the first time, not been so alone in her terror.

"I don't just know them," he said quietly. "I *am* them."

Saint's heart skittered to the edge of the precipice and fell into the deep sea below. It was freezing outside, but a hot flush was spreading across her chest and up her neck, and her ears and fingertips burned with the heat of it.

"Explain," she said. "Now."

"I told you our mother was forced into an arranged marriage," he said. She didn't move. "The marriage was to Lorenzo Barbarone."

"Your father is Lorenzo Barbarone," she said.

"My mother ran away when we were young, and she gave us her name," he continued. "He wasn't in my life long and he wasn't a nice man when he was, but..."

"You knew..." she whispered. "You knew this the whole time and you kept it from me, why?"

Dante choked on his next words. "There's more," he said.

"*More.*" Hot tears spilled down her cheeks, but Saint barely registered that she was crying. This man who had given her *everything* had been keeping the most important thing secret the whole time. "What more could there possibly be?"

"My mother," he said, his voice hard as steel now, and Saint realized she knew what he was going to say before he said it. "He killed my mother."

Between them, a silence fell that was as unclimbable as the chasms between the mountains, that stretched between them broad as the night and dark as the sky above, but there were no glimmers of hope in that blackness, nothing to guide her way. Everything she thought she knew was twisted and warped, and this man who had done everything in his power to keep her safe was no longer the haven she had believed him to be.

"Is that why you agreed to help me?" she asked quietly. "All those weeks ago, when I told you what happened, you didn't even hesitate. Did you want revenge?"

"No." His voice was firm and strong, and she couldn't help herself, she believed him. "I wanted to keep you safe. I wanted... I couldn't save my mother, but I thought it was my second chance to save *someone*."

That she understood. It made sense, in the kind of way grief could make sense, and try as she might, she couldn't fault him for wanting to help, for seeing their crossed paths as a kind of fate, a kismet that could give him salvation.

"You should have told me," she whispered. "I deserved to know."

"You did," he said. "And Niccolo's right, I was being a coward. I wanted to keep you here as long as I could."

Suddenly, the words from earlier made sense.

And this should make it pretty easy for you to leave in the morning.

He wasn't telling her this secret to clear the air between them. He wasn't telling her this truth so they could take the next step into their future together without anything holding them back. He was telling her this so she'd leave.

"You're pushing me away," Saint said, aware her voice was rising, aware and unable to stop it. "You're trying to get me to leave."

Dante didn't say a word, and that was damning enough all on its own.

"I can forgive you your secrets," she said. "I can hate them and hate that you kept them from me, but they are your secrets, but this..." She waved her hand at him. "This fucking sacrifice thing that you're doing, don't think I don't see right through you."

"It's not a sacrifice," he said. "You deserve a fresh start, with someone young, someplace new."

"Pull the age card on me one more time, Dante, try it."

He quieted, and she took the opportunity to look him straight in the eyes.

"Tell me the truth this time," she said. "All of it. Are you trying to get me to leave in some valiant effort to love me by letting me go?"

Again, he kept quiet, until. "You deserve better."

Saint practically shrieked with frustration. "You are *infuriating*. All this time I've been thinking you didn't want me as much as I wanted you and you were trying to be some kind of white knight. I didn't ask for it, Dante." She backed down the step on the porch, suddenly needing air, needing space from him. "I have been telling you not to put me on a pedestal since the day we met. I am truly sorry for what happened to your mom, but don't you dare use it as a way to push me out or whatever the *fuck* it is you're doing. Stop trying to save me from myself and just fucking admit that you're scared to love again so you're sabotaging this thing before it can hurt you."

It felt like she was swallowing glass, the words choking her as they lodged in her throat, but Saint knew she had to say them, or be haunted by them forever. "You're so afraid of someone walking away from you that you don't even let them get close. You walk away first—or push them away."

"Saint." She could see the entire universe in his eyes now, guilt, grief, pain, but it didn't matter how he felt if he wasn't willing to try.

"I'm not scared, Dante. Not of this thing or the way you make me feel, but I'm not begging, because I deserve better—and I finally understand that. If you want to be brave, come find me. Otherwise, I'll be gone by morning and you can find some other sad little broken *angel* to protect."

"It's my job to keep you safe." The Dante who had her heart was just there, twin flames of passion and pain, and she knew he believed that. That it was the only role he played. But as much as he had kept her safe, as much as he saved her life, there were some choices he didn't get to make for the both of them.

"No," she said. "It's not. I'm a grown woman capable of making my own decisions. And right now, that decision involves walking the *fuck* away from you."

Chapter Forty-Three

"That went well," Niccolo said from around the corner of the cabin. He was barely visible in the glow of his cigarette, just long hair and an overly large nose being stuck where it didn't belong.

"You told me I had to tell her the truth," Dante said, knowing he sounded petulant, knowing he was *wrong* but still needing someone else to blame it all on. His brother was close by and a very easy target.

"She didn't give a shit about that," Nic said. "She cared that you were making her choice for her."

"Isn't that what you did all those years ago?" Dante challenged.

"Yes," Niccolo replied, surprising Dante with his easy admission. "But that was different."

"How?"

"You were a child and literally my responsibility," Niccolo explained. "It was a matter of life and death. And—" He paused, because even the most tormented

Italian men were not strangers to a touch of drama. "We didn't speak for ten years."

"Right."

His brother had sacrificed everything and it had been the right call in the moment, for them. But making the decision for Saint, when every choice in her life to that point had been made for her, her parents' accident, her grandmother's illness, quitting school, running away for her life. He was just adding another thing to the list of things she hadn't been able to choose for herself.

"You want to give her a real choice?" Niccolo asked. "You have to let yourself be one of those choices."

And fuck if that wasn't terrifying. Because if he put himself on the table and she said no…

It would still be better than never trying. It would still very much be worth the risk of asking. He hadn't been protecting just her, with this fucked idea to send her packing. He'd been protecting himself, too, against the pain of seeing another person he loved leave, against the possibility of having his heart broken again.

But the possibility of having his heart broken was part of what made love so remarkable, it was part of what made love hopeful. Part of what made love *brave*. He had called her brave for so many reasons in the past weeks, for staying alive, for caring for her grandmother, for starting up with the lifestyle she knew nothing about. But telling him how she felt, taking the first step to him when he'd been slowly backing away, that was the fucking bravest thing of all.

"I have to go."

He was down the steps and halfway across the path, ignoring the calls from his friends, and focusing only on what he was going to say to Saint when they found each other, only what he was going to offer as collateral for his bruised and battered heart, true words he'd been terrified to say. He wasn't pushing her away now, not when he could finally admit that he wanted her in his life more than he feared her walking away. Not when he could finally tell her the whole truth.

I love you.

Those were the words on the tip of his tongue, the words he was about to shout to the mountaintop for everyone to witness, when he heard a sound that made his blood run cold.

It was the sound of a gun resonating through the Montana mountain air. It clicked with a type of finality that made time stop and the air freeze in place and his heart drop to his gut. He knew that sound — had known enough of the violence of his father's life and then his brother's — had tasted that violence himself before life had given him a different path, and there was something so unmistakable about the threat of violence in the strike of metal on metal that Dante knew it couldn't be anything other than what it was — what it meant.

"Well, well, well, if this isn't a family reunion."

And the sound of that voice, of the one that haunted his dreams, coated his memories in a film of soot and fear, that turned soft, childhood anger into rivulets of volcanic rage that threatened to take over everything, that was unmistakable too. Unmistakable and dangerous as all hell.

Abandon all hope, ye who enter here.

"Padre."

There was a certain irony in the fact that Dante had long stopped believing in God. He had no father now, not the father above and not the father standing before him with his gun to Saint's belly.

"Imagine my surprise when I find out that Berto had been shipped back to the city," Lorenzo Barbarone said. "From Montana."

When Maria had run, she had taken the boys as far as she could from the big city to the tiny mountain town, and it hadn't been lost on Dante that Saint's path had been the same, her car breaking down in the same town where his mother had found her temporary refuge. Perhaps, yes, that had been why he had helped her from the start, looking at her now, panic in her eyes but an abject stillness in her body that belied a staggering inner strength, Dante knew that wasn't why he had stuck around. That wasn't why they had connected or why they had spent the last week in each other's arms or why he knew he would lose himself to save her, no matter the cost.

"You found me."

"I wasn't looking for you, *figlio*," Lorenzo said. "But it is a pleasant surprise to, how do you say, kill two birds with one stone."

"Take me instead of her," Dante said, the words final and undeniable on his tongue. It would be the work of a second to trade places with Saint, though he knew his father would never allow such a trade. Lorenzo would always take care of loose ends. It was why Dante had been essentially orphaned at sixteen.

"Saint, look at me. Please." Her icy blue eyes were nearly gray now, pale and colorless and devoid of emotion, and Dante knew in his very marrow he would do whatever it took to bring the light back to his angel. "You're mine. Today and always. And I will do whatever it takes to keep you in my life."

"Dante…" She struggled against his father's hold, tears streaming down her pale cheeks. "I shouldn't have said those things."

"Don't," he replied. "I'm the one who needs to apologize to you. For everything. I'll do whatever it takes to get that chance."

He turned back to his father and repeated his plea, "*Padre, per favore*. Take me."

"You're like her, you know," his father said. "She bargained for your lives, you and the *bastardo*."

"You called."

Niccolo appeared from the other side of the cabin, his hands in his pockets, his long hair blowing in the cold mountain wind.

"Three birds." His father's laugh was cruel. "I've been looking for you for a long time."

"I can't say the same," Niccolo replied. "You stopped mattering a long time ago."

"I suppose I'll have to show you how much impact I can really have," Lorenzo said. And he struck the side of his gun against Saint's head.

She crumpled to the ground, falling at Lorenzo's feet with a puff of air, and Dante lunged for his father.

Niccolo got there first, grabbing Lorenzo's wrist of the hand holding the gun and charging for his open side. With the impact of two large men, Lorenzo lost his footing, but only for a breath, stumbling back and gaining the upper hand to kick Dante in the head with a force so resounding it made stars burst behind his eyes and his breath seize in his tightening chest. Fine. He would crawl if he had to, he would do whatever it took, *whatever* it took to keep Lorenzo from ever hurting another person he loved.

Because he loved Saint.

There was no denying that. The only reason he'd been able to for so long was because he had been lying to himself, had been pushing her away before she could leave him, had been trying to play the valiant knight in an effort to protect them both. It hadn't worked, of course. She had known before he had. Niccolo had known. Hell, no doubt his friends had known from a shared glance. Because there was no denying it. Not for a second longer, as she lay crumpled on the trail, her body still and a thin line of blood trickling from her temple. If it weren't for the slight rise and fall of her chest, Dante would have worried that she was gone, but for the moment, he had more pressing matters to attend to.

And when those pressing matters were managed, he would tell her the truth. Every damn word of it.

He pushed off the ground, the breath slowly returning to his chest—far too slowly, but there wasn't a second to wait. Lorenzo and Niccolo were caught in a tangle of metal and wool and leather, the glint of Lorenzo's gun, the shine of Niccolo's knife, harsh and metallic in the light of the full mountain moon. Dante took advantage of his father's distraction, coming up behind him and yanking on his arm, pinning it behind him with a shove. The father in his memories had been big—larger than life—but this Lorenzo was older, not nearly as strong, smaller even than himself and Niccolo, and he pressed his advantage, locking his other arm around his father's throat as Niccolo grabbed the gun free, the sight of which was enough to send the weight of the world throttling off his back.

"I've got him," Niccolo said. "Go check on Saint!"

Dante shifted, allowed Niccolo to take hold of his father's bound arms and crossed to the trail to where she lay still, way, way too still on the barren path, that stream of blood spilling across her silver hair, staining her beauty with the heavy weight of violence, and making Dante's gut clench. He lifted her into his arms, pressing two fingers to the pulse point at her wrist and waiting until he heard the strong, powerful throb of blood there. She was alive. Injured and bleeding, but alive. And his father...

Dante glanced up to where Lorenzo Barbarone stood, at the exact moment Lorenzo broke free from Niccolo's hold and grabbed for the weapon hanging from Niccolo's belt. A thousand things happened all at once. Dante shouted, a shot rang through the mountain air, and Niccolo doubled over with a grunt of pain, reaching for his abdomen, just as Lorenzo fell from his grip and stumbled over a rock, falling hard.

"I've got him." Ash was running up the mountain. "I've got him, D..."

The world was beginning to spin around Dante and the hard hit he'd taken with the heel of Lorenzo's shoe was catching up to him, making his vision double and blur, making it difficult to see where Ash's black leather jacket started and Niccolo's began.

His brother wasn't breathing. *Why wasn't his brother breathing?*

Ash's harried shouts were growing distant, like Dante was hearing them through the end of a long tunnel or under the surface of the water, and then he couldn't make out what Ash was saying at all, just the tone that wrenched at Dante's heart, because his brother couldn't be gone, not now, not when they had finally found each other again, not when he was about to have everything that he had always wanted — a true family again.

The very last though he had before his vision tunneled to nothing and the sound disappeared from his ears completely, was that he had to tell them both. He had to tell them both that he loved them.

Chapter Forty-Four

The room was bright, far, far too bright, and the thought passed like a dandelion on the breeze that she might be dead. It wasn't as shocking or dangerous as Saint had always thought death might be. It wasn't as comfortable either. Her arms were cold, and the lights were so bright, and she *hurt*. Surely if she was dead, she wouldn't hurt all over, her belly scratched and scraped, arms sore as though they'd been bound, and her head...

Her head felt like it might burst open, split on the rocks like the tidal waves of a hurricane. If this was death, she must have done something truly horrendous in her life without realizing it because there was an agony *beat, beat, beating* against her skull...

"Careful there, sweetie. Open your eyes slowly, that's right."

The light was too bright to open her eyes, but at further coaxing, Saint cracked one eye and then the other. The room was...she didn't know what the room was. She didn't recognize the light blue walls or the horrendous painting of flowers across from her.

Dante would never have a painting of flowers.

Dante.

Dante.

She pushed off the bed, her arms *burning* from the effort, only to be gently pushed back into the pillows.

"Not so fast, sweetie," the same voice from just out of sight. "You got a nasty head injury, and we need to make sure there's no lasting damage."

No *shit* she had a head injury. It felt like her thoughts were trying to escape out of every orifice in her face. But that didn't matter. She needed to find Dante, she needed to find him and tell him that—

That she was sorry. That she was asking what he couldn't. He might have been terrified to ask for more, but she wasn't, not anymore. She was done waiting for choices to take her, for her life path to be carved out by circumstances beyond her control. It was time for her to take the reins and grab her future with both hands.

When Lorenzo Barbarone had her bound, with the gun pushed against her stomach, all she had been able to think was that she hoped Dante didn't come. She hoped he didn't try to save her, that he got out alive.

Because the clarity of the cold metal on her skin had offered an irrevocable truth. She loved him. She liked Montana, spending time with his friends, the studio. But Dante had well and truly claimed her, and for days, perhaps weeks, it had been building to the inevitable. She loved him, and she would never miss another opportunity to tell him so.

She moved and it felt like her brain stayed in place while the rest of her body shifted.

Grab life by the reins slowly. Carefully.

"Where is he?" she managed to ask. She could finally open her eyes almost all the way, though the light made the throbbing in her head positively explosive, but she needed to know what was happening, to her, to him, no matter how much it hurt. Beside her, a pretty older woman in a pair of green scrubs was checking a clipboard and glancing at the machines next to the bed. *Machines. Nurse.* She was in a hospital. And Dante was...

"Where is he?" Panic was rising in her chest and making her dizzy, making her heart beat so fast it set off the beeping on the machine beside her. "Where is he?"

"Who?" the nurse asked, her voice not unkind.

"The— My..." The man she loved. "Black hair, tattoos, so pretty."

Her head wasn't working right. Because she knew his name, could see in her mind's eye, but talking seemed out of reach, like her memories were a little fuzzy and back to front. Perhaps it was from the injury. Perhaps it was from the medication. She didn't care about any of it. She only cared about him.

"They brought him in for surgery," the nurse said, in that same overly kind, placating tone. "We'll know soon."

"What happened?" She didn't know. How was it possible she didn't know? She could remember the fear of coming across the second in command of the Barbarone family, could remember seeing the panic in Dante's eyes when he saw them, but after that...

What had happened after that?

She couldn't remember. Dante had been watching her with such naked pain in his eyes, and now she understood it in a way that made her blood heat and her body hurt for reasons that had nothing to do with injuries or medications. She needed to know he was all right, needed to see him again, to tell him she forgave him, that she was sorry for what she said, to tell him she would fight for the future they could have.

You're mine. Today and always. And I will do whatever it takes to keep you in my life.

Before she even realized she was moving, Saint had pulled the wires free from her arm, feeling only the slightest sting from the needle, not nearly enough to deter her from making slow progress to the door, despite the nurse's protests. She pushed the door open and headed out into the hallway, desperately looking for something, a clue, a sign as to where he might be... She pushed herself, harder than she should have, not doubt, but each step she took got her closer to Dante, to...

"You have to come back." The nurse was on her now, a gentle but firm grip on her arm, and Saint tried to push her off, the sob rising in her chest, frustration and fear and panic. What if she never got the chance, what if she only knew how much she cared when it was way too late to do anything? How could she be asked to start her life over again when she had only just found what she had been missing, in time to lose it all again?

"I need to see him." She pulled away, aware of the hysteria rising in her chest, aware that she was making a scene and not giving a shit. Only one thing mattered now and that was telling Dante how she felt.

"Sweetie, I don't want to have to call security, but I will..."

"Please." It came out as a sob, but there was nothing for it. She had no control at the moment, not over the rising pressure in her chest, not over the power of her heart to propel her forward, to make her burn the world if that was the only option left. "*Please*, I need to see him."

"Saint." The voice was so familiar, so close to her memory, but she couldn't quite place it, not in this strange hospital, not with these white and blue walls spreading down as far as she could see, making the room seem to shift and vertigo send the ground sliding out from under her bare feet. Fuck, her feet were cold against the tile, and her head was pounding in time with her heart, a bursting, panicked pain that told her she was still alive — and she was going to suffer for that truth. "Saint, wait."

She pushed off the seeking arms, the nurse wasn't going to take her back. She wasn't going back to that sterile room until she saw him.

"Saint, Dante is okay. Just breathe."

A calming hand stroked circles on her back, and it made the paper-thin gown stick to her skin, cooling the hot sweat that had taken over, but making it a little easier to take the next breath, and the next.

"He's okay?" she choked out.

"He's okay." The voice was so familiar that it didn't matter if she couldn't see the person behind her, her head pounding too much to turn or even glance her eyes. "I can take you to him, but you just need to breathe for me."

Saint took a deep breath, struggling to get it past the lump that had formed in her throat and the tightening of her chest, but the next breath was easier, and then the next, and finally, soon, she was taking in the air she needed to see against the din of her head pain. Slowly, she turned, catching sight of Morgan beside her, a worried expression on her pretty face.

"There are you," Morgan said, her voice calm and gentle. "You gave us a bit of a scare there, love."

"He's okay?" Saint asked. It seemed to be the only thing she was capable of saying.

"A little banged up," Morgan said, moving her hand from Saint's back to her arm, maybe to keep her from bolting again, maybe to keep her from falling down. "But alive, Saint."

"The nurse said he was in surgery…" Her brain was so foggy, the pain or meds or confusion taking over everything. "That he's fighting for his life."

"His brother," Morgan said on a soft sigh. "Niccolo took a knife to the gut in the fight. They brought him right to the OR."

Her chest squeezed, emotions mixing and threatening to spill over. Relief that Dante was okay, that she wouldn't lose her chance, but sadness for Niccolo, gratitude, fear, hope to a god she no longer believed in that Dante wouldn't have to bury a brother.

"Can you take me to him?" she asked, suddenly feeling so incredibly tired, her legs starting to wobble and shake, even her feet feeling too weak to keep her standing.

Morgan took her arm more strongly then and slowly guided Saint a few doors down the hallway. It was difficult to walk, each step feeling like a million miles, until finally Morgan pushed the door open and showed Saint into another hospital room.

Dante was sitting up, a very stern nurse standing vigil by his bed, Caleb, Reece and Van squeezed into the tiny hospital room. Even in her confused state, Saint could still find it funny how much these big cowboys took up space, their very presences enough to impose. Or to protect.

"Dante."

She practically fell on the bed, helped down only in the last minute by Morgan's strong hand.

"*Ciccina.*" His voice was raspy, and the side of his head was patched with a large bandage, but he was *alive.* And he was hers. She was going to make sure of it. "I wanted to see you but..." He glanced over at the stern looking nurse.

"You can't walk," the nurse said. "And you can't see straight."

Saint laughed, not even realizing she was capable until the sound escaped her lips. "Neither can I," she said.

"We make for quite the pair," he replied. Distantly, Saint heard Morgan ushering the guys out of the room, heard them tittering about wanting to stick around and see what happened, but finally following her out into the hall. When the stern nurse left with a final warning, Saint and Dante were left entirely alone in the small room.

"I'm so sorry," he said, reaching out a wired hand to stroke the side of her face. She leaned against his touch, feeling the connection and the comfort like a balm, needing a lifetime more of it. "I should never have tried to push you away or make your choice for you."

"You were scared," she said. "I understand that."

"Not you, my brave girl," he said. "You never run scared."

"I ran scared all the way to Montana."

"You *survived.*" His voice held awe, and not for the first time, she was struck by just how much Dante could see her for who she really was. "You could survive anything."

"Not losing you," she said, the words a painful truth on her tongue. "I thought you were the one in surgery and I..." Tears were falling freely now, hot on her cheeks. "I didn't know what I would do if I didn't tell you how I felt."

"You could survive it," he said. "But you'll never have to."

That made her heart skitter and jump and she held his gaze, a million questions running through her mind.

"I should have told you a thousand times," Dante said, "from the day you fell into my life you changed me, *ciccina*. You bring a lightness to the room, joy to the dark days. You're brave and brilliant and so incredibly capable and I've been so terrified to risk losing you that I made up all these reasons to push you away so I wouldn't have to tell you the truth."

"And what truth is that?" She didn't dare hope, even as it bloomed a beautiful thing in her chest.

"That I love you. That I have been falling in love with you since the day you asked me to kiss you in the studio, since the day you trusted me with your secrets, since the moment you submitted my touch. I love you, and I'm not running from it, not anymore. Not ever again."

Saint gasped against the tears clogging her throat and making it difficult to speak, but some things were worth the fight.

"I love you too," she whispered. "I won't wait for you to ask, I won't let the choices be made for me. I'll be brave for us too, and fight every day to show you how much I love you."

And with that, she leaned down and kissed him, the familiar taste of him invading her senses, overpowering the sterile brightness of the hospital, pushing away any and everything until the moment the monitor started beeping and she finally pulled back.

"Hospital gowns aren't going to cover a damn thing," Dante murmured in her ear. "But don't think I won't make up for the embarrassment the second we get home."

Home.

Home. His apartment. His cabin. His suite at The Ranch. It didn't matter where they set up shop, where they called theirs, the studio, the back of her little sedan, as long as she was with him, for good this time, it was home.

"I can't wait," she whispered.

She was just about to steal another kiss when the door pushed open, and Ash stepped into the hospital room. His face was grim, the darkest she had ever seen his normally humorous expression, and her heart lurched at the possibilities behind the intensity in his pretty eyes.

"Niccolo," she managed. "Is he?"

Ash stood straighter than she had ever seen, and for a moment Saint thought that maybe the word had crumbled all around them despite everything.

"He's okay," Ash said, as if tasting the words for the very first time, the air rushing out of his lungs in a single push. "He's going to be okay."

Dante murmured something under his breath in Italian, and while Saint still didn't know enough to interpret its meaning, there was no denying that it was a prayer. Someone had been watching out for them that day. Even if that someone was each other.

"I'm going to take him back to Colorado after this," Ash said. "He's going to need to recover for a while, and the brothers can watch him." He seemed to realize what it was he had said, and gave Dante a nod.

"I know he'd like it if you visited, D." He caught sight of their entwined fingers. "If you both did."

"We will," Saint said. "As soon as we can."

Ash nodded, the pained expression just edging out of the corner of his eyes, and for a fleeting, insane moment, Saint had to wonder if maybe there was more than brotherly affection and the fear for his captain staining him with such hurt.

"You should know," Ash continued, "that Lorenzo is dead. He didn't survive the shot."

She had *so* many questions about what had happened when they had been trapped on that mountaintop, but for the moment, they could wait. Lorenzo Barbarone, the man whom she had seen commit cold-blooded murder, the one who had chased her halfway across the country, Dante's *father*, was gone.

"Will Nicco be charged?"

"Sheriff says it's a clear case of self-defense," Ash replied. Not his sister. The Sheriff. "We'll let you know when there's more to know."

"Thank you," Saint said. "For everything."

"It's what we do," Ash replied, his eyes finally taking on some of the familiar humor she'd so come to expect from him. "We take care of family."

And that was what she had become, Saint realized, as Ash finally left, and the room flooded with Dante's friends—Caleb, Reece, Van, Skylar, Morgan and Rhylee. After a while, a beautiful couple joined them who Saint recognized from the papers, who were introduced as Gabriel and Emerson. Bastion Kane video called Dante from an empty stage before his show, ribbing the hell out of him and flirting the hell out of her until they were both crying from laughing so hard.

Late in the night, just as visiting hours were winding down, there was a knock on the door and the most elegant man she had ever seen walked in, leaving two bodyguards out in the hall.

"Your Royal Highness," Dante said, to the hoots and hollers of the others. "I didn't realize my getting injured was a matter of state."

"I was in the area," the man introduced as Rafe said quietly, the tone of his voice smoothing, lilting with a soft accent she couldn't quite place.

"Liar," Dante said, his face breaking out in a grin. "*Ciccina*, the crown prince. Rafe, come meet my girl."

His girl. She was his girl. And he was hers, in all the ways that mattered, connected through adventure and mishap and self-sabotage and threats against their lives, and everything that had tried to come between them and ultimately brought them closer together. Forever. She would make sure of it.

Epilogue

"Now this is a good old-fashioned cowboy Christmas," Dante said, hanging the last ornament on the tree in the front hall of the Ranch.

"I don't think classic cowboy Christmases have dildo ornaments," Saint said, glancing between the many, *many* sex-toy themed ornaments he'd hung on the tree next to the bar. Instead of a star on top, there was a large multi-pronged rainbow butt plug that lit up when Dante pressed the center.

"*Au contraire,*" he said. "All the best cowboys have dildo trees."

"I'm going to have to argue that," Caleb said, walking into the room, Skylar at his side. "I have never had a dildo tree."

"Then you're missing out." Dante settled next to Saint on the sofa and looked at the tree. It was ghastly, if she were being honest, a mishmash of profane toys in so many different colors, sparkly anal beads, a light up dildo blinking against a lowering branch. She loved it.

And she loved him.

"This is the best Christmas tree I've ever seen," Saint said, resting her head on his shoulder and taking in the familiar scent of him. In the days they had been in the hospital, they had been kept apart, and now, nearly a month later, she still couldn't get close enough. Dante didn't seem to mind at all, taking his nursemaid duties very seriously, and keeping her trapped in bed until all hours of the night and day.

"*Mmm,* it'd be better if you were all wrapped up waiting for me on Christmas morning," he said, leaning over to steal a kiss.

Saint laughed, thinking of the costume she had waiting back in their room. Having girlfriends was *amazing.* Having girlfriends that shared her lifestyle was...everything. She could ask their advice, learn from their experiences, and share some of the more tantalizing details of her nights—and mornings and afternoons—with Master Dante and only get the same in return. They understood, each of their own masters asking the same or similar of their play as Master Dante asked, and while they hadn't yet played in public—and given Master Dante's protectiveness over her, she wasn't certain they ever would—Saint continued to feel like she was part of something bigger than herself, a lifestyle that honored consent and love and played with power and trust, one that made her feel safer than she ever had felt, and bolder than she had ever thought possible.

She grabbed a stray bow from the stacks of Christmas decorations and stuck it on his chest.

"You're my Christmas present, Sir," she whispered, the word so easy on her lips, so natural after weeks of comfortable play, and she still loved the way that it made his eyes spark and his body tighten below her. Saint knew she would continue to love it. Forever.

"*Mmm,* Christmas has come early this year," he said, standing and lifting her from the couch in one fluid motion. Saint barely registered Skylar and Caleb's laugh, or the arrival of Morgan and Reece and Rhylee and Van, as Master Dante whispered sinful promises into her ear, making her giggle and blush.

"Not too early, I hope, Sir," she said with a laugh.

"Maybe not at all if you keep that up, angel," he said, his voice taking that dark drop that she knew meant danger was coming. Danger and sweetness and pleasure and...

Love.

She loved this man. She loved the mountains and the apartment they shared over his studio and her work as an apprentice and the art classes she took at the local college and his friends. She loved Nicco and Ash, who were at that moment on the way back to Montana, after several weeks of healing. She loved her life.

And she very, very much loved Dante.

At this moment, however, she loved Master Dante even more.

"That tree is horrendous," she heard Reece say, as Master Dante carried her out of the main room and down the hall to his suite. She had hung colored lights along the windows the night before, and soft holiday music played from the speakers, setting the perfect scene for the night she had planned for them.

"Permission to change, Sir," Saint asked, when he finally carried her into the living quarters.

"Be quick," he said, "and take off more than you put on."

She dashed into the en suite, grabbing the bag that she had stashed earlier in the day with her latest purchase, and pulling it on quickly. She didn't doubt that he would come looking for her if she took too long and this gift was much better as a surprise. With one final look at her hair and a last dash of lip gloss, Saint stepped out into the suite.

Master Dante took one look at her and his eyes went dark, that hooded, desperate expression that she knew meant danger of the most delicious kind.

"My little Christmas elf," he said, taking stock of her red velvet mini dress, trimmed with white fur, the black heels, the candy cane stripe stockings, and the jaunty red hat that sat to the side of her head. "Have you come to give me my Christmas present?"

"I have, Sir," she whispered, loving the effect the outfit had on him, loving that he was so responsive to her games, even as she was still learning all the ways she might please him. "But you'll have to come get it."

He had her pinned to the large picture window with her hands above her head in an instant, his body warm and so incredibly masculine, and the sheer power of his strong stance enough to make her pussy throb and her nipples pebble into hard points.

"Where should I look for it?" he asked, using his free hand to push the mini skirt up, his fingers warm and seeking across her sensitized bare skin, and Saint couldn't help but buck into him, but lean into his touch as he teased and explored. "Is my gift here?" He slid further up, teasing around her aching pussy as Saint did her best to hold back against the pressure and need. Her best wasn't all that impressive, because she wanted him, filling her, taking her, giving her everything he had to offer.

"I think I need a better look," Master Dante said, before dropping to his knees and pushing her skirt up. In the next motion, he had his mouth on her pussy and was eating her like his life depended on it, like he couldn't get enough, like her pleasure was the only thing in the world that mattered to him. And with each stroke and lick and suck, he forced her to even greater heights of that pleasure, pushing her right up against the edge of her release, good sense clouding her judgment, her fingers searching for purchase on the cool glass but finding none, just the overwhelming, unignorable pleasure that coursed through her until Saint was quite certain he was going to keep her on the edge right until she begged for mercy.

She wasn't above begging.

"Master Dante, please," she whimpered. "Please let me come."

He just kept stroking his finger in and out, pushing her higher and closer to that impossible edge until she was teetering there, ready to fall, when he pulled back. His lips were slick with her desire and his eyes blazed hot and demanding, and that made Saint's desire ratchet up even higher.

"You do deserve it, little Christmas elf?" he asked.

"Yes, Sir," she whispered.

"Why?"

"I picked out the perfect present for you," she practically whimpered. "You just need to find it."

He slipped his hand around to cup her ass and hold her in place, and when he brushed her, Dante stilled, his eyes somehow burning brighter, hotter, more intense than she'd seen all day.

"My little angel," he said. "Did you prepare this pretty little ass for me?"

"Yes, Sir," she said, unable to keep the pride from her voice. She wanted to make him happy, to make him proud of her and all she did right in their shared scenes, and she had been fantasizing about what he would do when he found her gift for days.

"Yes, Sir," she said, never taking her eyes from him, "I filled myself in the shower this afternoon. On my hands and knees, pretending it was you." And it had been one of the hottest solo experiences of her life. Nothing compared to what he was about to do to her, no doubt.

"Did you come while you stretched your tight ass for me?" he asked, each word sounding gritted and rough. "Did you tighten around the toy while your pussy clenched and squeezed?"

"I didn't come," Saint whispered. "I didn't think you'd want me to."

"You're right," Master Dante replied. "Your pleasure belongs to me, your orgasms belong to me. Your ass"—he tapped the toy the smallest amount, but it made her pussy flood with pleasure—"belongs to me."

"Then claim it, Sir," she begged. "Please."

He stood and turned her until she was pressed against the window, then he flipped her skirt up so he could inspect her handiwork. She wondered what he saw, looking at the candy-striped plug in her ass, and if he wanted more as much as she did. He twisted the toy slightly and Saint gasped, the sensation overwhelming to her already sensitized body, but nothing compared to the sensation of Master Dante's intense, needy gaze upon her, and everything that meant.

"Soon," he promised. "We have all the time in the world. Today, I just want to feel how tight you are around my cock with this lovely little present in your ass." He brushed the plug again and Saint nearly jumped out of skin, again when he ran his hand through her wetness, each touch bringing her back to that invisible edge he seemed so keen on denying her.

"Yes, Sir," she whispered, "thank you, Sir."

"You know I can't deny you anything," he replied. He stepped back and she could hear the sound of his zipper, and then his swollen cock was pushing against her entrance, and he was right, it was so incredibly tight with the toy and Master Dante's impressive cock, and it felt so incredibly *right*, to be stretched by him, owned by him, taken and claimed so completely by the man she loved.

"Take your pleasure," he said, thrusting hard inside her and pinning Saint's hands at her back to keep her in place. Maybe she shouldn't have loved the restraints so much, but she did, loved the way he controlled her movement and her escape, how he was the one in charge and she was entirely at the mercy of his touch. "Take it again and again until I tell you to stop, *ciccina*."

And with another thrust, she did, her body hitting the wall and crashing through, spiraling down into an explosive, white-hot bliss that made stars burst before her eyes, that made her pussy pulse around him and the toy feel somehow even bigger in her ass. And then, just as quickly, the heat of the last release still barreling through her, Saint burst all over all again, swelling and squeezing around his cock, the knowledge that Master Dante was close to his release making her wild, sending her bucking and thrusting as much as she could, making Saint whimper and moan, especially as she felt another release coming hard and fast, and this time, she knew she was going to take him with her.

She squeezed hard, found his rhythm, and followed thrust for thrust for thrust, taking, taking, taking, until Master Dante muttered a sharp curse in Italian, squeezed her hands tighter, and spilled hot, thick cum into her waiting pussy. The sensation was enough to overwhelm her one last time, and she followed him, crying out his name and sinking into the sweet, incredible abyss of pleasure.

Master Dante pulled out slowly, then carefully removed the toy, before gently wiping her down with a warm towel. Then he guided Saint to the warm, cozy bed she had come to call her own in this place she never wanted to say goodbye to. The place she would never have to say goodbye to.

Dante joined her on the bed, and she noticed he had something in his hands.

"I have a present for you, too," he said, handing her a small box, and Saint's heart leapt in her throat. They hadn't done anything by the book, not the falling love or the falling in bed, or dating or living together, but they had done it on their terms, and now, if she could read the tension in his body right, the final piece of the puzzle was just about to fall into place. "Open it."

Inside the box were two silver bracelets. They were subtle, delicate, with intricate linework that wove organically, like the vines of a plant, and they were adorned with small blue and purple stones. The color of both their eyes, she realized. She also realized they connected, with a subtle locking mechanism that would keep her wrists pinned together, if that was what Master Dante wanted.

"One day," Master Dante said slowly, "when you're ready, I'll mark these bonds to your skin with my ink so every time you look at them you know who you belong to. But for now, angel, *ciccina*, my Saint, I ask with these bracelets—will you wear my binds and be my submissive, and only mine?"

She didn't hesitate, not for a second, not when she had been wanting it all these weeks.

"Yes, Master," she whispered, loving the word on her tongue. Not Master Dante. Master. Hers and only hers.

His deep purple eyes glowed and glistened the slightest, and he lifted the bracelets free, attaching one around each wrist.

"Merry Christmas, *ciccina*," he said. "My life changed the day you showed up in this town, and I cannot wait to see what our future holds. I love you."

"Merry Christmas," she murmured back. "I love you today and I will love you every day to come."

And thence we came forth to see again the stars.

Outside, it began to snow. But inside, Saint and Dante held each other close, warm and safe in each other's arms, and very much in love.

Sign up for our newsletter and find out about all our romance book releases, eBook sales and promotions, sneak peeks and FREE romance books!

Want to see more from this author?
Here's a taster for you to enjoy!

Triple Diamond:
The Lovin' is Easy
Gemma Snow

Excerpt

"A *what?*"

Against the din of the ancient window air conditioner chugging into the room, Madison's voice had a tinny, almost petulant sound. But of all the things she had expected from the impromptu meeting with some family estate lawyer she'd never heard of, *this* wasn't it.

"A *ranch*, Ms. Hollis," Mr. Sidney replied, the tone of his voice indicating that he'd picked up on her confusion and ensuing frustration with the afternoon's events and that, frankly, he didn't care. "The Triple Diamond Ranch in Wolf Creek, Montana, to be exact."

Madison rubbed her hands over her face and tried to make sense of everything. Mr. Sidney had contacted her a week prior about a will left to her by some uncle on her mother's side, an uncle she'd never heard of, from a mother who'd been gone some eighteen years now. She took a deep breath, trying a different tack.

"Are you certain this is my uncle" — she glanced at the stack of legal documents two inches thick on the desk before her — "Mason?"

Mr. Sidney peered down at her over the wire rim of his thin glasses — a remarkable feat, given that she had at least two inches on the man, who sat short and boney in the chair across the desk.

"Mr. Mason Westerly King first arranged this inheritance with Sidney and Sidney nearly two decades ago," he replied. "We've had ample time to determine and confirm your identity, Ms. Hollis."

Madison resisted the urge to roll her eyes, but only just. Mr. Sidney's attitude came on the tail of what had already been the week from hell. She sighed, her heavy breath spilling out of her mouth like a deflating hot air balloon. *It's only Wednesday.*

"Mr. Sidney, I'm afraid I still don't quite understand. What am I supposed to do with a ranch" — she gestured with her hand — "I don't know, eight, ten hours away from here?"

He gave a slow blink. "My advice, Ms. Hollis, is to go inspect the ranch yourself. You have all the information on the mineral rights and past financial records. Once you get the lay of the land, you can determine whether you wish to sell or keep the property. But otherwise, after I get your signature on these forms, I'm afraid there's not much else I can help you with."

Madison did scowl that time, but with her head bent over the stack of papers while signing the requisite lines, he couldn't see it. She was perfectly pleased to be done with Mr. Sidney for good, but he was wrong about one major thing. She wasn't going to decide whether or not to keep the ranch — she had decided the very first time he had mentioned the word *inheritance.* No, the second she got out to Montana, she would sell the damn thing and be done with it. Maybe then everything would go back to normal. *Ha. Yeah, right.*

About the Author

Gemma Snow loves high heat, high adventures and high expectations for her heroes! Her stories are set in the past and present, from the glittering streets of Paris to cowboy-rich Triple Diamond Ranch in Wolf Creek, Montana.

In her free time, she loves to travel, and spent several months living in a fourteenth-century castle in the Netherlands. When not exploring the world, she likes dreaming up stories, eating spicy food, driving fast cars and talking to strangers. She recently moved to Nashville with a cute redheaded cat and a cute redheaded boy.

Gemma loves to hear from readers. You can find her contact information, website details and author profile page at https://www.firstforromance.com

ENTWINED PUBLISHING